the
HARLEM READER

ALSO BY HERB BOYD

*RACE AND RESISTANCE: AFRICAN AMERICANS
IN THE TWENTY-FIRST CENTURY*

*AUTOBIOGRAPHY OF A PEOPLE: THREE
CENTURIES OF AFRICAN AMERICAN HISTORY
AS TOLD BY THOSE WHO LIVED IT*

*BROTHERMAN: THE ODYSSEY OF BLACK MEN
IN AMERICA—AN ANTHOLOGY*
(WITH ROBERT L. ALLEN)

A CELEBRATION OF NEW YORK'S

MOST FAMOUS NEIGHBORHOOD,

FROM THE RENAISSANCE YEARS

TO THE TWENTY-FIRST CENTURY

 THREE RIVERS PRESS • NEW YORK

EDITED BY *Herb Boyd*

the HARLem reaDer

FOREWORD BY HOWARD DODSON

TO A FEW OF HARLEM'S MOST DEVOTED BOOK LOVERS: ARTURO SCHOMBURG, LEWIS MICHAUX, RICHARD B. MOORE, REGINA ANDERSON ANDREWS, JEAN BLACKWELL HUTSON, ERNEST KAISER, AND UNA MULZAC.

Complete text for permissions appears on pages 313–316.

Copyright © 2003 by Herb Boyd

Published by Three Rivers Press, New York, New York.
Member of the Crown Publishing Group, a division of Random House, Inc.

www.randomhouse.com

Photograph on page v is used by permission of the Library of Congress, Prints & Photographs Division, FSA/OWI Collection, reproduction number LC-USW3-031097-C.

THREE RIVERS PRESS is a registered trademark and the Three Rivers Press colophon is a trademark of Random House, Inc.

Printed in the United States of America

DESIGN BY ELINA D. NUDELMAN

Library of Congress Cataloging-in-Publication Data

The Harlem reader : a celebration of New York's most famous community / edited by Herb Boyd ; foreword by Howard Dodson.—1st ed.

   1. Harlem (New York, N.Y.)—Miscellanea. 2. Harlem (New York, N.Y.)—History—Miscellanea. 3. Harlem (New York, N.Y.)—Biography. 4. New York (N.Y.)—Miscellanea. 5. New York (N.Y.)—History—Miscellanea. 6. New York (N.Y.)—Biography. 7. African Americans—New Yo--rk (State)—New York—Miscellanea. 8. African Americans—New York (State)—New York—History—Miscellanea. 9. African Americans—New York (State)—New York—Biography. I. Boyd, Herb, 1938–
F128.68.H3 H33   2003
974.7'1—dc21   2002151280

ISBN 1-4000-4681-5

10 9 8 7 6 5 4 3 2 1

First Edition

JUKE BOX LOVE SONG

Langston Hughes

I could take the Harlem night
and wrap around you,
Take the neon lights and make a crown,
Take the Lenox Avenue busses,
Taxis and subways,
And for your love song tone their rumble down.
Take Harlem's heartbeat,
Make a drumbeat,
Put it on a record, let it whirl,
And while we listen to it play,
Dance with you till day—
Dance with you, my sweet brown Harlem girl.

CONTENTS

CONTENTS

xii

FOREWORD

Everyone, it seems, has an impression of Harlem, an image of Harlem, a story about Harlem, a romance with Harlem. Ask and they are quick to give you their thoughts, perspectives, views. Some are so in love with Harlem that they cannot discuss it rationally. Others are so disenchanted that they cannot see, feel, know its spirit, passions, hidden beauties, and allures. However vivid those impressions, perspectives, and enchantments are, most people do not take the time to write them down. As a consequence, their unique ideas and views are not available to the general public.

The good news is that while most people didn't take the time to record their perspectives, many did. Herb Boyd's *The Harlem Reader* is a judicious selection of published texts by writers who knew/know Harlem. They reflect the ever-changing, ever-evolving public consciousness of Harlem as a community, a center of cultural creativity, and an icon of the best and worst that urban black America has produced.

As would be expected, there is ample representation of work written during and about Harlem's first heyday—the 1920s. It was during that decade that Harlem earned its reputation as the cultural capital of black America. At once a magnet that drew people of African descent from the four corners of the black world, and a cauldron in which the diverse cultural, political, and social traditions were molded into a new Negro renaissance, the Harlem of the 1920s captured the public's imagination and inspired thousands to put pen to paper and comment on its lives, activities, and mysteries. The literary legacy of the Harlem Renaissance of the 1920s has continued to attract the attention of contemporary writers and scholars.

Venetria K. Patton and Maureen Honey recently compiled and edited *Double-Take: A Revisionist Harlem Renaissance Anthology* (2001). This six-hundred-page collection seeks to bring to light the voices of black women writers of the Harlem Renaissance era, drawing heavily on the era's contemporary periodicals and anthologies where they were more frequently published. Containing an almost equal number of male and female contributors, the anthology includes essays, poetry, short stories, and dramatic works.

A Renaissance in Harlem (1999), compiled and edited by Lionel C. Bascom, features a collection of "lost essays of the WPA" by Ralph Ellison, Dorothy West, and others, documenting Harlem life during the Renaissance and the Great Depression. Selected from manuscripts in The Library of Congress's WPA Writers Project Collection, they were based on interviews with Harlemites conducted between 1936 and 1940. Recent collections of work by prominent Harlem Renaissance figures and institutions have also expanded the body of published sources on the Renaissance. Two readers on W. E. B. DuBois by David Levering Lewis (1995) and Eric J. Sundquist (1996) include significant Harlem references. Jeffrey B. Perry's *A Hubert*

Harrison Reader (2001) tracks this significant, but under-appreciated, Renaissance figure's life and thought, much of which was Harlem centered or Harlem inspired. Carla Kaplan's *Zora Neale Hurston: A Life in Letters* is a collection of some five hundred letters by Hurston, a leading Renaissance figure. When added to such compilations as Nathan Huggins's *Voices from the Harlem Renaissance* (1976), David Levering Lewis's *The Portable Harlem Renaissance Reader* (1994), and Sondra Kathryn Wilson's *The Crisis Reader* (1999) and *The Opportunity Reader* (1999), individuals looking for authentic first-person commentaries on the Harlem Renaissance will find an abundance of materials in print and available for research and study.

Harlem as a subject of public attention and commentary did not start with the Renaissance. And it did not end in the era of the Great Depression. As *The Harlem Reader* shows, people were writing about Harlem as early as the nineteenth century. They have continued to do so down to the present day. The writers Boyd has selected to include in his *Harlem Reader* span two centuries and represent some of the most significant social, political, and cultural African-American voices of the twentieth century.

Scholarly voices like those of W. E. B. DuBois, David Levering Lewis, Harold Cruse, and John Henrik Clarke are here, as are Harlem political activists Marcus Garvey, Hubert Harrison, James Weldon Johnson, Adam Clayton Powell Jr., J. Raymond Jones, and, of course, Malcolm X. Visual and performing artists Gordon Parks Sr., Ossie Davis, Ruby Dee, Sidney Poitier, and Duke Ellington are voices in *The Harlem Reader*, as are poets and writers such as Langston Hughes, Piri Thomas, Sonia Sanchez, James

Baldwin, Maya Angelou, Michele Wallace, and Willie Per-domo. Harlem subjects of the writings range from 409 Edgecombe and Voudou MacBeth to the Cotton Club, the 369th, Strivers Row, the Garvey Movement, the Abyssinian Baptist Church, and the Harlem Renaissance itself. Characterized by spirited, insightful, critical yet celebratory writing, the essays, articles, short stories, and poetry included in *The Harlem Reader* are a perfect introduction to the issues, events, and personalities that have made Harlem one of America's (and the world's) most unique communities. Read the *Reader!* Immerse yourself in Harlem! Celebrate Harlem!

Howard Dodson, Chief Curator,
Schomburg Center for Research in Black Culture

INTRODUCTION

Ever since the Dutch farmer Andries Hudde received a patent giving him the right to possess, bargain, or depose a tract of land just north of New Amsterdam, the place now known as Harlem has always been a magnet. Whether it was potentially arable soil for European immigrants in the early seventeenth century, or a haven for black Southerners fleeing the ravages of the boll weevil or Klansmen two hundred years later, Harlem has been a lure of hope and possibility. It has been a crucible of aspirations, a Valhalla of promise, and has produced enough myth and lore to command shelves of books about its legend.

Over the last half-century, Harlem has been perpetually under the microscope and called everything from an angel to a harlot, a community of endless bounty to a ghetto on the verge of exploding, like Langston Hughes's "dream deferred." It has been picked apart by historians and sociologists, analyzed by psychiatrists, glorified by ministers and poets, and its stories anthologized, particularly those from the "Renaissance," in which the intent was to at least present an aspect of Harlem's multifaceted realities. Most of the books on Harlem have focused mainly on the 1920s, when there was a great harvest of literary expression and artistic endeavors. At last count there were more than three dozen delightful books on the Harlem Renaissance, but only a few that touched on political, economic, and cultural development during the succeeding two generations.

There has been a spate of fiction anthologies, poetry collections, and the kaleidoscope of expressions compiled in recent times by the late John Henrik Clarke, the Schomburg Center, and the Studio Museum. But nowhere is there a book that stretches beyond the halcyon twenties into the world of the learned scholars, novelists, and ordinary "griots" so that you can feel Harlem's unique pulse, see those hues of humanity, smell the seductive aroma wafting from a thousand restaurants and street vendors, and hear the countless tongues trying to talk above the music blasting from boom boxes and store speakers. To capture Harlem's diversity, its many moods and attitudes, the way it continues to be a mecca for the tourist and resident, requires a whole choir of voices—voices that know how to harmonize, and a voice that knows how to solo and sing its own sweet song.

The Harlem Reader is an attempt to orchestrate such a multitude of voices, to gather some of those vital impressions, those precious gems languishing in articles, essays, narratives, poems, memoirs, and diaries, and blend them with fresh accounts offered by living storytellers, some famous and some not so famous. The book is not categorically, chronologically, or thematically constricted, but tries to create a mosaic of impressions about personal experiences, organizations, institutions, and the dramatic moments that are at the core of Harlem's ever-evolving history.

HOME ON THE GRANGE

ALEXANDER HAMILTON

Alexander Hamilton was born in 1757 on the island of Nevis, in the Leeward group, British West Indies. He was the illegitimate son of a common-law marriage between a poor itinerant Scottish merchant of aristocratic descent and an English–French Huguenot mother who was a planter's daughter. Through the efforts of his aunts, he arrived in the American colonies in 1772, later enrolling in what was to become Columbia University. During the Revolutionary War, he was only in his early twenties but quickly distinguished himself as a chief aide to General Washington. He would earn similar distinction five years later as a lawyer. After the war, Hamilton served Washington as the first secretary of the treasury and staked his place as one of the principal architects of Federalism, which advocated a strong central role for the national government. He wrote more than half of the legendary *Federalist Papers* (1787) and also penned Washington's famous farewell speech at the end of his second term. Hamilton was a major player in American politics for many years. No presidential election could escape his influence. Years of bitter political rivalry with Aaron Burr led to a duel. On July 11, 1804, Burr shot and mortally wounded Hamilton, who died a day later, at forty-seven. Two years before his death, Hamilton and his family moved into the Grange, a country home he had built in a rural part of Manhattan not far north of New York City. But the expenses involved, and investments in northern land speculations, seriously strained his finances. The Grange occupied some thirty-two acres of farmland in what is now Harlem in New York City. He had hoped to raise some produce to help defray costs, but it did not work out that way. Over three years of farming on the Grange, selling strawberries, cabbages, and asparagus, he earned only eighteen dollars in profits.

"The greatest part of my little farm will be dedicated to grass," he said upon acquiring the property. ". . . Because there must be some public fools who sacrifice private to public interest at the certainty of ingratitude and obloquy—because my *vanity* whispers I ought to be one of those fools and ought to keep myself in a situation the best calculated to render service—because I don't want to be rich and if I cannot live in *splendor* in Town . . . I can at least live in *comfort* in the country and I am content to do so."

THE AFRO-AMERICAN REALTY COMPANY

GILBERT OSOFSKY

From *Harlem: The Making of a Ghetto* (1963)

Not until Philip Payton organized his realty company was Harlem officially launched as a cohesive community. Payton was a clever businessman and a visionary who knew a hot piece of property when it fell into his hands. Gilbert Osofsky probes the beginning of Harlem meticulously, culling precious gems of history from miles of research.

Payton's activities in Harlem real estate reached a high point in 1904 with his founding of the Afro-American Realty Company. The company had its genesis in a partnership of ten Negroes organized by Payton. This partnership specialized in acquiring five-year leases on Harlem property owned by whites and subsequently renting them to Negroes. In 1904, Payton conceived of reorganizing this small concern into a regular real estate corporation, capable of buying and constructing homes as well as leasing them. The company, incorporated on June 15, 1904, was permitted to "buy, sell, rent, lease, and sub-lease, all kinds of buildings, houses . . . lots, and other . . . real estate in the City of New York. . . ." It was capitalized at $500,000 and authorized to issue 50,000 shares at ten dollars each. Ten of the eleven original members of the all-Negro Board of Directors subscribed to five hundred shares each. The company began with an estimated capital of $100,000. . . .[1]

The Afro-American Realty Company was founded with high hopes of success—hopes which proved unfounded. At first, the corporation seemed to have sound financial backing and the support of eminent members of the Negro community. "The personnel of the Board of Directors of the company is bound to commend it to the respect, trust and confidence of even the most skeptical of our race," its prospectus stated. "Most of them are men who have made a success in their individual lives and are well-known in New York City for their ability, worth and integrity.[2] Early company transactions were profitable and tended to verify Payton's optimistic judgments. In 1904, for instance, the Afro-American Realty Company sold three of its newly acquired houses on West 135th Street to a white real estate concern, the Hudson Realty Company. Hudson Realty proceeded to evict its Negro tenants in order to replace them with whites. Payton, in turn, "blocked the game" by buying two other houses on the same street and evicting the white tenants in them. Within a short time, he was able to repurchase the original three (at 40, 42 and 44 West 135th Street), "filling the houses with Afro-Americans." These first highly publicized transactions boosted the reputation of the Realty Company. They "gave great publicity to the exis-

---

1. "Certificate of Incorporation of the Afro-American Realty Company Filed and Recorded June 15, 1904" (New York City Hall of Records).
2. The Afro-American Realty Company, Prospectus (New York, 1904), 7 (original in New York City Hall of Records).

tence of the Afro-American Realty Company," the *New York Age* concluded in 1905.[3]

Payton did not let the company rest on its laurels. To attract financial support from the Negro working class he advertised regularly in the Negro press and promised the average investor much more than he was able to fulfill later. (The prospectus offered profits of seven to ten percent, but the weekly advertisements omitted the seven).[4] Investment would not only yield "Tempting Profit," Negroes were told, but it was also their obligation to support an enterprise which would help end "relentless race prejudice": "To-day is the time to buy, if you want to be numbered among those of the race who are doing something toward trying to solve the so-called 'Race Problem,'" it was argued. The anticipated success of the company would become a symbol of Negro business acumen and would end racial segregation in urban housing: "A respecting, law-abiding Negro will find conditions can be so changed that he will be able to rent, wherever his means will permit him to live," the Prospectus maintained. Race prejudice would be turned into "dollars and cents" for Negroes, not whites.[5] Although public reports showed stocks being sold rapidly, privately the company found it necessary to hire a salesman to drum up business at a commission of twenty percent. And stocks were sold, usually

---

3. E. F. Dycoff, "A Negro City in New York," 949–50; *New York Age*, December 21, 1905; L. B. Bryan, "Negro Real Estate in New York" (WPA research paper, Schomburg Collection), 2–3.

4. See the *New York Age* in 1905 and 1906 for advertisements.

5. Prospectus, 3–7.

to individuals who could afford only a few shares at a time.[6]

The Realty Company promised the world and delivered little. It had hopefully been incorporated for fifty years, but folded after four. During its short and hectic existence it was racked with internal dissension. In four years there were three major reorganizations of its Board of Directors and officers. James C. Thomas and James E. Garner severed connections with the company in its first year. Wilford H. Smith was later influential in bringing suit against Payton for fraud. The final reorganization, in 1906, left Payton as president and general manager. It was formal recognition of the power he had wielded since the founding of the corporation.

6. Fred R. Moore to Emmett J. Scott, December 27, 1905. Washington. Papers, Box 29.

HARLEM TOWN

**SARAH L. DELANY AND A. ELIZABETH DELANY,
WITH AMY HILL HEARTH**

From *Having Our Say:
The Delany Sisters' First 100 Years* (1994)

Not only did the Delany sisters share an apartment when they first settled in Harlem; they were practically inseparable over the rest of their long lives. Both were graduates of Columbia University who became prominent professionals, and neither had "husbands to worry us to death." Bessie practiced dentistry and Sadie taught home economics at several schools. With wit, humor, and intelligence, the sisters often astounded listeners with their vivid recollections of their years in Harlem, particularly the glorious twenties and harrowing thirties. They combined their resourceful memories in the book *Having Our Say*, which was later adapted to the stage with a successful run. They lived long enough to enjoy several years of celebrity. Bessie, at 104, died in her sleep on September 25, 1995, and Sarah died in January 1999 at 109.

We made our first trip to New York City with our Mama in 1915. We took the train from Raleigh to Norfolk, then took a boat to New York, which cost us eight dollars each. The boat left Norfolk in the afternoon. We slept on cots on the open deck, and woke up just as the boat pulled into New York harbor.

Somebody asked us if we remembered seeing the Statue of Liberty as we pulled into the harbor. Tell you the truth, we didn't care too much about it. The Statue of

Liberty was important to white European immigrants. It was a symbol to them. We knew it wasn't meant for us.

On that first visit, we could not get over the size of New York. Papa had been there once, and had tried to describe it, but it was beyond our imagination. The bridges and buildings were on a massive scale compared to anything we had ever seen.

And there were so many different kinds of people, from all over the world. In North Carolina, there were white people, Negroes, and Indians. That was it. In New York, there were Irish people, German people, Jewish people, Italian people, and so on. So many different white people! And they ate different foods, and you could smell strange things cooking when you walked by people's apartments in the nice weather when their windows were open. And you'd hear these voices, speaking languages—well, you could only guess what exotic place they were from, and what they were saying.

You could buy anything in New York. We had thought we were so sophisticated, being from Raleigh, where you could get things like fruit from Florida shipped in by train. That was a big deal! But in New York, Raleigh seemed pretty small.

On that first trip we stayed with friends of the family for a few days, then we went home. But we wanted more! So when we returned to Raleigh, we talked to Papa about us moving to New York to attend college. Our brother Harry was already there, working as a Pullman porter, saving money to attend New York University. By then we were grown women, twenty-four and twenty-six years old, and toughened up by our rural teaching years. So when a Presbyterian minister asked Mama, "Aren't y'all afraid to let those girls go up to Harlem-town?" Mama said, "No, I'm not afraid to let my girls go anywhere. We've taught them right from wrong and if they don't do what's right, there's nothing we can do about it."

So we had Mama and Papa's blessing, sort of. Of the two of us, it was Sadie who made the move first, in 1916, followed by Bessie a year and a half later. Eventually, all of us Delany children, except Lemuel, moved to New York City.

Now, it was awfully hard to find an apartment in Harlem then. There were a lot of colored folks coming to Harlem at the same time, looking for a new life. So looking for an apartment was like a full-time job in itself. You'd have to go from one place to the next, and the super would say, "There's no room now, but come back next month and see." And you'd come back, but somebody had always beat you to the punch.

So, it was common for people to take in boarders. Our brothers were boarding over at the Williamses' house, and we Delany girls boarded with the Scotts. The Scotts were a West Indian family, rather well-to-do. Mr. Scott worked in a white bank, which was absolutely unheard of for a colored man in those days, but he was very light. Like many West Indians, Mrs. Scott was a follower of Marcus Garvey. She would drop whatever she was doing and run off to his parades and meetings.

A lot of the West Indian Negroes thought they were better than American Negroes, and the American Negroes thought they were better than the West Indian Negroes.

One thing about the West Indian Negroes at that time was that the ones who came to Harlem to go to school were a better class than the ones who came to get jobs. There was some silly tension.

Mrs. Scott had taken us in as a favor to Mrs. Russell, who lived across the street and ran a boardinghouse, only it was full. Mrs. Russell had been a pupil of Mama's. But Mr. Scott really didn't want us "boarders" living in his home, and so the whole time we lived at the Scotts we never once ate in the dining room. They made us eat in the kitchen. It wasn't ideal, but it was the best we could do.

Our brother Lucius was the first one of us to get an apartment and he let us all move in with him. So there we were—Sadie, Bessie, Julia, Hubert, and Lucius—living together in a three-room apartment at 2505 Seventh Avenue at the corner of 145th Street. This was in about 1919.

Our share of the rent was nine dollars each.

We were packed like sardines in that apartment, and the neighbors across the airshaft complained about us. They were colored people like ourselves. Well, they apparently had the idea these nice-looking colored girls were entertaining these nice-looking colored boys. They thought we were running a fast house! We don't know why it didn't occur to them that we were brothers and sisters, except they must have had unclean minds. So we had a little talk with the super and straightened out the whole mess.

On the ground floor of our building there was a butcher shop owned by Mr. Steinberg, who was a Jewish man. He was very encouraging to all of us Delanys. He would see us come and go to classes, or to our jobs, and he would say good-naturedly, "Now, hurry up! Don't be late!" He was very pleased that we were getting an education.

Poor Lucius! It was his apartment, but his sisters were the boss. Sadie was the oldest, and therefore the head of the household. It worked like this: When a decision had to be made, Sadie had the last word, but Bessie kept everybody in line. Now, Lucius was the best-looking one in the family. He was so good-looking the women would go crazy. And for a while, there was this girl who was flirting with Lucius who just about annoyed us all to death. She would ring the buzzer, and when we'd run down five flights of stairs from our apartment to open the door, there would be no one there. We finally figured it out, and Bessie straightened Lucius right out. She said, "Lucius, our Mama and our Papa trusted us to come live here. We must behave in an adult fashion. We must not let them down!" And Lucius listened. He was a good brother. That girl didn't come around anymore.

Still, it wasn't always easy living with our brothers. They would take our brand-new stockings and wear them on their heads at night, to straighten their hair. Ooohweee, did that ever make us mad!

The only brother who wouldn't mind us one bit was Manross, when he'd come to visit. He was stubborn as a mule. He took after Mr. Miliam, our white grandpa. He even looked like him, only he was colored and Mr. Miliam was white as a lily. If you tried to tell Manross what to do, he'd just stare at you.

Manross was in the ROTC at Shaw University in Raleigh, and the next thing we knew, he had gotten swept up into World War I. Funny thing about that war, it happened overseas but it created bloodshed among us here at home. A lot of white people did not think colored men would serve our country with dignity. They thought they'd be cowards. Well, they didn't know Manross!

Like Manross, all the colored veterans came back just as proud as they could be, strutting around Harlem and everywhere else in the country in their uniforms. Manross and his buddies thought they had proved themselves. They thought they would surely come home and be treated like citizens. Manross was very disappointed, because white folks sometimes gave him dirty looks or made nasty remarks when he'd wear his uniform. Manross said, "What more do I have to do to prove I'm an American, too?"

But a lot of white people were mad. They were saying, "Who do these colored boys think they are?" There were riots in Harlem, and lynchings in the South, because white people wanted to put us back in our place.

While this mess was going on, we just worked like dogs, trying to improve ourselves, and counting our blessings that we had the chance. As far as we were concerned, Harlem was as close to Heaven as we were going to find on this Earth.

BOYHOOD IN HARLEM

THOMAS C. FLEMING

From *Reflections on Black History,*
an unpublished memoir

When my father sent for me to join him in Harlem in 1916, he was working as a cook on a coastal freighter between New Haven and New York. He was glad to have me living with him. But most of the time he was traveling, and I couldn't stay in his apartment alone; I was too young to handle it. So he took me to a woman who kept children of working parents, and he boarded me out. About six black kids were living there, sleeping two in a bed. The woman put me in bed with a kid who had chicken pox, and I got it. There were a lot of poor people living in Harlem then, most of them working people. Most black men worked in service jobs—cooks, waiters, janitors, bootblacks. Harlem already had the largest black population of any city in the country, but I don't remember a single black bus driver, subway worker, street sweeper, or garbage collector. There might have been one or two.

In the three years that I attended public school in Harlem, I never saw a black teacher; they were all white. You did see a few black policemen and firemen, but they were so uncommon that everybody knew who they were.

Most black women worked as domestics—not only in New York, but all over the United States. Most of the time the women were more educated than the men. I think it's because the girls stayed at home longer, and listened to their mothers better. Boys often dropped out of school as low as the fourth or fifth grade, and some didn't go at all.

Harlem then had a lot of poor Italian immigrants, who were still arriving in large numbers, along with Jews and others from Eastern Europe, and a smattering of people from the Caribbean islands. As these groups came in, the middle-class whites started getting out.

Blacks lived primarily on the west side of Harlem, between Lenox Avenue and Seventh Avenue, and the Italians dominated the east side of Fifth Avenue, in East Harlem. Up above us, on Morningside Heights, was a large concentration of Irish.

I think most blacks realized they were segregated, because they were confined to living in that area. Not by any law, but because most property owners outside of that area would not rent or sell to them.

For self-protection, you had to be a member of a boys' gang in the block where you lived. It might be just for the kids on your side of the street, and right across the street might be a different gang. When you came out of the house, you generally stayed with your fellow gang members.

There were two rivers where you could swim in the summertime, the Harlem River on the east and the Hudson River on the west. The Harlem River was the better place, but between us and the swimming hole were the Italians. They didn't want us or the Irish coming through their territory. So we formed an alliance with the Irish gang. All the kids carried a stick or some other weapon, but not guns. When we crossed Fifth Avenue, here came all the Italian kids, armed the same way we were. We had to fight our way to the river. Some kids stayed on shore to keep the Italians back. We'd throw rocks at each other. They called us nigger, and we would shout, "Oh you guinea, oh you wop, oh you two-cent lollipop!"

THOMAS C.
FLEMING

WE RETURN FIGHTING

DAVID LEVERING LEWIS

From *When Harlem Was in Vogue* (1979)

With two Pulitzer Prizes on his mantel for his phenomenal
research on the life of W. E. B. Du Bois, David Levering Lewis
(1936–   ) has few peers in the realm of African-American history.
Long before he sat down to be totally consumed by Du Bois's gar-
gantuan achievements, Lewis devoted considerable time and
thought to the Harlem Renaissance. His *When Harlem Was in
Vogue* is deemed among the best books on the period, and this
vignette, in which he recalls the return of the Hell Fighters to
Harlem at the end of World War I, is excerpted from that work.

On a clear, sharp February morning in 1919, on New
York's Fifth Avenue, the men of the Fifteenth Regiment of
New York's National Guard marched home to Harlem.
Their valor under fire (191 unbroken days in the trenches)
was legendary. Almost as acclaimed were the triumphs of
their regimental band, under the command of Lieutenant
James Reese Europe. Big Jim Europe's band, its instru-
ments bought through a tin-can millionaire's generosity,
had conquered French, Belgian, and British audiences as
utterly as his regiment had overwhelmed Germans in
battle, leaving crowds delighted and critics mystified by
the wail and wah-wah of the "talking trumpet." (So much
so that when the proud, skilled musicians of France's

Garde Républicaine failed to reproduce these unique sounds, suspicious experts examined one of Europe's horns for some hidden valve or chamber. The logic-bound French concluded that the talking trumpet was a Negro anomaly, musical magic beyond their ken.) European fascination with jazz had started with Jim Europe's band. White America already remembered the band from times before the war, when it had teamed up with Vernon and Irene, the dancing Castles, to make dancing a national pastime and help, as preachers vainly fumed and Puritan parishioners unlimbered, to revolutionize the nation's mores.

But today, February 17, was no occasion for the syncopated beat of ragtime. Lieutenant Europe's men, with Bill "Bojangles" Robinson as regimental drum major, were playing martial music for a victory march, for a heroes' ascent through Manhattan to Harlem. Thirteen hundred black men and eighteen white officers moved in metronome step behind Colonel William Hayward, still limping from a wound suffered at Belleau Wood, out of Thirty-fourth Street into Fifth Avenue. They marched in the tight formation preferred by the French Army, a solid thirty-five-foot square of massed men, sergeants two paces in front of their platoons, lieutenants three paces ahead of sergeants, captains five paces ahead. They had been called "Hell Fighters" by the admiring French in whose 16th and 161st divisions they had served for almost ten months. Officially, they were still the United States's 369th Infantry Regiment, the only unit of the war allowed to fly a state flag, the only American unit awarded the

Croix de Guerre, and, as the French High Command's supreme mark of honor, the regiment chosen among all Allied forces to lead the march to the Rhine.

New York Mayor John F. Hylan was enjoying the sun in Palm Beach that day, and the city fathers had declined to proclaim an official holiday; but high-ranking dignitaries were present and most New Yorkers gave themselves the day off. "I just had to see these boys," one middle-aged white spectator told a reporter. "I never will get another opportunity to see such a sight, and I can get another job."

"Swinging up the Avenue," the New York Times front page reported, the men of the 369th "made a spectacle that . . . might explain why the Boches gave them the title of Blutlustige Schwarze Männer—bloodthirsty black men." Colonel Hayward and Lieutenant Europe (the sole Afro-American officer) were objects of special attention by the crowds, but the hero of the moment was a coal dealer from Albany, Sergeant Henry Johnson, the first American to win the Croix de Guerre. Running out of ammunition, Johnson had killed four of the enemy with a bolo knife and captured twenty-two. The Croix de Guerre (with star and palm) gleamed from the sergeant's tunic as he stood, waving graciously, in the open limousine provided by the city. "New Yorkers," the Times continued, "were mightily impressed by the magnificent appearance of these fighting men."

The staccato of leather on Fifth Avenue macadam rose and fell to the deafening counterpoint of applause. At 60th Street, the command of "eyes right" was given as the regiment passed the official reviewing stand. Governor and Mrs. Alfred E. Smith received the salute with appropriate expressions of gravity and pleasure, as did the secretary of state for New York, Francis Hugo, and Acting Mayor Moran. Representing Newton D. Baker, President Wilson's secretary of war, was Emmett Scott, special adviser on Afro-American affairs and the deceased Booker T. Washington's protégé. Rear Admiral Albert Gleaves and General Thomas Barry saluted briskly. Mr. and Mrs. William Randolph Hearst and department-store tycoon John Wanamaker applauded. That doyen of plutocrats, Henry Clay Frick, could be seen waving a flag from the window of his 73rd Street palace. From another window close by, Mrs. Vincent Astor and several society ladies waved these brave men along to their Harlem neighborhoods.

It was James Weldon Johnson, an official of the National Association for the Advancement of Colored People (NAACP), whose eye and pen gave the parade its best measure in the *New York Age*, one of Afro-America's leading newspapers:

The Fifteenth furnished the first sight that New York has had of seasoned soldiers in marching order. There was no militia smartness about their appearance; their "tin hats" were battered and rusty and the shiny newness worn off their bayonets, but they were men who had gone through the terrible hell of war and come back.

The tide of khaki and black turned west on 110th Street to Lenox Avenue, then north again into the heart of Harlem. At 125th Street, the coiled white rattlesnake insignia of the regiment hissed from thousands of lapels, bonnets, and windows. A field of pennants, flags, banners, and scarves thrashed about the soldiers like elephant grass in a gale, threatening to engulf them. In front of the unofficial reviewing stand at 130th Street, Europe's sixty-piece band broke into "Here Comes My Daddy" to the extravagant delight of the crowd. At this second platform, Harlem notables and returning heroes beheld each other with almost palpable elation and pride. No longer now in the dense, rapid-stepping formation learned from the French, ranks opened, gait loosened. "For the final mile or more of our parade," Major Arthur Little recalled, "about every fourth soldier of the ranks had a girl upon his arm—and we marched through Harlem singing and laughing."

Colonel Hayward shouted a command: the march halted. The Hell Fighters were home. They had come, as thousands of other returning Afro-American soldiers came, with a music, a lifestyle, and a dignity new to the nation—and soon to pervade it.

THE CLASS STRUGGLE

W. E. B. DU BOIS

From *W. E. B. Du Bois Reader* (1995)

No long introduction is necessary when discussing the scholarship and research of W. E. B. Du Bois (1868–1963); by any estimate it was prodigious and exhaustive. He lived a long and productive life, and nothing of significance occurred during his lifetime at which he didn't level a comment. Years before he adopted a communist outlook, he used the tools of Marxism to analyze social and political phenomena, as he does here in an article in *Crisis* magazine, the house organ of the NAACP, which he founded and edited.

Ten years ago [in 1911] the Negroes of New York City lived in hired tenement houses in Harlem, having gotten possession of them by paying higher rents than white tenants. If they had tried to escape these high rents and move into quarters where white laborers lived, the white laborers would have mobbed and murdered them. On the other hand, the white capitalists raised heaven and earth either to drive them out of Harlem or keep their rents high. Now between this devil and deep sea, what ought the Negro socialist or the Negro radical or, for that matter, the Negro conservative do? Manifestly there was only one thing for him to do, and that was to buy Harlem; but the buying of real estate calls for capital and credit, and the institutions that deal in capital and credit are capitalistic institutions.

If the Negro had begun to fight capital in Harlem, what capital was he fighting? If he fought capital as represented by white big real estate interests, he was wise; but he was also just as wise when he fought labor which insisted on segregating him in work and in residence.

If, on the other hand, he fought the accumulating capital in his own group, which was destined in the years 1915 to 1920 to pay down $5 million for real estate in Harlem, then he was slapping himself in his own face. Because either he must furnish capital for the buying of his own home, or rest naked in the slums and swamps. It is for this reason that there is today a strong movement in Harlem for a Negro bank, and a movement which is going soon to be successful. This Negro bank eventually is going to bring into cooperation and concentration the resources of fifty or sixty other Negro banks in the United States, and this aggregation of capital is going to be used to break the power of white capital in enslaving and exploiting the darker world.

Whether this is a program of socialism or capitalism does not concern us. It is the only program that means salvation to the Negro race. The main danger and the central question of the capitalistic development through which the Negro American group is forced to go is the question of the ultimate control of the capital which they must raise and use. If this capital is going to be controlled by a few men for their own benefit, then we are destined to suffer from our own capitalists exactly what we are suffering from white capitalists today. And while this is not a pleasant prospect, it is certainly no worse than the present actuality. If, on the other hand, because of our more democratic organization and our widespread inter-class sympathy we can introduce a more democratic control, taking advantage of what the white world is itself doing to introduce industrial democracy, then we may not only escape our present economic slavery but even guide and lead a distrait economic world.

W. E. B.
DU BOIS

23

WITNESS TO THE HARLEM RENAISSANCE

JAMES WELDON JOHNSON

From *Along This Way* (1933)

There are many books, reports, and eyewitness accounts of the Harlem Renaissance, but other than Langston Hughes, James Weldon Johnson (1871–1938) was clearly the most versatile of the period's numerous writers and artists. No matter the genre—essay, novel, short story, song lyrics, autobiography, or poetry—Johnson had few equals, black or white. His diverse interests and skills gave him the edge he needed to comment on the times and two of the era's most talked-about books.

The two books about Harlem that were most widely read and discussed were Carl Van Vechten's *Nigger Heaven* and Claude McKay's *Home to Harlem*. Mr. Van Vechten's novel ran through a score of editions, was published in most of the foreign languages, and aroused something of a national controversy. For directly opposite reasons, there were objections to the book by white and colored people. White objectors declared that the story was a Van Vechten fantasy; that they could not be expected to believe that there were intelligent, well-to-do Negroes in Harlem who lived their lives on the cultural level he described, or a fast set that gave at least a very good imitation of life in sophisticated white circles. Negro objectors declared that the book was a libel on the race, that the dissolute life and characters depicted by the author were non-existent. Both class of objectors were wrong, but their points of view can be understood.

Negro readers of the book who knew anything knew that dissolute modes of life and dissolute characters existed in Harlem; their objections were really based upon chagrin and resentment at the disclosures to a white public. Yet, Mr. McKay's book dealt with low levels of life, a lustier life, it is true, than the dissolute modes depicted by Mr. Van Vechten, but entirely unrelieved by any brighter lights; furthermore, Mr. McKay made no attempt to hold in check or disguise his abiding contempt for the Negro bourgeoisie and "upper class." Still, Home to Harlem met with no such criticism from Negroes as did Nigger Heaven. The lusty primitive life in Home to Harlem was based on truth, as were the dissolute modes of life in Nigger Heaven; but Mr. Van Vechten was the first well-known American novelist to include in a story a cultured Negro class without making it burlesque or without implying reservations and apologies.

Most of the Negroes who condemned Nigger Heaven did not read it; they were topped by the title. I don't think they would now be so sensitive about it; as the race progresses it will become less and less susceptible to hurts from such causes. Whatever the colored people thought about Nigger Heaven, speaking of the author as a man antagonistic to the race was entirely unwarranted. Carl Van Vechten had a warm interest in colored people before he ever saw Harlem. In the early days of the Negro literary and artistic movement, no one in the country did more to forward it than he accomplished in frequent magazine articles and by his many personal efforts in behalf of individual Negro writers and artists. Indeed, his regard for Negroes as a race is so close to being an affectionate one, that he is constantly joked about it by his most intimate friends. His most highly prized caricature of himself is one done by Covarrubias in black-face, and presented to him on his birthday. Mr. Van Vechten's birthday, that of young Alfred Knopf, and mine, fall on the same day of the same month. For four or five years we have been celebrating them jointly, together with a small group of friends. Last summer we celebrated at the country place of the Knopfs. In a conversation that Blanche Knopf, Lawrence Langner, and I were carrying on, something about the responsibility for children came up. Mr. Van Vechten interrupted Mrs. Knopf with an opinion of his own on the subject, to which she retorted, "Carl, you don't know anything about it, because you are not a parent." Mr. Van Vechten responded with, "You're mistaken; I am the father of four sons." And Alfred Knopf flashed out, "If you are, they must be the four Mills Brothers." Mr. Van Vechten joined in the outburst of laughter. From the first, my belief has held that *Nigger Heaven* is a fine novel.

THE GARVEY MOVEMENT

JOHN HENRIK CLARKE

From *Harlem USA* (1971)

For practically five decades Dr. John Henrik Clarke (1915–1998) was the doyen of black history and culture among the radical intellectuals, particularly those with a nationalistic tendency. From his arrival in Harlem in 1933 from Georgia, his vast knowledge on just about everything pertinent to the black world made him a popular speaker and sought-out adviser, which made his death all the more calamitous. Even so, he left behind volumes of material that will take scholars years to properly catalog. He had a thorough grasp of Marcus Garvey and his Universal Negro Improvement Association; what follows is a portion of it.

The early twenties was a time of great change and accomplishment in the Harlem community. It was a period when Harlem was literally "put on the map." Two events made this possible—a literary movement known as the Harlem Renaissance, and the arrival in Harlem of the magnetic and compelling personality, Marcus Garvey. Of the numerous black manassehs who presented themselves and their grandiose programs to the people of Harlem, Marcus Garvey was the most tempestuous and flamboyant. Garvey came to the United States from Jamaica, British West Indies, where he was born. He had grown up under a three-way color system—white, mulatto and black. Garvey's reaction to color prejudice and his search for a way to rise above it and lead his people back to Africa, spiritually if not physically, was the all-consuming passion of his existence.

Marcus Garvey's glorious, romantic and riotous movement exhorted black men to reclaim and rebuild their African homeland and heritage. Garvey came to the United States as a disciple of Booker T. Washington, founder of Tuskegee Institute. Unfortunately, Booker T. Washington died before Marcus Garvey reached this country. Garvey had planned to raise funds and return to Jamaica to establish an institution similar to Tuskegee. In 1914 he had organized the Universal Negro Improvement Association in Jamaica. After the failure of this organization, he looked to the United States, where he found a loyal group of followers willing to listen to his message.

Garvey succeeded in building a mass movement among American blacks while other leaders were attempting it and doubting that it could be done. He advocated the return to Africa of all people of African descent. To transport them from the United States, he organized, very rashly and incompetently, a steamship company called the Black Star Line. Garvey and his movement had a short and spectacular life span in the United States. His movement took really effective form in 1921, but by 1926 he was in a federal prison, charged with misusing the mails. From prison he was deported home to Jamaica. This is, briefly, the essence of the Garvey saga.

The self-proclaimed Provisional President of Africa never set foot on African soil. He spoke no African language. But Garvey managed to convey to members of the black race everywhere (and to the rest of the world) his passionate belief that Africa was the home of a civilization which had once been great and would be great again. When one takes into consideration the slenderness of Garvey's resources and the vast material forces, social conceptions and imperial interests which automatically sought to destroy him, his achievement remains one of the great propaganda miracles of this century.

Garvey's voice reverberated inside Africa itself. The King of Swaziland later told Mrs. Marcus Garvey that he knew the names of only two black men in the Western world: Jack Johnson, the boxer who defeated the white man Jim Jeffries, and Marcus Garvey. From his narrow vantage point in Harlem, Marcus Garvey became a world figure.

IN HIS OWN WORDS

From *The Philosophy and Opinions of Marcus Garvey,*
edited by Amy Jacques Garvey (1992)

In a book that captures the essence of his ideology and political outlook, Marcus Garvey (1887–1940) summarizes the events that preceded his arrival in the United States after the death of his mentor, Booker T. Washington; the founding of the Universal Negro Improvement Association and the Black Star Line; and some of the machinations of the district attorney's office to destroy him and his organization.

I got in touch with Booker Washington and told him what I wanted to do. He invited me to America and promised to speak with me in the Southern and other States to help my work. Although he died in the Fall of 1915, I made my arrangements and arrived in the United States on March 23, 1916.

Here I found a new and different problem. I immediately visited some of the then so-called Negro leaders, only to discover, after a close study of them, that they had no program, but were mere opportunists who were living off their so-called leadership while the poor people were groping in the dark. I traveled through thirty-eight States and everywhere found the same condition. I visited Tuskegee and paid my respects to the dead hero, Booker Washington, and then returned to New York, where I organized the New York division of the Universal Negro Improvement Association. After instructing the people in the aims and objects of the Association, I intended returning to Jamaica to perfect the Jamaica organization, but when we had enrolled about eight hundred or one thousand members in the Harlem district and had elected the officers, a few Negro politicians tried to turn the movement into a political club.

Seeing that these politicians were about to destroy my ideals, I had to fight to get them out of the organization. Then it was that I made my first political enemies in Harlem. They fought me until they smashed the first organization and reduced its membership to about fifty. I started again, and in two months built up a new organization of about 1,500 members. Again the politicians came and divided us into two factions. They took away all the books of the organization, its treasury and all its belongings. At that time I was only an organizer, for it was not then my intention to remain in America, but to return to Jamaica. The organization had its proper officers elected, and I was not an officer of the New York division, but President of the Jamaica branch.

On the second split in Harlem thirteen of the members conferred with me and requested me to become President for a time of the New York organization so as to save them from the politicians. I consented and was elected President. There then sprang up two factions, one led by the politicians with the books and the money, and the other led by me. My faction had no money. I placed at their disposal what money I had, opened an office for them, rented a meeting place, employed two women secretaries, went on the street of Harlem at night to speak for the movement. In three weeks more than two thousand new members joined. By this time I had the Association incorporated so as to prevent the other faction using the name, but in two weeks the politicians had stolen all the people's money and had smashed up their faction.

The organization under my Presidency grew by leaps and bounds. I started *The Negro World*. Being a journalist, I edited this paper free of cost for the Association, and worked for them without pay until November, 1920. I traveled all over the country for the Association at my own expense and established branches until in 1919 we had about thirty branches in different cities. By my writings and speeches we were able to build up a large organization of over two million by June, 1919, at which time we launched the program of the Black Star Line.

To have built up a new organization, which was not purely political, among Negroes in America was a wonderful feat, for the Negro politician does not allow any other kind of organization within his race to thrive. We succeeded, however, in making the Universal Negro Improvement Association so formidable in 1919 that we encountered more trouble from our political brethren. They sought the influence of the District Attorney's office of the County of New York to put us out of business. Edwin P. Kilroe, at that time an Assistant District Attorney, on the complaint of the Negro politicians, started to investigate us and the association. Mr. Kilroe would constantly and continuously call me to his office for investigation on extraneous matters without coming to the point. The result was that after the eighth or ninth time I wrote an article in our newspaper, *The Negro World*, against him. This was interpreted as a criminal libel, for which I was indicted and arrested, but subsequently dismissed on retracting what I had written.

During my many tilts with Mr. Kilroe, the question of the Black Star Line was discussed. He did not want us to have a line of ships. I told him that even as there was a White Star Line, we would have, irrespective of his wishes, a Black Star Line. On June 27, 1919, we incorporated the Black Star Line of Delaware, and in September we obtained a ship.

The following month (October) a man by the name of Tyler came to my office at 56 West 135th Street, New York City, and told me that Mr. Kilroe had sent him to "get me," and at once fired four shots at me from a .38-caliber revolver. He wounded me in the right leg and the right side of my scalp. I was taken to the Harlem Hospital, and he was arrested. The next day it was reported that he committed suicide in jail just before he was to be taken before a City Magistrate. . . .

SPRINGTIME IN HARLEM

ROI OTTLEY

From *New World A-Coming* (1943)

Roi Ottley (1906–1960) was a prominent African-American journalist who recycled his articles and research into a fabulous chronicle of Harlem's past from its beginnings to the middle of World War II. This chapter is taken from his book *New World A-Coming*, which, as he notes in the book's introduction, might have been better called *Inside Black America*. Ottley's keen sense of observation and colorful writing style evokes a Harlem in splendid bloom.

Negro life began to assume new dimensions in the decade following the First World War, which served to give Harlem its unique reputation. For everywhere there seemed to be gaiety, good feeling, and the sound of jazz, ushering in an era of incredible doings. The rhythm of life seemed to beat to the clink of glasses and the trump of drums. From the windows of countless apartments, against a glow of dull red lights, silhouetted figures rocked and rolled to mellow music. Harlem was dancing to the syncopations of Fletcher Henderson's band and listening to the moanin' low of Bessie Smith. Urchins were happily tricking dance steps on the sidewalks. Laughter was easy, loud.

Hundreds of honky-tonks prospered, and money seemed to flow from everyone's pockets as easily as laughter from their lips. Policy kings, hot-stuff vendors, and bootleggers were the peers of any man. Harlem's Imperial Elks Number 127 of the Independent, Benevolent, and Protective Order of Elks of the World erected a sumptuous clubhouse costing $300,000, and beturbaned A'Lelia Walker, daughter of a former laundress, startled the community with a "million dollar wedding"—actually costing forty thousand dollars.

Harlem had entered an era of noisy vitality. Much of what happened was stimulated by jazz, war, and easy money. The phenomenal boom in property values had made a few enterprising Negroes wealthy. Some real estate operators acquired large sums by the so-called "Negro-scare racket"—a scheme in which Negro tenants, none too prepossessing, were moved into fashionable neighborhoods where white people lived, with the result that the alarmed residents bid for the properties of these racketeers at outrageous prices.

Few Negroes traded in bigotry—most of them earned money the hard way. There was, for instance, Pig Foot Mary, huge and deep-voiced, who had trailed her migrant customers to Harlem. Early in the fall of 1901, she drifted into New York from the Mississippi Delta penniless, and within a week after her arrival set up a business in front of a popular San Juan Hill saloon. Mary, whose real name was Lillian Harris, after earning five dollars as a domestic, spent three for a dilapidated baby carriage and a large wash-boiler, and invested the balance in pigs' feet. Hot pigs' feet showed an immediate profit.

From early morning until late at night, swathed in starched checked gingham, she remained at this stand for sixteen years. Beyond two cotton dresses, her worldly goods were a mounting bank account. Mary was saving enough money, she often said, to purchase a place for herself in an old folks' home for respectable colored people. Concern about her old age vanished when she moved to Harlem, opened her business at 135th Street on Lenox Avenue, and three weeks later married John Dean, owner of an adjoining newsstand. He persuaded her to purchase a $44,000 apartment-house building, which she sold six years later to a Negro "underground specialist" (undertaker) for $72,000. Though unable to read or write, Pig Foot Mary became one of the community's shrewdest businesswomen. Her subsequent dealings in real estate brought her bank account up to $375,000—an ample sum for old-age security.

Substantial incomes were earned as well by prizefighters, who by and large had little concern about tomorrow. Lanky "Keed" Chocolate, a former Havana bootblack, dazzled Harlem with yellow automobiles, purple suits, and riotous living. Tiger Flowers, a Bible-totin' Baptist deacon, contributed lavishly to the collection plates of Negro churches. Harry Wills, the powerfully built "Black Panther," managed to get many lucrative matches by proclaiming the fact that the champion, Jack Dempsey, had drawn the color line. And there was free-spending Battling Siki, the clowning black Senegalese who stunned the boxing fans by beating the adored Georges Carpentier, and later startled blasé Paris by careening along the boulevards in a high-powered automobile with a lion tied to it. He showed up in the Negro capital to continue the revels begun in the cafes of Montmartre, finally meeting a violent death in Hell's Kitchen at the hands of white hoodlums.

Theatrical people, too, were large money-makers. Florence Mills, the graceful and beloved "Little Blackbird," delighted downtown audiences in *Dixie to Broadway*. The phonograph recordings of Bert Williams, a Ziegfeld star, still were best-sellers. Charles Gilpin, an intense brown man, once an elevator operator and trainer of pugilists, was acclaimed as the star of *The Emperor Jones;* while big Paul Robeson was appearing in *All God's Chillun Got Wings*, which had a decidedly controversial interracial theme. Roland Hayes, a sensitive and gifted tenor from Fisk University, had triumphantly mounted the concert stage. Bandmaster Lieutenant "Jim" Europe, a robust, bespectacled figure who had introduced jazz to war-weary Paris, was back and a popular figure at the Winter Garden with his Clef Club orchestra. And hardly had jazz assailed the ears of New York when jovial W. C. Handy arrived with a satchel of music that proved to be a new and popular motif. His "Yellow Dog Blues" and "St. Louis Blues" were sung by wailing blues singers in every dive, joint, and basement cabaret—places which, incidentally, did a bouncing business.

The Sugar Cane Club, operated by Edwin Smalls, today owner of Smalls' Paradise, was typical of the era's off-the-beaten-path joints. At the bottom of a steep flight of stairs at 135th Street and Fifth Avenue was a damp, dimly lit cellar, with two-dozen-odd tables surrounding a tiny dance floor. From one side a five-piece band beat out rhythms, while each player in turn would "take a Boston"—that is, execute some unexpected riffs. (None of the musicians could read music, nor did the lack of knowledge seem important.) To such music, the patrons, mostly Negroes, would stand and shuffle their feet—dancing on a dime, it was called—while others did the aptly titled bump and mess-around.

There also were the entertaining waiters, who, while they sang, threaded their incredible way through packed houses, twirling trays aloft, balancing them precariously on one or two fingers, while they danced skillfully between the tables; the journey ended, they executed a dexterous flourish of the tray, an intricate flurry of taps, and deposited a pitcher of raw gin before the customers. "Yeah, man!" Nights when business was lively the lights would be extinguished and a spotlight focused on a rotating mirrored chandelier which cast its myriad reflections across the features of Ethel Waters, who sang here before she became known to white audiences. Usually singing a down-to-earth blues, she would in an aloof yet personal manner give a double-entendre version in the colorful idiom of Harlem, as she moved from table to table, patting a cheek here, squeezing a hand there:

> Rent man waitin' for his forty dollars.
> Ain't got me but a dime and some bad news.
> Bartender, give me a bracer, double beer chaser,
> 'Cause I got the low-down, mean, rent man blues.

Negroes mostly sought their entertainment at house-rent parties, a distinctly Harlem innovation that became the vogue in other Black Belts of the country. Saturday night was the big night. Thursday night also was a favorite—"sleep-in" domestic workers usually had time off and were free to pitch and carry on, but found their small salaries inadequate for cabarets. Usually admission to house-rent parties was fifteen cents. What was spent once inside was another matter. A small bare room with a red glow for light served as the "ballroom," where the strenuous business of rug-cuttin' was performed. The only furniture was a piano from which a "box-beater" extracted close harmonies and "jump rhythms," or "gutbucket," which is now called boogie-woogie. In the kitchen pots of chitterlings and pigs' feet stood ready for the hungry revelers. A jug of corn was a staple for such affairs, sold at a makeshift bar in the hallway in half-of-a-half-pint portions called "shorties." Then there would be goings-on until daybreak, and rent next day for the landlord.

House-rent parties attracted a large transient trade, such as Pullman porters, interstate truck drivers, servants of footloose white folks, and innocent Negro tourists to the Black Metropolis. Additional business was promoted among that army of people who crowded the streets at night, seeking adventure and companionship in preference to remaining in dingy and ill-ventilated rooms. They found their way to these get-togethers through little business cards which were distributed by the "madams" to drum up trade. Only colored people were handed these "invitations," for during Prohibition any white face might be that of an enforcement agent; and moreover, the local police appeared more diligent in raiding these places, sometimes called "Buffet Flats," than known gin mills, or speakeasies, which flourished on almost every street corner. Here is a typical bit of doggerel sales talk:

There'll be brownskin mammas,
High yallers too,
And if you ain't got nothin' to do
Come on up to Mary Lou's.
There'll be plenty of pig feet
And lots of gin;
Jus' ring the bell
An' come on in.

A Barefoot Prophet, so called because winter and summer he strode the streets in bare feet, was a frequent house-rent party visitor. A towering man, with a luxuriant mane of white hair, a flowing beard, and a long heavenly robe, he was an eternal beacon along Harlem's highways. He, whose calling cards identified him as Elder Clayborn Martin, was a beloved figure in the community. This giant carried the "Word" to gin mill, cabaret, tavern, and poolroom. At the last place he often paused to shoot a game, quote a few passages of the Scriptures, and take up a collection, then disappear in the night.

His origin was obscure. Some said he came from Virginia. For more than fifty years, at any rate, he yearly wended his way from New York to Virginia, walking the entire distance. At an early age—he once told me after marking a cross on my forehead with ointment—he had received a divine message: "Take off your shoes, for this is Holy Ground. Go preach my gospel!" And he literally obeyed, preaching sermons that possessed almost a fable quality:

"Our world is like a fox, brethren, like a fox that catch his foot in the trap of the Devil. Fox knows, brethren, that if he stays long enough in the Devil's trap, the Devil will kill him with a long stick. So the fox gnaws off his foot, and leaves the foot for the Devil and goes home on three legs and praises God he's gittin' home at all. . . . Now, brethren, you see what I mean. We's got sin and we's got sinners, and better than that the sinners should lead us into the Devil's traps, we must cut them off. . . ."

As Prophet Martin lay dying in Harlem Hospital, at the age of eighty-six, he sent out his last call, pinned to a candy box and written in his own shaking hand: "Help Bury the Prophet." Hundreds heeded his last message.

Life in Harlem seemed to provide easy pickings, so that all the fabulous characters produced in Black America and elsewhere at one time or another descended on this happy hunting ground. The outlanders heard that gravy ran in the gutters and all one had to do was reach down and sop it up with biscuits. One of the arrivals, for instance, was Casper Holstein, a penniless immigrant, who became a prosperous "policy banker." From his income, he established a fund for yearly awards to outstanding Negro artists and writers, and contributed thousands of dollars for social welfare in his native Virgin Islands. His curious career was cut short by white gangsters who kidnapped him and extorted fifty thousand dollars. The impeccable Baron Wilkins, flashy gambler and cabaret host, was another importation. He moved his night club uptown from the Black Bohemia area and became wealthy in catering to the white-quality trade. If his origins were obscure, certainly his end was clear—he was sensationally shot to death by "Yellow" Charleston, a dope addict.

Until the police department, in one of its periodic drives of righteousness, brought to an end the unique entertainment in which black and white cavorted, the annual ball of the Hamilton Lodge of Odd Fellows was perhaps the most bizarre feature of the period. It was the sort of affair in which men dressed as women and women dressed as men and was usually held at Rockland Palace, a dance hall capable of holding eight thousand persons. These people, who packed the place, came from all sections of the country to walk in the fashion parade. Prizes were given to the best dressed. Negro and white men, bewigged, powdered, rouged, and wearing flowing gowns, competed without racial incident.

Harlem loves spectacles. In those days Aubrey Lyles, star of *Shuffle Along* and later *Runnin' Wild*, drove a long red automobile with solid ivory trimmings that made Negroes gasp. It was the first car seen in the community which had the comforts of a Pullman car. The back seat slid down to make a bed.

Behind the driver's seat were a bar and icebox. Somewhat later, Jules Bledsoe, who sang "Old Man River" in *Show Boat*, broke into the limelight with an expensive, high-powered motor, driven by a white chauffeur in livery. He explained to the complete satisfaction of Harlem, so Langston Hughes relates, that he had a white uniformed chauffeur so that the white public could tell which was the chauffeur and which the owner of the car.

The Black Metropolis was the *Vogue!* Stimulated by the contemporary craze for Negro jazz, Negro musical shows—*Shuffle Along* and *Runnin' Wild*—and Negro dances—Charleston and Black Bottom—many Bohemian whites made nightly sallies to the section. Carl Van Vechten contributed much to the community's reputation as a diverting hot spot with the publication of his novel, *Nigger Heaven*, which had considerable popularity in the twenties. But the section of Harlem that these people came to know was, after all, no more than a brown-skinned edition of life in New York—though perhaps more intense, literal, and noisy. White visitors to Harlem were in fact as much a part of the show as Negroes themselves, and much of the entertainment, at times unorthodox, was seasoned to suit their tastes.

Many night clubs catered to white patrons exclusively and, curiously enough, drew the color line. For example, Negroes were barred from the Cotton Club, the widely advertised "Aristocrat of Harlem." A pair of massive doormen stood at the entrance to reinforce the rule. On one occasion W. C. Handy, accompanied by Gene Buck of ASCAP, was barred admittance—this in spite of the fact that his music was the feature of the show. While few were wealthy enough to pay the club's exorbitant cover charge, Negroes still resented the restrictions; nor were they taken in by the distribution of Christmas baskets by the Cotton Club owners.

But the theatrical people aspired to appear there. For one thing, the club was famous for its high-yaller chorus; and so lucrative was it as a source of income that white girls often passed as light-complexioned Negroes to procure employment. It was here, too, that Duke Ellington and Cab Calloway made reputations as orchestra leaders.

National attention soon was focused on Harlem, and, to Negroes everywhere, the community became the symbol of opportunity. Wave after wave of migrants teemed into Harlem. The Black Metropolis was indeed coming of age. It had its own schools, newspapers and magazines, labor unions, hotels, hospitals, restaurants, churches, and a multitude of organizations and societies like the Elks and Masons. At first glance, Harlem gave the impression of being self-sufficient, a community unto itself. Actually, it was no more self-sufficient than it is today. Its people were dependent on the financial, commercial, and industrial arteries of the dominant white group for its very life's blood. It was this dependence, as well as economic and social restrictions, that helped to give Negro life its distinct character.

The spectacular Back-to-Africa Movement, which noisily explored the fascinating abstraction of an African utopia and stirred millions of Negroes to wild enthusiasm, was the high note of the period. It was led by the amazing Marcus Garvey, who preached with wonderful zeal of a Black House as opposed to a White House; a Black Congress as opposed to a White Congress; of Black Generals, Black Aristocracy, and a Black God, that swept Negroes along a mighty wave of Black Nationalism. Its mammoth meetings, colorful parades, gorgeous uniforms, and heavy rituals received amazing acclaim and caused Black America to pour its wartime earnings into the stupendous scheme of African redemption. By its operations the mind of the Negro is revealed in many of its subtle shadings and manifestations. If we get a grasp of this movement, a phenomenon that cannot be accounted for by purely intellectual processes, the realities of today are thrown into more searching perspective.

HARLEM IN THE SPOTLIGHT

HUBERT HARRISON

Excerpt from "Harlem's Neglected Opportunities:
Twin Sources of Gin and Genius, Poetry and Pajama Parties,"
Amsterdam News, November 30, 1927

Hubert Harrison (1883–1927) was deemed by many a "walking encyclopedia." Given his vast knowledge and varied interests, Harrison probably earned this reputation quite rightly. In Harlem's precincts he was unparalleled as a speaker, able to cite chapter and verse on political, philosophical, and literary affairs with accuracy and profundity. It was in radical politics that he truly shone, and the collection of essays compiled and edited by Professor Jeffrey Perry is a testament to his versatility and insight. In this excerpt, written near the end of his life, Harrison draws a bead on the negative features of Harlem, demanding more civic consciousness on the part of his neighbors.

Ever since the literary gents from Greenwich Village "discovered" Harlem as the twin source of gin and genius, poetry and pajama parties, the spotlight of publicity has been playing on it. But, as we see in the theatre, a spotlight often shows an object in false colors. And so it is with Negro Harlem, which is something of a cross between Hell's Half Acre and a Fool's Paradise. It is a modern community facing modern problems, and in it the germs of a modern social intelligence are afloat on the abyss—as elsewhere.

Some of its aspects are promising, while others are frankly depressing. In a later article I shall have much to tell of Harlem's splendid promise; in the present article I confine myself to those features that are "not so good" in the hope that we may bend our moral muscle to the task of collective self-improvement.

THE BUG IN THE QUEEN'S BED

The modern Harlemite lives in one of the most beautiful sections of New York, with spacious avenues, splendid apartments, wonderful theatres and all the social accessories that minister to comfort, self-respect and luxury. Yet he often reminds the critical outsider of the bug in the queen's bed who looks around at the manifold glories of period upholstery, snowy linen and gorgeous curtains and purrs contentedly: "See how elegantly I'm situated." But the poor bug had nothing to do with the grandeurs of which he boasts, and has to make himself very scarce when the chambermaid comes around. Despite our boasted advantages, it was left to Negro Harlem in the days immediately preceding the Elks' Convention to show the rest of Negro America that we have been lying down contentedly under a legal prohibition which, even in Richmond, Virginia, did not exist for Negro Elks. And it is generally known that the lack of hotels among us was primarily responsible for the fact that hundreds of Negro Elks were accommodated in certain large hotels downtown which will not ordinarily receive Negroes.

But the white man knows full well when and where the dollars drop. In fact, it is quite certain that white people made more money off the Elks' Convention than colored people did. And this was by no means the fault of the Elks' entertainment committee, but was due to general conditions in Harlem which indict us all equally.

Another curious feature of Harlem life is revealed when one observes the managers of such large-scale enterprises as exist in Harlem, the heads of the big social service institutions and most of the prominent leaders, have come from other cities—many of them quite recently.

Doubtless this is due in part to the fact that Harlem, like the rest of New York, is largely populated by people who were born elsewhere. But when one notes the manifest mutual envy, jealousy and hatred existing among Negroes and Negro groups in Harlem, one is tempted to attribute the phenomenon partly to that cause. I have heard it said, in places as far apart as Chicago and Lynchburg, that "Harlem Negroes hate each other harder than any other Negroes in the country."

CAN WE PULL TOGETHER?

The first duty which any community owes to itself is that of social cohesion, of collective sticking together, and it seems that in this respect Harlem is still neglecting one of its greatest opportunities. A public opinion is not always susceptible of statistical proof, or even of statistical preservation, but ten minutes' casual conversation with any Negro in Harlem will acquaint one with the general belief that we are backward in this respect. Some lay it to the inevitable social consequences of metropolitan life. "For safety's sake," they say, "you can't afford to be as friendly with people in a big city as in Chittling Switch, Mississippi." There is some truth to that. And yet—Chicago is a very big city.

Some have laid it to the diversity of origins of the Harlem population, which makes it hard for the West Indian to "understand" the American, for the Bostonian to sympathize with the Virginian, or for the New Yorker to properly appreciate the chap from Charleston. I have my own idea of the matter, and I give it here for what it may be worth.

As I see it, any population as marked as is the Negro obeys the law of social pressure in its formative stage. The convergent pressure from outside tends to make its units stick together, while the removal of that pressure makes them fly apart. The Jews in Europe and the Negroes in the South are cases in point.

Now, despite all our talk, the cities of New York and Boston are those in which the least pressure of prejudice is put upon the Negro masses. And those cities are precisely the ones in which the Negro, by himself, has accomplished least. The complete deduction is one which I would rather not draw. But many Harlemites have drawn it themselves.

EDUCATIONAL OPPORTUNITIES GOING TO WASTE

Whatever hatred we may nourish against the white man of the South for hindering us educationally, none of it will lie against the white man of New York. In South Carolina, $10.34 is spent annually for the education of each white child and $1.70 for the education of each colored child. In six counties of Georgia the annual cost of a Negro's education was, in 1915, 39 cents.

If the Negro from South Carolina or Georgia doesn't know his place in the world, he has a very good excuse. But the white man of New York offers to the Negro child as good an education as that offered the white child—and it is a free gift. Grammar school, high school and college are absolutely free. Evening schools and evening colleges are the same.

When the Negro's free college course is completed, he can start teaching in any school in the city. Six of my friends are teaching in high schools that I would call "white," but there are neither white nor black schools in New York—only public schools.

And what does the young Harlem Negro do with this wealth of opportunity? You can see him on any summer's night out on the sidewalk gyrating and contorting himself like a pet monkey, doing the "Charleston" or the "black bottom." The Jew overflows City College, while the Harlem Negro in whose very mouth the building is situated musters about twenty-five or thirty. Recently the Board of Education started enrolling students for an evening high school at P.S. 139 (in West 140th Street). The minimum required was five hundred. They enrolled 197. Naturally, they had to close down the school.

The Public Library recently acquired the Schomburg collection, a large number of books on every phase of Negro life, history, art and culture. Harlem's interest in it is so great that when a white man from Hungary wanted to talk with me, I took him there, because we would not be disturbed by anyone!

In order to draw people there, the librarian had transferred to that department newspapers, which many go up to read. At this point I must pay a tribute to the young Negro women of Harlem. They use the library (downstairs); they read and study, they go to high school in far greater numbers than the young men. What that promises for the future it isn't pleasant to contemplate.

In respect to music, I have space for just one remark: the College of the City of New York, through Professor Baldwin, furnishes every Sunday afternoon, from November to May, an organ recital which is attended by thousands of music lovers from all over the city. It is entirely free; it is within easy walking distance, just over the hill. Yet one never finds ten Negroes at any time.

NEGRO HARLEM AN ECONOMIC WASHOUT

In a business sense, Negro Harlem is peculiar. For all our bluff and bluster we have no Negro bank. Chicago has three. Negro business, for the most part, still goes on crutches—except for the undertaker, the barber, and perhaps the realtor, who is generally the economic jackal for the white real estate lion. Chicago has many streets full of Negro businesses. We have had no life insurance companies. Chicago's Negro not only organized and perfected several, but one of them has reached out and annexed New York as a business colony of Chicago. This annexation was celebrated by a big dinner in March at the Renaissance Casino. What Harlem needed was a day of mourning—but no one seemed to see that.

The banking situation is symbolic of the general economic situation. Some millions of Negro dollars are lent out by the white bank to white businessmen to perfect the strangle-hold of white business on the pockets of the community. So that, until a Negro bank arises in Harlem, the thrift of Harlemites becomes a means of harnessing them more hopelessly to the chariot wheels of white business.

In the meanwhile, our local attempts to organize large-scale businesses generally end in failure. From shoe store to department store they go down in disaster, while a half-hostile public looks on, grinning at the failure which its support might have changed to success.

In the long list of Harlem's neglected opportunities there is not one as tragic as this one of Negro business. Of course, it can be "explained." But one wonders whether, in this case, "explaining" helps us any.

While productive business struggles under such handicaps, the business that panders to ephemeral pleasure flourishes in our faces. They are the poolrooms, the night clubs and cabarets, the dance halls, the numbers, the Italian rum shops—all these make money for their proprietors.

HAVE WE A CIVIC SENSE?

The total picture is not, of course, all black. I am merely giving here the darker side of a civic reality. But these things are true. And, being true, it behooves us to give over bragging about things that were not contributed by us and get down to brass tacks. The small army (or shall I say company?) of homeowners constitute our best civic asset. But Brooklyn beats us hollow in that respect. And, after all, the development of a civic sense is a duty which devolves upon the entire community.

An illustration may help to make this clear: The beauty of Harlem's two main avenues, Seventh and Lenox, is largely the product of the trees, which serve to set them off during the summer months. Four years ago certain official Dogberries began to chop these trees down, first lopping off branches here and there and later laying the trees themselves low in spots. And in all that time not a word of protest has come from our local organizations, whether of rent-payers or homeowners. If there existed in Harlem even an embryonic civic consciousness, such a thing would have been challenged long ago.

And yet it is out of the development of a civic consciousness, of each citizen's organic relationship to the community and the community's responsibility for each citizen, that the Greater Harlem will arise. The newer Harlem will not neglect the opportunities which now lie around us on every hand, challenging the manhood within us to rise to the level of our social needs.

RINGTAIL

RUDOLPH FISHER

From *The Short Fiction of Rudolph Fisher,*
edited and introduced by Margaret Perry (1987)

"Ringtail" is a derisive term that was often combined with "monkey chaser" to insult West Indians who had migrated to Harlem in the 1920s. In many of his short stories, Rudolph Fisher (1897–1934) was very much concerned about the complexity of urban development in Harlem, especially the too often troubling social and political relations between different groups. In this short story he captures the low-intensity turmoil between African-Americans and the immigrants who came mainly from the British West Indies.

The pavement flashed like a river in the sun. Over it slowly moved the churches' disgorged multitudes, brilliant, deliberate, proud as a pageant, a tumult of reds and blues and greens, oranges, yellows, and browns; from a window above, outrageous, intriguing, like music full of exotic disharmonies; but closer, grating, repellent, like an orchestra tuning up: this big broad-faced, fawn-colored woman in her wide, flappy leghorn hat with a long cerise ribbon streaming down over its side, and a dress of maize georgette; or that poor scrawny black girl, bareheaded, her patches of hair captured in squares, her beaded cobalt frock girdled with a sash of scarlet satin. But whether you saw with pleasure or pity, you could have no doubt of the display. Harlem's Seventh Avenue was dressed in its Sunday clothes.[1]

And so was Cyril Sebastian Best. To him this promenade was the crest of the week's wave of pleasure. Here was show and swagger and strut, and in these he knew none could outvie him. Find if you could a suit of tan gabardine that curved in at the waist and flared at the hips so gracefully as his own; try to equal his wide wing-collar, with its polka-dot bow-tie matching the border of the kerchief in his breast pocket, or his heavy straw hat with its terraced crown and thick saucer-shaped brim, or his white buckskin shoes with their pea-green trimmings, or his silver-topped ebony cane. He challenged the Avenue and found no rival to answer.

Cyril Sebastian Best was a British West Indian. From one of the unheard-of islands he had come to Trinidad. From Trinidad, growing weary of coin-diving, he had sailed to Southampton as kitchen boy on a freighter, acquiring en route great skill in dodging the Irish cook's missiles and returning his compliments. From Southampton he had shipped in another freighter to New York under

---

1. Strolling was an integral part of life in Harlem, as described by James Weldon Johnson: "The masses of Harlem get a good deal of pleasure out of things far too simple for most other folks. In the evenings of summer and on Sundays they get lots of enjoyment out of strolling. Strolling is almost a lost art in New York; at least, in the manner in which it is so generally practiced in Harlem. Strolling in Harlem does not mean merely walking along Lenox or upper Seventh Avenue or 135th Street; it means that those streets are places for socializing. . . . One saunters along, he hails this one, exchanges a word or two with that one, stops for a short chat with the other one. . . . This is not simply going out for a walk; it is more like going out for adventure." *Black Manhattan* (New York: Atheneum, 1968), 162–63.

a cook from Barbados, a man who compunctionlessly regarded all flesh as fit for carving; and Cyril had found the blade of his own innate craftiness, though honed to a hair-splitting edge, no match for an unerringly aimed cleaver. The trip's termination had undoubtedly saved his life; its last twenty-four hours he had spent hiding from the cook, and when the ship had cast anchor he had jumped overboard at night, swimming two miles to shore. From those who picked him up exhausted and restored him to bodily comfort he had stolen what he could get and made his way into New York.

There were British West Indians in Harlem who would have told Cyril Sebastian Best flatly to his face that they despised him—that he would not have dared even address them in the islands; who frequently reproved their American friends for judging all West Indians by the Cyril Sebastian Best standard. There were others who, simply because he was a British West Indian, gathered him to their bosoms in that regardless warmth with which the outsider ever welcomes his like.

Among these latter, the more numerous, Cyril accordingly expended. His self-esteem, his craftiness, his contentiousness, his acquisitiveness, all became virtues, certainly not eliminating or modifying any of them. He became fond of denying that he was "colored," insisting that he was "a British subject," hence by implication unquestionably superior to any merely American Negro. And when two years of contact convinced him that the American Negro was characteristically neither self-esteemed nor crafty nor contentious nor acquisitive, in short was quite virtueless, his conscious superiority became downright contempt.

It was with no effort to conceal his personal excellence that Cyril Sebastian Best proceeded up Seventh Avenue. All this turnout was but his fitting background, his proper setting; it pleased him for no other reason than that it rendered him the more conscious of himself—a diamond surrounded with rhinestones. It did not occur to him as he swung along, flourishing his bright black cane, that any of the frequent frank stares or surreptitious second glances that fell upon him could have any origin other than admiration—envy, of course, as its companion in the cases of the men. That his cocky air could be comic, that the extremeness of his outfit could be ridiculous, that the contrast between his clothes and his complexion could cause a lip to curl—none of these far winds rippled the complacency of his ego. He had studied the fashion books carefully. Like them, he was incontrovertibly correct. Like them, again, he was incontrovertibly British; while these Harlemites were just American Negroes. And then, beyond and above all this, he was Cyril Sebastian Best.

The group of loud-laughing young men near the corner he was approaching had not regard for the Sabbath, appreciation for the splendor of Seventh Avenue, or respect for any particular person who might pass within earshot. Indeed, they derived as great a degree of pleasure out of the weekly display as did Cyril Sebastian Best, but of a quite different sort. Instead of joining the procession, they preferred assembling at some point in its course and "giving the crowd the once-over." They enjoyed exchanging loud comments upon the passers-by, the slightest quip provoking shouts of laughter; and they possessed certain stock subtleties which were always sure to elicit merriment, such as the whistled tune of "There she goes, there she goes, all dressed up in her Sunday clothes!" A really pretty girl usually won a surprised "Well, hush my mouth!" while a really pretty ankle always occasioned wild embraces of mock excitement.

An especially favored and carefully reserved trick was for one member of the group to push another into a stroller, the latter accomplice apologizing with elaborate deference, while the victim stood helpless between uncertainty and rage. In Harlem, however, an act of this kind required a modicum of selectivity. The group would never have attempted it on the heavy-set, walnut-visaged gentleman just passing, for all of his suede spats and crimson cravat; but when Cyril Sebastian Best lilted into view the temptation was beyond resistance.

"Push me!" Punch Anderson pleaded of his neighbor. "Not yet, Meg. Wait a minute. Now!"

The impact sent Cyril's cane capering toward the gutter; his hat described progressively narrower circles on the sidewalk; and before Punch could remove his own hat and frame his polite excuse Cyril's fulminant temper flashed. Some would have at least considered the possibility of innocent sincerity; others, wiser, would have said nothing, picked up their things, and passed on; but Cyril Sebastian Best reacted only to outraged vanity, and the resultant cloudburst of vituperation staggered even the well-informed Punch Anderson.

"Soft pedal, friend," he protested, grinning. "I'm apologizing, ain't I?"

More damnation. Epithets conceived over kitchen filth; curses born of the sea; worded fetor.

Punch's round-faced grin faded. He deliberately secured the West Indian's hat and cane and without a word handed them to him. Cyril snatched them out of Punch's hand as if from a leper and flung out a parting invective—a gem of obscenity. Punch's sense of humor died.

"Say that again, you black son of a simian, and somebody'll be holding an inquest over you!"

In the act of raising his hat to his head, Cyril said it again. Punch's fist went through the crown of the hat to reach the West Indian's face.

A minute later Cyril, tears streaming, polka-dot kerchief growing rapidly crimson with repeated application, was hurrying through the unbearable stares of gaping promenaders, while in his ears seethed the insult: "Now get the hell out o' here, you ringtail monkey-chaser!"[2]

II

The entrance of the Rosina wears an expression of unmistakable hauteur and you know it immediately to be one of the most arrogant of apartment houses. You need not stand on the opposite side of the Avenue and observe the disdain with which the Rosina looks down upon her neighbors. You have only to pass between her distinguishing gray-granite pillars with their protective, flanking grille-work and pause for a hesitant moment in the spacious hall beyond: the over-immaculate tiled floors, the stiff, paneled mahogany walls, the frigid lights in their crystalline fixtures, the supercilious palms, all ask you at once who you

---

2. Ringtail monkey-chaser: pejorative term for a West Indian, or someone from the tropics, who is dismissed even further by the expression ring-tail, which meant a criminal or, at least, a tramp.

are and what you want here. To reach the elevator you must make between two lordly, contemptuous wall-mirrors, which silently deride you and show you how out of place you are. If you are sufficiently courageous or obtuse, you gain the elevator and with growing discomfiture await the pleasure of the operator, who is just now occupied at the switchboard, listening in on some conversation that does not concern him. If you are sufficiently unimpressed or imprudent, you grumble or call aloud, and in that case you always eventually take to the stairs. Puff, blow, rage, and be damned. This is the Rosina. Who are you?

What more pleasurable occupation for Cyril Sebastian Best, then, than elevator and switchboard operator in the Rosina? If ever there was self-expression, this was it. He was the master of her halls, he was the incarnation of her spirit; in him her attitude became articulate—articulate with a Trinidadian accent, but distinctly intelligible, nonetheless. There were countless residents and their callers to be laughed at; there were endless silly phone-talks to be tapped at the switchboard; there were great mirrors before which he could be sure of the perfect trimness of his dapper gray-and-black uniform; there were relatively few passengers who absolutely required the use of the elevator, and most of those tipped well and frequently. It was a wonderful job.

Cyril's very conformity with his situation kept him ordinarily in the best of humor, the rendering of good service yielding him a certain satisfaction of his own. It was therefore with a considerable shock that one resident, flatteringly desirous, as she thought, of Cyril's aid in facilitating a connection, heard herself curtly answered, "Ah, tell de outside operator. Whaht you t'ink I keer?"—and that a familiar caller in the Rosina, upon being asked, "Whaht floor?" and answering pleasantly, "Third, as usual," heard himself rebuked with " 'As usual'! You t'ink I am a min-dreader, 'ey?"

Clearly Cyril Sebastian Best was in no obliging mood to-day.

Nothing amused, nothing even interested him: neither the complexion of the very dark girl who persisted in using too much rouge with an alarmingly cyanotic result, nor the leprously overpowered nose of the young lady who lived in fifty-nine and "passed" for white in her downtown position. He did not even grin at the pomposity of the big yellow preacher who, instead of purchasing ecclesiastic collars, simply put his lay ones on backward.

Cyril sat before the switchboard brooding, his memory raw with "monkey-chaser" and "ringtail." Now and then a transient spasm of passion contorted his features. In the intervals he was sullen and glum and absorbed in contemplated revenge.

"Cyril! Aren't you ever going to take me up? I'm starving to death!"

He looked up. Hilda Vogel's voice was too sweet, even in dissatisfaction, not to be heeded; and she was too pretty—fair, rougelessly rosy, with dimpled cheeks and elbows. How different from the picture just now in his mind!

Cyril had secret ambitions about Hilda. Like himself, she was foreign—from Bermuda; a far cry, to be sure, from Trinidad, but British just the same. And she was sympathetic. She laughed at his jests, she frankly complimented his neatness, she never froze his pleasantries with silence, nor sneered, nor put on airs. One day, during their frequent ascents, she had paused for as long as five minutes at her landing to listen to his description of the restaurant he was going to own someday soon. It couldn't be meaningless. She saw something in him. Why shouldn't he have ambitions about her?

"Cyril! How'd you hurt your lip?" she asked in the surprise of discovery as the car mounted.

Merely that she noticed elated him; but he would have bitten the lip off rather than tell her. "I bump' into de door doonsteers."

"Shame on you, Cyril. That's an old one. Do I look as dumb as that?"

He was silent for three floors.

"Goodness! It must have been something terrible. Oh well, if you ignore me—" And she began humming a ditty.

She had never been so personal before. Had his soul not been filled with bitterness, he might have betrayed some of those secret ambitions at once, right there between floors in the elevator. As it was, he was content with a saner resolution: he would ask permission to call Wednesday night. He was "off" Wednesdays.

"You soun' quite happy," he observed, to make an opening, as he slid back the gate at her floor.

"You said it!" she answered gaily, stepping out; and before he could follow his opening her dimples deepened, her eyes twinkled mysteriously, and she added, "I may be in love—you'd never know!" Then she vanished down the hallway with a laugh, while the speechless Cyril wondered what she could mean.

III

In the flat's largest room a half-dozen young men played poker around a dining-table. A spreading gas-dome of maroon-and-orange stained glass hung low over the table, purring softly, confining its whitish halo to the circle of players, and leaving in dimness the several witnesses who peered over their shoulders. One player was startlingly white, with a heavy rash of brown freckles and short kinky red hair. Another was almost black, with the hair of an Indian and the features of a Moor. The rest ranged between.

A phonograph in a corner finished its blatant "If You Don't I Know Who Will," and someone called for the "West Indian Blues."

"That reminds me, Punch," said Meg Minor over his cards. "Remember that monk you hit Sunday?"

"Never hit anybody on Sunday in my life," grinned Punch across the table. "I'm a Christian."

"Punch hit a monk? Good-night! There's gonna be some carvin' done."

"Name your flowers, Punch!"

"'Four Roses,' for Punch!"

Meg went on through the comments: "He's an elevator-boy at the Rosina up the Avenue."

"What'd you hit him for, Punch?"

"Deal me threes, Red," requested Punch, oblivious, while Meg told the others what had happened.

"Serves you right for actin' like a bunch of infants," judged Red. "Punch in the Post Office and you supposed to be studyin'—what the hell are you studyin' now, Meg?"

"Serves us right? It was the monk that got hit."

"Hmph! D'you think that's the end of it? Show me a

monk that won't try to get even and I'll swallow the Woolworth Building."

"Well, we were just feeling kind o' crazy and happened to meet up with that bunch of don't-give-a-kitty kids. It was fun, only—"

"Bet fifteen cents on these four bullets," said Punch.

"Call!"

"Call!"

"You stole the last pot, bluffin'," calculated Eight-Ball, nicknamed for his complexion's resemblance to the pool ball of that number. He tossed a blue chip into the growing pile.

"Have to protect my ante," decided his neighbor, resignedly.

"I'm a dutiful nephew, too," followed Meg.

Punch threw down three aces and a joker and reached for the pile of chips.

"Four bullets sure 'nough!"

"An' I had a full house!"

"The luck o' the Nigrish. Had a straight myself."

"Luck, hell. Them's the four bullets that monk's gonna put into him."

"Right. Get enough for a decent burial, Punch."

"Deal, friend," grinned the unruffled Punch. "I'm up."

"On the level, Punch," resumed Meg, "keep your eyes open. That little ape looks evil to me."

"Aw, he's harmless."

"There ain't no such thing as a harmless monkey-chaser," objected Red. "If you've done anything to him, he'll get you sooner or later. He can't help it—he's just made that way, like a spring."

"I ain't got a thing for a monk to do, anyhow," interjected a spectator. "Hope Marcus Garvey[3] takes 'em all back to Africa with him. He'll sure have a shipload.

Eight-Ball finished riffling the cards and began to distribute them carefully. "You jigs[4] are worse 'n ofays,"[5] he accused. "You raise hell about prejudice, and look at you—doin' just what you're raisin' hell over yourselves."

"Maybe so," Red rejoined, "but that don't make me like monks any better."

"What don't you like about 'em?"

"There ain't nothin' I do like about 'em. They're too damn conceited. They're too aggressive. They talk funny. They look funny—I can tell one the minute I see him. They're always startin' an argument an' they always want the last word. An' there's too many of 'em here."

"Yeah," Eight-Ball dryly rejoined. "An' they stick too close together an' get ahead too fast. They put it all over us in too many ways. We could stand 'em pretty well if it wasn't for that. Same as ofays an' Jews."

"Aw, can the dumb argument," said Meg. "Open for a nickel."

"Raise a nickel."

---

3. Marcus Garvey (1887–1940) was the major proponent and leader of the "Back to Africa" movement in the United States and later in England. Born in Jamaica, BWI, the group he headed and brought to fame was the Universal Negro Improvement Association. Many intellectuals derided Garvey, but his magnetic personality impressed the masses.

4. Jig: a black. A variant term for "boogy," which itself derives from a contraction of Booker T. Washington. Both terms were used by and of blacks only.

5. Ofay: a white. "Fay" is said to be the original term and "ofay" a contraction of "old" and "fay." [Ed.: Another interpretation concludes that "ofay" was derived from Pig Latin, a fun language among African-Americans that placed the emphasis on the first syllable of a word, put the word's first letter at the end, and added "ay." Thus, "foe," the enemy for black folks, became "ofay."]

"Who was the pretty pink you were dancin' with the other night, Punch?" inquired the observer behind him.

The lethargic Punch came to life. "Boy, wasn't she a sheba?[6] And I don't even know her name."

"Sheikin'[7] around some hey?"

"Nope. My sister Marian introduced me. But I'm so busy looking I don't catch the name, see? When I dance with her she finds out I don't know it and refuses to tell. I ask if I can come to see her and she says nothing doing—wouldn't think of letting a bird call who didn't even know her name."

"Really got you goin', hey?"

"Damn right, she did. I ask Marian her name afterwards and she won't come across either. Says she's promised not to tell and if I really want to locate the lady nothing'll stop me. Can y' beat it?"

"Why don't y' bribe Marian?"

"If you can bribe Marian I can be President."

"All right, heavy lover," interpolated Meg impatiently. "You in this game?"

Punch discovered then that he had discarded the three queens he had intended to keep, and had retained a deuce and a fivespot.

"Well, cut me in my neck!" he ejaculated. "Did you see what I did?"

The man behind him laughed. "Boy, you're just startin'," he said. "Wait till you locate the pink!"

The gloomy dinginess that dimmed the stuffy little front room of the Rosina's basement flat was offset not so much

---

6. Sheba: a queen of a woman; a real "good-looker."
7. Sheikin': chasing women; womanizing.

by the two or three one-bulb lights in surprisingly useless spots as by the glow of the argument, heated to incandescence. Payner, the house-superintendent, whose occupancy of these rooms constituted part of his salary, had not forgotten that he was a naturalized American of twenty years' standing, and no longer fresh from Montserrat; but Barbadian Gradyne had fallen fully into his native word-throttling, and Chester of Jamaica might have been chanting a loud response to prayer in the intervals when the others let his singsong have its say.

"No people become a great people," he now insisted, with his peculiar stressing of unaccented syllables, "except where it dominate. You t'ink de Negro ever dominate America? Pah!"

"Africa," Gradyne lumberingly supported him, "lot de only chance. Teng mo' years, mahn, dis Harl'm be jes like downg Georgia. Dis a white mahn's country!"

"Back to Africa!" snorted Payner. "Go on back, you b'ys. Me—I doan give a dahm f' all de Garveys an' all de Black Star liners[8] in Hell. I stay right here!"

"You t'ink only for you'self," charged Chester. "You t'ink about you' race an' you see I am right. Garvey is de Moses of his people."

"Maybe so. But I be dahm' if Moses git any my money.

---

8. Black Star liners: "Garvey made a four months' tour of the West Indies in a Black Star liner, gathering in many converts to the movement, but no freight for the vessel. Of course, the bubble burst. Neither Garvey nor any one with him knew how to operate ships. . . . So the Black Star Line . . . collapsed in December 1921. The Federal Government investigated Garvey's share-selling scheme and he was indicted and convicted on a charge of using the mails to defraud." (Johnson, Black Manhattan, 255–56).

Back to Africa! How de hell I'm goin' back where I never been?"

Neither Gradyne's retaliative cudgel nor Chester's answering thrust achieved its mark, for at that moment Cyril Sebastian Best broke unceremoniously in and announced: "De house is pinch!"⁹

Like a blast furnace's flame, the argument faded as swiftly as it had flared.

"Where you was raised, boy? Don't you got no manners a-tall?"

Cyril banged the door behind him, stuck out his chest, and strutted across the room. "I tell you whaht I hahve got," he grinned.

"A hell of a nerve," grunted Gradyne.

"An' I tell you whaht I'm goin' get," Cyril proceeded. "I'm goin' get rich an' I'm goin' get married."

"How much you pays, 'ey?" asked Chester.

"Pays? For whaht?"

"For you' licker. You's drunk as hell."

"Den I stays drunk all 'e time. I got de sweetes' woman in de worl', boy—make a preacher lay 'is Bible downg!"

"Who it is?"

"Never min' who is it." But he described Hilda Vogel with all the hyperbole of enthusiasm.

Gradyne inspected him quizzically. "Dat gel mus' got two glass eyes," he grinned.

"Or else you have," Payner amended.

"How you know she care anyt'ing about you?" Chester asked.

---

9. Pinch: a cheat.

"I know." Cyril was positive. "She tell me so dis ahfter-noon in de elevator. I been makin' time all along, see? So dis ahfternoon when I get to de top floor I jes' staht to pop de question an' she look at me an' roll 'er eyes like dis, an' say, 'I may be in love!' an' run like hell downg de hall laughin'! Boy, I know!"

Payner and Chester and Gradyne all looked at him with pitying sympathy. Then Chester laughed.

"You cahn't tell anything by that, mahn."

"I cahn't, 'ey? Why not?"

"You had de poor girl too far up in de air!"

IV

"Did you see the awful thing Harriet wore?"

"Did I? Who in the world made it?"

"Noah's grandmother."

"And that King Tut bob—at her age!"

"Maybe she's had monkey glands—"

Cyril, listening in at the switchboard, found it very uninteresting and leaving off, deigned to take up three passengers who had been waiting for five minutes in the elevator. When he reached the street floor again, the instrument's familiar rattle was calling him back.

"Apartment sixty-one, please."

Something in the masculine voice made Cyril stiffen, something more than the fact it sought connection with Hilda Vogel's apartment. He plugged in and rang.

"Can I speak to Miss Vogel, please?"

"This is Miss Vogel."

"Miss Hilda Vogel?"

"Yes."

The masculine voice laughed.

"Thought you'd given me the air, didn't you?"

"Who is it, please?" Cyril noted eagerness in Hilda's voice.

"Give you one guess."

"My, you're conceited."

"Got a right to be. I'm taking the queeniest sheba in Harlem to a show to-night, after which we're going to Happy's and get acquainted."

"Indeed? Why tell me about it?"

"You're the sheba."

Hilda laughed. "You don't lose any time, do you, Mr.—Punch?"

"I don't dare, Miss—Hilda."

Cyril, bristling attention, shivered. Despite its different tone, he knew the voice. A hot wave of memory swept congealingly over him; he felt like a raw egg dropped in boiling water.

"How did you find out I was—me?"

"Oho! Now it's your turn to wonder!"

"Tell me."

"Sure—when I see you."

"I think you're horrid."

"Why?"

"Well, I've got to let you come now or I'll die of curiosity."

"Dark eyes, but a bright mind. When do I save your life?"

"Are you sure you want to?"

"Am I talking to you?"

"You don't know a thing about me."

"More'n you know about me. I looked you up in *Who's Who!*"

"Now you're being horrid again. What did you find?"

"You work in the Model Shop on the Avenue, you live with your ma and pa, and you're too young and innocent to go around with only girls, sheikless and unprotected."

"How do you know I'm sheikless?" Cyril's heart stumbled.

"You're not—now," said the audacious Punch.

The girl gasped. Then, "You didn't find out the most important thing."

"To wit and namely?"

"Where I am from."

"Nope. I'm more interested in where you're going."

"We're—" she hesitated gravely. "I'm—Do you—object to—foreigners?"

It was Punch's gasp. "What?"

"There! You see, I told you you didn't want to come."

"What are you talking about?"

"We're—I'm a Bermudan, you know."

Punch's ringing laugh stabbed the eavesdropping ears. "I thought you were an Eskimo, the way you froze me that night."

"You're not—prejudiced?"

"Who, me? Say, one of the finest boys down at the P.O. is from Bermuda. Always raving about it. Says it's Heaven. Guess it's the place angels come from."

She was reassured. "Not angels. Onions."

"I like onions," said Punch.

"What time are you coming?"

"Right away! Now!"

"No. Eight."

"Seven!"

"Well—seven-thirty."

"Right."

"Good-bye."

"Not on your life. So long, Hilda."

"So long, Punch."

"Seven-thirty."

"Seven-thirty."

The lift was full of impatient people audibly complaining of the delay. The only response from the ordinarily defiant Cyril was a terrific banging open and shut of the gates as he let them out, floor by floor. His lips were inverted and pressed tightly together, so that his whole mouth bulged, and his little eyes were reddened between their narrowed lids.

"I may be in love—you'd never know." He had thought she was encouraging him. He would have made sure that next day had there not been too many people in the car. Fortunately enough, he saw now; for she had been thinking of the ruffian whose blow still rent his spirit, whose words still scalded his pride: "Now get the hell out o' here, you ringtail monkey-chaser!"

He had seen Counselor Absalom. Absalom had said he couldn't touch the casino witnesses, no money, prolonged litigation. Absalom hadn't even been sympathetic. Street brawls were rather beneath Absalom.

Cyril slammed the top gate and reversed the controlling lever. As the car began to drop, something startled him out of his grim abstraction: the gate was slowly sliding open. It had failed to catch, recoiling under the force with which he had shut it. Yet the car was moving normally. The safety device whereby motion was possible only when all the gates were shut had been rendered useless—perhaps by his own violence just now. He released the lever. The car halted. He pushed the lever down forward. The car ascended. He released it. The car halted again. He pushed the lever down backward. The car descended. Its movements were entirely unaffected.

Cyril paused, undecided. For a long moment he remained motionless. Then with a little grunt he rose again and carefully closed the open gate. His smile as he reached the ground floor was incarnate malevolence, triumphant.

V

Meg Minor was following a frizzly bobbed head and a bright-red sweater up the Avenue. In the twilight he wasn't sure he knew her; but even if he didn't—he might. Introductions were old stuff. If the spark of attraction gleamed, blow on it: you might kindle a blaze.

As he crossed a side street an ambulance suddenly leaped from nowhere and rushed at him with terrifying clangor. He jumped back, the driver swore loudly, and the machine swept around the corner into the direction Meg was going.

"Swore like he was sorry he didn't hit me," he grinned to himself. "Must be out making patients or something. Where's that danger signal I was pacing?"

The red sweater had stopped in the middle of the next block. So had the ambulance. When Meg reached the place, a gathering crowd was already beginning to obstruct passage. Since the sweater had halted, Meg saw no reason for going on himself, and so, edging as close to it as he could, he prayed that the forthcoming sight might make the girl faint into his arms.

He paid no attention to the growling buzz about him. There was a long wait. Then the buzz abruptly hushed and the crowd shifted, opening a lane to the ambulance. In the shift Meg, squirming still nearer to the red sweater, found himself on the edge of the lane.

Two men, one in white, came out of the house, bearing a stretcher covered with a blanket. As they passed, Meg, looking, felt his heart trip and his skin tingle. He stared forward.

"Punch! For God's sake—"

"Stand back, please!"

"It's Punch Anderson, Doc! What—what—is he—?" Meg pressed after the white coat. "Doc—good Lord, Doc—tell me what happened! He's my buddy, Doc!"

"Tried to hop a moving elevator. Both legs—compound fractures."

Doors slammed. The ambulance made off with a roar and a clamor. Meg stood still. He did not see the bright red sweater beside him or hear the girl asking if his friend would live. He was staring with mingled bewilderment and horror into the resplendent entrance of the Rosina. And, as he stared, the sound of the ambulance gong came back to his ears, peal upon peal, ever more distant, like receding derisive laughter.

NIGHTS AT THE COTTON CLUB

DUKE ELLINGTON

From *Music Is My Mistress* (1973)

Edward Kennedy Ellington (1899–1974) is best known as the Duke, and he carried the name with all the elegance and style the title implied. He was an extraordinary musician who left countless compositions to the American treasury of song. Harlem was always a special place for this native of Washington, D.C., and in several memorable ways he helped to extend the community's legend and legacy during his days at the Cotton Club, which he evokes here.

So far as we were concerned, the engagement at the Cotton Club was of the utmost significance, because as a result of its radio wire we were heard nationally and internationally. In 1929 we appeared simultaneously at the Cotton Club and in Florenz Ziegfeld's *Show Girl*, which had a Gershwin score and introduced "An American in Paris" and "Liza." This was valuable in terms of both experience and prestige. The following year, Irving Mills succeeded in arranging for us to accompany Maurice Chevalier at the Fulton Theatre and play a concert selection of our compositions. This was about the only time I ever used a baton! In 1930, too, we went to Hollywood to appear in *Check and Double Check*, a film featuring the then-popular radio team of Amos 'n' Andy. The big song in it was "Three Little Words" by Harry Ruby and Bert Kalmar, but an instrumental of mine called "Ring Dem Bells" also became very popular. It was taken up by other bands, and for a considerable time it was a much-requested item. We hired Cab Calloway's band to play for us in the Cotton Club while we were away. We were going out to make some money, and the condition under which we could go was that we paid him.

Later that year, in the fall, we had a six-piece recording date. Mills never lost his liking for the original small-combo sound, even when the big band had made its mark. On this occasion, as usual, the night before was the time for me to write and think music. I already had three tunes and, while waiting for my mother to finish cooking dinner, I began to write a fourth. In fifteen minutes, I wrote the score for "Mood Indigo." We recorded it, and that night at the Cotton Club, when it was almost time for our broadcast, Ted Husing, the announcer, asked, "Duke, what are we going to play tonight?" I told him about the new number, and we played it on the air, six pieces out of the eleven-piece band. The next day, wads of mail came in raving about the new tune, so Irving Mills put a lyric on it, and royalties are still coming in for my evening's work more than forty years later. Husing, incidentally, was a beautiful cat with an up-to-the-minute awareness then known as "hip." He was radio's number-one announcer, and he did a great deal for us.

When we had made "Black and Tan Fantasy" with the growl trombone and growl trumpet, there was a sympa-thetic vibration or mike tone. That was soon after they had first started electrical recording. "Maybe if I spread those notes over a certain distance," I said to myself, "the mike tone will take a specific place or a specific interval in there." It came off, and gave that illusion, because "Mood Indigo"—the way it's done—creates an illusion. To give it a little additional luster for those people who remember it from years ago, we play it with the bass clarinet down at the bottom instead of the ordinary clarinet, and they always feel it is exactly the way it was forty years ago.

The Cotton Club was a classy spot. Impeccable behavior was demanded in the room while the show was on. If someone was talking loud while Leitha Hill, for example, was singing, the waiter would come and touch him on the shoulder. If that didn't do it, the captain would come over and admonish him politely. Then the headwaiter would remind him that he had been cautioned. After that, if the loud talker still continued, somebody would come and throw him out.

The club was upstairs on the second floor of the northeast corner of 142nd Street and Lenox Avenue. Underneath it was what was originally the Douglas Theatre, which later became the Golden Gate Ballroom. The upstairs room had been planned as a dance hall, but for a time the former heavyweight champion, Jack Johnson, had run it as the Club De Luxe. It was a big cabaret in those days, and it would seat four to five hundred people. When a new corporation took it over in the twenties, Lew Leslie was put in charge of producing the shows, and the house band was led by Andy Preer, who died in 1927.

Sunday night in the Cotton Club was the night. All the big New York stars in town, no matter where they were playing, showed up at the Cotton Club to take bows. Dan

Healy was the man who staged the shows in our time, and on Sunday night he was the MC who introduced the stars. Somebody like Sophie Tucker would stand up, and we'd play her song "Some of These Days" as she made her way up the floor for a bow. It was all done in pretty grand style.

Harlem had a tremendous reputation in those days, and it was a very colorful place. It was an attraction like Chinatown was in San Francisco. "When you go to New York," people said, "you mustn't miss going to Harlem!" The Cotton Club became famous nationally because of our transcontinental broadcast almost every night. A little later, something similar happened with Fatha Hines at the Grand Terrace in Chicago. But in Harlem, the Cotton Club was the top place to go.

The performers were paid high salaries, and the prices for the customers were high too. They had about twelve dancing girls and eight show girls, and they were all beautiful chicks. They used to dress so well! On Sunday nights, when celebrities filled the joint, they would rush out of the dressing room after the show in all their finery. Every time they went by, the stars and the rich people would be saying, "My, who is that?" They were tremendous representatives, and I'm darned if I know what happened to them, because you don't see anybody around like that nowadays. They were absolutely beautiful chicks, but the whole scene seems to have disappeared.

The nucleus of the band was the group I had had at the Kentucky Club. Harry Carney had joined us during the summer, and he went in with us. We also had Ellsworth Reynolds, a violinist who was supposed to be the conductor, but he really wasn't as experienced in show business as we were after playing all those shows downtown in the Kentucky Club. So I started to direct the band from the piano, without baton or any of that stuff, for I understood what they were doing more than anyone else in the band.

The music for the shows was being written by Jimmy McHugh with lyrics by Dorothy Fields. Later came Harold Arlen and that great lyric writer, Ted Koehler. They wrote some wonderful material, but this was show music and mostly popular songs. Sometimes they would use numbers that I wrote, and it would be these we played between shows and on the broadcasts. I wrote "The Mystery Song" for the Step Brothers in rehearsal. It was part of their act, not part of the show. The different acts were presented individually as well as in the ensemble. After the Step Brothers came the Berry Brothers, and later on the Nicholas Brothers.

Sometimes I wonder what my music would sound like today had I not been exposed to the sounds and overall climate created by all the wonderful and very sensitive and soulful people who were the singers, dancers, musicians, and actors in Harlem when I first came there.

During the Prohibition period, you could always buy good whiskey from somebody in the Cotton Club. They used to have what they called Chicken Cock. It was in a bottle in a can, and the can was sealed. It cost something like ten to fourteen dollars a pint. That was when I used to drink whiskey as though it were water. It seemed so weak to me after the twenty-one-year-old corn we had been accustomed to drinking down in Virginia. That was strong enough to move a train, but I paid no attention to this New York liquor. I just drank it, never got drunk, and nothing ever happened.

The episodes of the gangster era were never a healthy subject for discussion. People would ask me if I knew so-and-so. "Hell, no," I'd answer. "I don't know him." The homicide squad would send for me every few weeks to go down. "Hey, Duke, you didn't know so-and-so, did you?" they would ask. "No," I'd say. But I knew all of them, because a lot of them used to hang out in the Kentucky Club, and by the time I got to the Cotton Club, things were really happening!

DUKE
ELLINGTON

THE HARLEM RENS

ARTHUR ASHE JR.

From *A Hard Road to Glory* (1988)

Besides being a superb athlete, Arthur Ashe (1943–1993) was one of the most learned men in sports, demonstrating his scholarship and writing skills in a popular autobiography and in a series of books chronicling the achievements of black athletes. The Harlem Rens is among the teams Ashe profiles in his comprehensive study of black sports in the nineteenth and twentieth centuries.

The two stellar men's squads—the New York Renaissance Big Five and the Harlem Globetrotters—came from New York City and Chicago, respectively. This came as no surprise since these cities' public school, club, YMCA, church, American Legion, and college teams were nationally recognized. It so happened that the rise and subsequent demise of these squads as basketball powerhouses fell almost neatly between the two World Wars.

The New York Renaissance, better known as the Rens, began as the Spartan Braves of Brooklyn. The Spartan Braves became the Spartan Five, and later still became the Rens in 1923. The Braves had joined New York City's Metropolitan Basketball Association (MBA) but the MBA in 1922 ordered the Braves to suspend Frank Forties and Leon Monde for a violation. The Spartans refused and were fined. The following year—the same year the YMCA held its first national event—the Braves' owner, Robert J. Douglas, took Forties and added four others to form the Rens. It was the first full-salaried, black professional basketball team.

Full credit must go to Douglas, who is now referred to as the father of black basketball. His keen eye for talent and sound business acumen enabled his squad to survive until the late 1940s. He was born on the Caribbean island of St. Kitts in 1885, and had brought with him to America those traits of perseverance and hard work that so typified the black West Indian immigrants. A. S. "Doc" Young went so far as to say that "never before, or since, in American sports history has an all-Negro team operated by Negroes earned the national acclaim that accrued to the Rens."

The Rens' first starting five were Hilton Slocum, Frank Forties, Hy Monte, Zack Anderson, and Harold Mayers. The team got its name from Harlem's Renaissance Ballroom on 135th Street and Seventh Avenue. To show they were to be taken seriously, the Rens won their debut game, 28 to 22, against the Collegiate Big Five on November 3, 1923. They finished the season with a 15–8 record.

The Rens soon had little difficulty finding opponents. Their main black rivals were the Harlem Globetrotters, the Chicago Hottentots with Joe Lillard, the Chicago Collegians, the Chicago Studebakers, and the Savoy Big Five. Other opponents included the Celtics, the Philadelphia Sphas, the Detroit Eagles, and the Akron Firestones. The most intense games were those against the Globetrotters and the Celtics. In the past such rivalries often led to violence on the court between teams. Before the rules changes of the 1930s and 1940s, play was often plodding. There was a jump ball after every basket, and everyone clogged the middle.

There was also heavy betting, poor officiating, and selfishness. Douglas saw this shortcoming early and insisted his players perform more like a team, with strict adherence to discipline and the good of the team over that of the individual. Things had gotten so out of hand earlier that the *Chicago Defender* editorialized for a change. "The first thing to be done to help make this game one of the cleanest and best played and liked of games," it said, "is to cut out some of the rough stuff. . . . Another big fault is gallery playing and what might be termed as clique playing. Players . . . sent into the game have been refused the opportunity to handle the ball. . . . The biggest and most important of all things is choice of referees."

The *New York Age* was just as adamant: "Some teams began to fight among themselves. By the end of the 1921 season, basketball in this city was in an unhealthy condition, although from outward appearances, the game was never more popular, or the clubs more prosperous." The Rens tried to compensate with teamwork. Noted the late Rens player Eyre "Bruiser" Saitch, "We didn't even have a coach! We didn't have positions; we played the man." He further claimed that after playing together so often, it was easier for the same five players to adjust one another. A man's position on the team in those days mattered less than now. A center—now the tallest player on a team— was so named in the 1920s only because he was used to jump-center at the beginning of a play. After that, positions made little difference.

Saitch did, however, deplore the necessity to combine the social with the athletic. A highly skilled athlete, he wanted to see the game stand on its own, but that never came to pass in the 1920s. "We had to have a dance afterwards or nobody would come to the damn thing . . . the Renaissance [Ballroom] was right across the street from The Red Rooster [nightclub]. . . . If you didn't get there by seven o'clock, you didn't get in the damn door. The big game didn't start until ten o'clock." Such was the case in the socio-athletic milieu of the nation's black cultural capital during the Harlem Renaissance period of the 1920s.

SONNET TO A NEGRO IN HARLEM

HELENE JOHNSON

From *The Norton Anthology of African American Literature,*
edited by Henry Louis Gates, et al. (1997)

Though she is vastly overshadowed by the literary contributions of her cousin Dorothy West, Helene Johnson (1906–1995) was a lyrical poet with a distinct sensuality and a muted sense of race pride. Her published works were few, but they fully disclose her ability to evoke powerful, personable images. A native of Boston, Johnson came to Harlem in 1926 and published a number of poems in the leading journals of the day.

You are disdainful and magnificent—
Your perfect body and your pompous gait,
Your dark eyes flashing solemnly with hate,
Small wonder that you are incompetent
To imitate those whom you despise—
Your shoulders towering high above the throng,
Your head thrown back in rich, barbaric song,
Palm trees and mangoes stretched before your eyes.
Let others toil and sweat for labor's sake
And wring from grasping hands their meed of gold.
Why urge ahead your supercilious feet?
Scorn will efface each footprint that you make.
I love your laughter arrogant and bold.
You are too splendid for this city street.

ON "GLORIA SWANSON"

BRUCE NUGENT

From *Gay Rebel of the Harlem Renaissance:
Selections from the Work of Richard Bruce Nugent,*
edited by Thomas Wirth (2002)

According to Thomas Wirth, an independent scholar, publisher, and bibliophile who has devoted years of tireless love rescuing Bruce Nugent from obscurity, "Nugent was a significant figure during the Harlem Renaissance." He composed a number of poignant vignettes while working for the Federal Writers' Project in the late 1930s. "Gloria Swanson" is among this collection, and Nugent found in Mr. Winston someone who came close to his own openly gay position during a time when such revelations were not in vogue. Nugent (1906–1987) was a versatile artist whose paintings, poems, and illustrations made him a popular favorite among what he termed the "niggerati." He was also a talented actor who performed in several notable plays of his day.

When "Gloria Swanson" came to New York and became one of the most popular "hostesses" to be found in any of the nightclubs, he had already left behind a colorful career in Chicago. Mr. Winston, who had adopted the name of the glamorous Gloria Swanson as his own, had been a darling of the underworld and sporting element in the Windy City. In 1928 he was hostess at the "Book Store," a speakeasy-nightclub which immediately grew in popularity once he became known as a permanent fixture there.

"Gloria" had been a perennial winner at the "drags" in Chicago. His net and sequin evening gowns were well-known, habitual and expected. As a matter of fact, there were very few persons who had ever seen him in male attire at all. Seldom coming on the street in the daytime, breakfasting when the rest of the world was dining, dining when the rest of the world was taking its final snooze before arising for the day, his public life was lived in evening gowns, his private life in boa-trimmed negligees. Prohibition was at its most successfully unsuccessful, crime was at its peak, graft was the order of the day, and life was lived at a highly accelerated pace. Winston—plump, jolly, and bawdy, with a pleasant "whiskey" voice, his every gesture and mannerism more feminine than those of any female, his corsets pushing his plumpness into a swelling and well-modeled bosom, his chocolate-brown complexion beautiful, and his skin soft and well cared for—was just the sort of playmate for the fast-living element.

He had the free, loud camaraderie that distinguished the famous Texas Guinan. Gangsters and hoodlums, pimps and gamblers, whores and entertainers showered him with feminine geegaws, spoke of him as "her," and quite enthusiastically relegated him to the female's function of supplying good times and entertainment. He could also cook.

His "Book Store" was a rendezvous protected by the fact that his "protector" was a big shot—a well-known underworld figure. All went well until his "boyfriend" had a fit of jealousy—a tantrum of violence during which he practically wrecked the joint. After that, all protection ceased. The police began raiding the place, but even that novelty began to wear thin, and soon it was no longer the same pleasure spot it had been before.

So "Gloria" came to New York, where he had little trouble in finding employment in a popular cellar night spot on 134th Street in Harlem. There he reigned regally, entertaining with his hail-fellow-well-met freedom, so perfect a woman that frequently clients came and left never suspecting his true sex. He sang bawdy parodies and danced a little, all very casually and quite impersonally, lifting modestly to just above the knee his perennial net and sequins or his velvet-trimmed evening-gown skirts, displaying with professional coyness a length of silk-clad limb.

He had come to New York at a time when male and female impersonation was at a peak as nightclub entertainment. Jean Malin was the toast of the notorious gangster "Legs" Diamond's Club Abby; the Ubangi Club had a chorus of singing, dancing, beribboned and berouged "pansies," and Gladys Bentley, who dressed in male evening attire, sang and accompanied herself on the piano; the well-liked Jackie Mabley, one of Harlem's favorite black-faced comediennes, habitually wore men's street attire; the famous Hamilton Lodge "drag" balls were becoming more and more notorious; and gender was becoming more and more conjectural. "Gloria Swanson"—with her loud, friendly expansiveness, her "boyfriends," furs, and evening gowns, her ever-ready wit and lace-draped apartment—easily became and remained queen of them all.

Remained queen, that is, until Mayor La Guardia's police began to object to the sexes confusing the less sophisticated denizens of New York with such indiscriminate interchange of habiliment and behavior.

"Gloria's" admirers could not even recognize "her" in

the masquerade forced upon him by this sudden tightening of the law. And masquerade of the most successful and impenetrable sort it most certainly was when "Gloria" wore male attire. Then, "never raining but it pours," the erstwhile glamorous "Gloria" became ill. The illness put an end to his attempt to readjust himself to the constriction forced upon his talents, and "she" was forced to withdraw from public life altogether.

THE ABYSSINIAN BAPTIST CHURCH

ADAM CLAYTON POWELL JR.

From *Adam by Adam:*
The Autobiography of Adam Clayton Powell Jr. (1994)

No name is as revered in the history of Harlem as Adam Clayton Powell Jr. (1908–1972). Nor is any church as famous as the Abyssinian Baptist Church, of which he was the pastor. The two are inextricably joined. Here Powell recalls a portion of the church's significant legacy and the role he assumed upon his father's retirement.

As early as 1911 my father caught the Harlem vision. Few Negroes then lived in Harlem; most were still concentrated in the Forties downtown. My father recognized that the restless push of business along Broadway and Seventh and Eighth Avenues in the Forties would eventually squeeze the Negro people out, and they would have to move uptown because there was no place between 40th Street and 135th Street where they were wanted or would be allowed to live.

A black leader had caught this same dream before my father. He was Marcus Garvey, the semiliterate, short, squat, heavyset Jamaican who, on his arrival in Harlem in 1914, said, "Where are your black lawyers? Where are your black judges? Where are your black mayors? Let us proceed now to set up a black empire in the United States." He immediately set up a Black United States within the

United States of America. He was the Black President and he had a Black Vice President, Black Cabinet, Black Congress, Black Army with Black Generals, Black Cross Nurses, a Black newspaper called *The Negro World*, a steamship line called the Black Star Line, and a Black religion with a Black God. Negroes all over the South and in the West Indies began to say, "Let's go to Harlem to see this Black Moses." Marcus Garvey was the first man to ever make "black" Negroes proud of their color.

One of the greatest thrills of my life when I was about ten or twelve years old was to sit at Garvey's feet, or roll down Seventh Avenue with him as he paraded in his white-plumed hat. But he was railroaded to prison in the United States, railroaded to prison in London via an agreement with the British government after his term was finished in the United States, and he died of a broken heart in London. But today if you go to Jamaica you will see in Queen Victoria Park a statue of Queen Victoria— and staring her straight in the face is a statue of the first hero of the Jamaican Republic, Marcus Garvey.

Father kept pushing to make the Abyssinian Church Harlem-minded. At last, when I was scarcely twelve years old, the church purchased land on 138th Street between Seventh and Lenox Avenues, and there, next door to Marcus Garvey's Black Freedom Hall, Daddy pitched his tent. For two summers, under that canvas, thousands were packed in every night as he preached. The membership of the church jumped to four thousand; tithing money increased to $35,000 a year; the regular offerings doubled. The Harlem push had picked up momentum.

In those days, from 137th to 138th Streets, and from

Seventh to Lenox Avenues, there was a farm where I played as a ten- and eleven-year-old. An Italian squatter lived on the hill on Seventh Avenue, and from the hill to Lenox Avenue he farmed, producing fresh vegetables that he sold in the neighboring community. He also kept a herd of goats. On the land the church later bought he allowed us to play baseball. One day when my father came to watch us play ball, he said, "This is the spot upon which I want to build our church!" And upon that rock he did build the church. Up to this time no Negro church in the United States had cost $100,000 except the Union Baptist Church of Philadelphia. Yet, on that rock my father built a church that cost almost $340,000. It was built of rock, steel, brass, and marble. Mr. P. was indeed quite a man!

On the first Monday in July 1922, the editor of the religious department of the *New York Journal-American*, Mr. Joseph Gilbert, wrote: "Work on what will be the largest Baptist Church in the country is now under way on 138th Street between Seventh and Lenox Avenues."

I helped to clear the land upon which the first tent was pitched. The land was cleared by volunteers from the church, and while they worked the ladies served them food. I ran back and forth with a pail of lemonade to refresh them as they toiled under the hot sun. Though still a boy, I helped to drive the first peg that put the guys of the tent in place. I stood by my father as the masons laid the cornerstone. I helped plan the gymnasium of the community center. Every step of the way I was part of the building of that Tudor-Gothic structure, even to running downstairs sometimes, late at night, to throw the switches that turned off lights the sexton had left burning. This was my church. It was my eternal mother.

On June 17, 1923, the new buildings on 138th Street near Seventh Avenue were completed at a cost of $334,881.86. The insurance today on these buildings is more than $1 million.

At one time sixty thousand dollars was needed to pay off the balance of the indebtedness. John D. Rockefeller Jr., a staunch Baptist and the major contributor to the Riverside Baptist Church, agreed to give the entire amount, but on condition that one member of the Board of Trustees be appointed by him. My father brought this news back to the United Boards of the church, which turned it down unanimously. Within four and a half years the church was free and clear of any mortgage and also from any outside control.

The church and the community center were too small from the first day they opened. The church was built of solid rock, Italian marble, windows imported from Germany and England. The community center, built as part of the main building, was packed from basement gymnasium to rooftop, morning and night, throughout the week.

Long before the concept of Social Security had been introduced by Franklin D. Roosevelt's New Deal, the Abyssinian Church bought and furnished a white limestone townhouse at a cost of forty thousand dollars. It was dedicated on July 4, 1926. Here all members of the church, when they were no longer able to work or support themselves, could live out their old age free of charge.

The church became so affluent that it was able to give one thousand dollars a year to the National Baptist Foreign

Missions Board; one thousand dollars to the building of the Medical Center in New York City; two thousand dollars to Virginia Union University; four thousand dollars to Fisk University; one thousand dollars to Tuskegee and Hampton. Nor did any new church ever come to Harlem to buy or to build without receiving a large financial gift from our church.

A school of religious education, set up under the supervision of Columbia University, included teacher-training as well as weekday and Sunday religious education classes. Adult education provided elementary English, citizenship, designing, dressmaking, home nursing, and business courses, and the famous school of dramatic arts directed by Richard B. Harrison, "De Lawd" of [the Broadway play] *The Green Pastures.*

When my father received the Harmon Award in January 1928, for notable achievement in religious service, Herbert Hoover, then President of the United States, sent him a personal letter of congratulation.

In September 1937, my father resigned and was named pastor emeritus with a pension for life. Under the ministry of my father, during his twenty-nine years the church budget, originally $6,000, was increased to $55,000; under my father's ministry and mine the original indebtedness of $146,000 was converted to the present assets of $400,000; the original membership was seven hundred, the present membership twelve thousand.

Because of the inauguration of two Sunday morning services early in my ministry, I was preaching to twice the number of people my father had reached. So many people passed through the community center, now named after my father, that a dean of theology from a West Coast university said, "You don't have to tell me that you work here. I can look at your floor, your walls, and your furniture and see that it is used."

We have never had enough room. Soon after I became pastor I closed down the ten-room penthouse apartment on the top floor of the church, turning it over to community activities. Within one week, that too was overcrowded. Social Security had by now been born and I asked the church to place our home for the aged, the white limestone townhouse, on the market because there were no more applicants. Rather than encumber the church with purchasing a house for the minister to live in, I asked the accountants to figure out the average yearly expense for maintaining a parsonage over the previous ten years and accepted that in lieu of a parsonage.

The Abyssinian Baptist Church reached another milestone early in 1961 when we finalized plans for the purchase of three YMCA buildings adjacent to the church, at a cost of approximately half a million dollars.

No important Negro has come to Harlem from any of the far corners of the earth without being honored at the Abyssinian Baptist Church. When Haile Selassie, Emperor of Ethiopia, came to the United States for the first time and decorated President Eisenhower, I also was decorated. The Emperor gave the Abyssinian Church, through me, a solid-gold seven-foot Coptic cross; the gold alone is worth twenty thousand dollars. The President of Liberia, the President of Haiti, the Acting President of Indonesia have worshiped in our auditorium. Before Ghana was known to the world, a young black seaman sailing in the

Merchant Marine and shipping out of New York visited the church. His name was Kwame Nkrumah, and he later became Prime Minister of that young country. Dr. Agokiane, who became a leading political figure in Nigeria, ofttimes worked with me back in the 1930s, worshiping in church and helping to picket stores that were not practicing democracy.

In November 1983, the Abyssinian Baptist Church will celebrate a hundred and seventy-five years of service to its people. I will be marking my seventy-fifth birthday. And as long as He is willing, we'll celebrate together as we have most Sundays since 1937.

THE HARLEM FOX

J. RAYMOND JONES

From *The Harlem Fox,* with John Walter (1989)

Professor John Walter has done a splendid job of taking memoir and interviews with the subject and breathing new life into a politician who was known as "the Harlem Fox." J. Raymond Jones (1899–1991) was never exactly sure why they called him the Fox, but it may have been a tribute to his ability to wangle all sorts of political concessions for his community. Equally shrewd and politically adept was Benjamin Davis, fondly recalled by the Fox. This piece reveals the confluence of mainstream and leftist politics that often coexisted in Harlem.

[Benjamin] Davis followed to a remarkable degree in the early footsteps of Adam Clayton Powell, because Powell, in his initial campaigns, enjoyed Communist support, breaking with them only after he was well entrenched in Congress. Powell's decision not to run for the City Council in 1943 gave Davis the opportunity to participate in electoral politics in New York City. In that year, Davis handily won a City Council seat, backed by the Communist Party, which was very popular in Harlem at that time. The Party had gone to great lengths stressing interracial harmony within its ranks, and proposing the possibility for an American future without discrimination, with Communism as the dominant ideology. A Black person could be whatever he or she wished to be. These claims were given much credence, for the Party had done a great job of propaganda with its defense of the Scottsboro Boys from 1932 on. Everybody knew of the Alabama case, and though the boys were represented by the International Legal Defense, everyone knew the Defense was an arm of the Communist Party.

In the City Council, Davis worked assiduously for his constituency. In fact, by 1947 he was already something of a folk hero, and in the same year he began to experience difficulties with the newspapers because of his Communist affiliation. Two years later he was arrested on the charge of conspiracy to overthrow the government of the United States. Although everyone knew this was a trumped-up charge, the kind injudiciously thrown at known Communists in those days, the Democratic Party and the Harlem leadership had to do something. I had supported Davis in 1943 and in 1945, but in 1947 I had him change his registration to Democrat to get my support. But the situation had radically changed in 1949. Now, because of growing anticommunism, the Mayor was against him, the Governor disliked him, and even Tammany Hall had abandoned him. In this environment I, too, had to withdraw my support. The question now became, Who can we run against him? Davis, a bona fide folk hero and an articulate politician, had an impeccable voting record. What was to be done?

Since by 1945 I was well entrenched in the leadership of Tammany Hall, and since next to Adam Powell I was considered one of the most powerful leaders in Harlem, the job fell to me to devise some means to defeat Davis at the polls in 1949. So into this drama I placed one of my own boys, Earl Brown. Like Davis, Brown was a Harvard man, except that Brown had attended Harvard College, and Davis, Harvard Law School. Brown, a Kentuckian, was also a southerner like Davis. After Harvard, Davis worked as a journalist for the Black newspaper, the *Amsterdam News*, and for a while as a reporter for *Life* magazine. Although I knew we would have to groom Brown, write his speeches, coach him, do everything, I thought he had a good chance to defeat Davis.

While I was planning the campaign, the City Council made every effort to expel Davis since by then he had been convicted in the courts for conspiracy. The City Council expelled him in the early fall of 1949, but the expulsion occurred before the election, in which he still had every right to run and campaign. Republican Governor [Thomas] Dewey, famous former prosecutor, did not want to have what he called "the stigma of Communism" in the hallways of government, and not surprisingly so, considering that his sights were again set on the White House, even after Truman's win.

We knew Brown could not win without the backing of Republicans, so we decided to make him a sort of fusion candidate. This was not such a farfetched idea in a situation like this because only four years before La Guardia had left office, and he had been essentially a fusion candidate throughout his career. We discussed the question of Republican support for Earl Brown with David B. Costume, the Republican New York County Leader, who said he had to check with Governor Dewey. He reported later that the Governor did not support the nomination of Earl Brown. He was not opposed to a fusion candidate, but he objected to Earl Brown because of Brown's constant criticism of his administration. Carmine DeSapio and I knew that Earl had criticized Governor Dewey, but we could not let the Governor's objection block Brown's election. We had to convince the Governor that he was objecting to the wrong Brown. At that time in Harlem there was another Brown, a street-corner orator from Chicago, whose first name I do not recall. His very fluent and most articulate orations, along with his well-clipped goatee, earned him the name "Billy Goat Brown." Since Earl had reported in the *Amsterdam News* on Billy Goat Brown's antics, we convinced Costume that the Governor must have confused the two and thought that our Earl Brown was giving him the business. This seemed reasonable to Governor Dewey and he endorsed our man.

All seemed set, but when we began exercises to ascertain the political potential of Mr. Brown, we found that not only was he unable to write a political speech, but he was also unable to deliver one with any élan, although he was a Harvard graduate and an editor of the *Amsterdam News*. So to the brilliant writer and Carver Club member Dr. J. Dayton Brooks fell the responsibility of writing speeches for Earl Brown. Since it had taken us so long to get the fusion coordinated, we began our campaign rather late, sometime in October. With elections in November, we had a very short, telescoped campaign.

Early in October, Earl Brown had occasion to go to California, and early one morning, around two o'clock or so, he awakened me with a call from Los Angeles. I wondered what bothered him so to call me at this hour. Brown was incoherent and I could not make head or tail of what he was talking about, but I got the impression that he had learned that somebody found something on him that would damage him in the campaign. He couldn't tell me what it was and left me in a quandary. "All right," I said, "when you know what is happening, let me know."

The next morning I began to worry seriously as my doubts about Earl intensified. I knew he was a compulsive gambler. I used to play cards with Edward Dudley, and a man about town in Harlem named Dick Thomas, and Brown himself, and I had noticed from time to time that Brown was not averse to playing a trick or two with the cards. I knew also that he favored the race tracks. I knew he always carried a tote sheet, bet regularly on the horses, and met the bookies in the morning before he went to the track. He was usually in debt to them. This I knew because he told us so.

That same morning I called in Dick Thomas, who always seemed to know everything, and asked him, "What is wrong with Brown?" He answered, "Ray, it's my fault. Benjamin Davis," he said, "told me that Vito Marcantonio was handling a contract with the Police Department to get Brown's record." Of course, I was stunned because I did not know what kind of problems Brown had. I didn't think they were anything really serious, but even a record of his gambling would have been enough to damage severely the campaign. Thomas told me that the police were not going to pass the information over to Vito, who was at that time the Communist Congressman from Harlem, until a better bid was made for it. I did not know what to do, so I went to see O'Dwyer and explained the problem. O'Dwyer was outraged that the Police

Department was involved with this kind of nonsense, and, being a man of action, picked up the phone right then and there to call the Chief Inspector. He told him in no uncertain terms that this sort of thing was absolutely against the law, against all rules and regulations, and as nominal chief of the Police Department, he would not stand for it. Anybody found to be involved in that sort of thing would be punished immediately. He then ordered an immediate investigation.

Later I learned that one detective had accepted money to compile damaging information on Earl Brown. When he discovered we knew of his activities, he decided to make amends right away. He sensed that he was in serious trouble. He confessed to the Mayor's investigator that he had taken some money to do this job, and needed to give the money back if he was to avoid being hurt by his outside employers. We could have left it at this, but we thought better of it, and decided it would be best if he were punished by the Police Department in the regular way. We sought the five hundred dollars for him to return to his "employers," and luckily were supported by a prominent, wealthy benefactor, eager to displace the Communists in Harlem, who had promised money to the Earl Brown campaign. All this was accomplished in a couple of days. About two days later, Brown returned from California and learned from his friend Dick Thomas that the heat was off.

In the meantime, Benjamin Davis became increasingly upset, because the information he expected to be out on Earl Brown was not forthcoming. He complained to Dick Thomas who promptly came to me and asked what I had done. Of course, I smiled and told him nothing. But Earl Brown, displaying a short memory and feeling confident, was making the rounds to collect his hard-earned campaign contributions. Inevitably, of course, he wound up on the benefactor's doorstep and was promptly told that his contribution had been given to me! That was a mistake, for Brown came raving into the Carver Club asking why I had stolen his money. I was nonplussed, but it soon became obvious that he was referring to the money that had saved his career. I should have laughed at the irony of the scene, but Brown was so angry he left no room for humor. Collis Crocker, my secretary, sensing that Brown was endangering himself, quickly grabbed him by the shoulders and hustled him out of my office. When it was all over, Crocker returned and said: "This is a situation where we should put as much distance as possible between us and that man." Brown was elected to the City Council that fall with a three-to-one majority, but as far as I was concerned he was no longer one of my people.

Brown's election in 1949 began an odd career which ended up satisfactorily for him, I suspect, but which would have caused me great psychological damage had I been in his shoes. He remained on the City Council until 1958, when he made the severe mistake of siding with the Tammany leadership of Carmine DeSapio against Adam Clayton Powell. It was this ironic development that caused my return to politics. I simply could not resist the chance to teach all of them, Brown, DeSapio, and the Tammany leadership, a severe political lesson.

OUR HARLEM

OSSIE DAVIS AND RUBY DEE

From *With Ossie and Ruby: In This Life Together* (1998)

**Ossie Davis (1917–) and Ruby Dee (1924–) are virtually in-
separable, and it was a good plan to have them combine their
thoughts and memories in a dual autobiography (joined at the
spine?). As they do throughout the book, the two take turns
here, offering their separate but related portraits of a community they helped define in the same way it defined them. In this
segment Ruby, a native of Harlem, is preparing to graduate
from junior high school; Ossie, a newcomer fresh from Georgia,
is fascinated by the charity of Father Divine.**

RUBY'S HARLEM

Harlem defined us, claiming our consciousness and, I
suspect, our subconsciousness. It was a place where pain
was understood without explanation; where joy was an
undercurrent when it wasn't loud and raucous; where
spirit was tested, and knowledge grew up through the
cement; where danger got its pulse and peace passed
understanding. Overcoming was the name of the game.
We plunged into the hot middle of things when picking
around the cool edges got tiresome. There we could
holler on the street corner without necessarily getting
locked up; ideas could find wings and maybe fly. There
love was perched to refuel on redemption.

In Harlem, the gangsters, after their fashion, looked after the neighborhoods where they lived and sent their children to school until Dutch Schultz and the Cosa Nostra bumped them off and left the streets exposed. It was where pimps, politicians, and crooks counted on the guileless-ness and the yearning, the trust and the hope of the people.

Right then, though, the diploma meant that it was time to get out of the house, and to acquaint our lungs and our brains with a different kind of air. I had not grown up thinking of Harlem as a "ghetto" or "slum." I didn't know those words. I didn't even think of it as an enclave of seg-regation, despite all the evidence of brutality and injustice that noisied up the atmosphere and people's lives.

Many years were to pass before I learned how many people had joined forces to split the cocoon that sent us nine wriggling, wide-eyed girls out of Harlem and into the big white world and other wider definitions of ourselves.

Most of the girls who graduated from junior high schools in neighborhoods like Harlem went to Julia Rich-mond, Wadleigh, or industrial or commercial high schools. They were good schools, but they didn't offer the demand-ing academic curriculum, nor did they have Hunter High School's reputation for providing direct access to Hunter College.

It so happened, however, that Mrs. Madelyn Hender-son, the mother of my friend Carlotta, felt that the chil-dren of Harlem were being shortchanged. She had a master's degree in clinical psychology and taught men-tally challenged children in the Little Italy section of New York City. Although fair-skinned, she never denied being black, but her associates considered her to be one of them, and so she often fielded slurs and innuendos about colored people. Active in the NAACP and the Urban League, she would form a group of children and take them downtown to solicit memberships and donations on the streets. Small wonder that she became president of the Parent Teacher Association at P.S. 136.

The fact that inner-city children were being shunted to less demanding schools impelled her to do something about it. She encouraged teachers and parents to insist on the right to compete for admission to the best schools available. Why not make it possible for students at P.S. 136 to take the entrance examination for Hunter High, a school known for its academic rigor, excellence, and concern? Surely those students on the rapid track, who had finished junior high in two rather than three years, should automatically take the test. I was among those students in the rapid classes.

OSSIE'S HARLEM

One such potential black messiah was Father Divine. He had a great big Heaven, as he called his establishments, on 126th Street, where a man could get a good meal for twenty-five cents. That's where we went first.

Father Divine was, in many ways, the exact opposite of Marcus Garvey. He was strictly non-militant, not deigning to confront the white man or anybody else. Rumor had it that Father Divine was God. Father refused to affirm or deny it. He did not come into the world to ask the question, but to provide the answer. And the answer was peace. He brought redemption to the sinner by completely ignoring the sin, but without all the sweat and frenzy.

There were several of Father's Heavens all over Harlem. They were clean, warm, neat, and full of angels proudly but quietly scurrying about their Father's business. The one on 126th Street was the second largest one. We made it our business to have dinner at one of the Heavens, not only because of the food, but even more so because of the pageantry.

In the midst of the Depression, when the U.S. government was trying to minister to the basic needs of the people, Father Divine proved a shining example of how to do it. He managed to feed the people and provide them with a clean, safe place to stay, but also he changed their lives, inside and out, for the better. His cult was not mysterious or mumbo jumbo; it was open for everyone's inspection. Loving Father Divine was about as easy as pie. Everybody in Harlem dropped in once in a while. Fiorello La Guardia, the mayor of the city of New York, was glad to visit with Father, and so was Eleanor Roosevelt.

The faithful would begin to pour into the restaurant in the late afternoon to wait for the arrival of Father, which was sure to take place before midnight. Also present were the curious, the voyeurs. . . .

There was usually a piano, and most every evening, a different somebody would be there plunking on the keys. Sometimes, a second talent would come in, have dinner, then join the piano player with his clarinet, trumpet, or sax. He'd play for a while and then be on his way to his gig. Men and women were forbidden to dance together, but nobody stopped you if you felt like taking the floor by yourself.

Often by ten o'clock at night, the place would be jammed. Then suddenly a tremor would run from corner to corner, signaling that Father was close by. Everything and everybody would stop in their tracks. The restaurant would be closed and all attention shifted to the main dining room, centered with a long table upon which twenty to thirty settings—plates with their gleaming crystal, linen, and silverware—were already in place. Officers, members, dignitaries, and staff, fluttering like nervous pigeons, would hurry themselves to the doorway. A few minutes more, then a furious joy would find tongue. People would be asked to kindly make way, and Father Divine, accompanied by Mother Divine, a young white woman from Canada whom Father had made his bride, would enter the room. Father would swiftly move to the head of the table, take his seat, and that was the signal for bedlam.

One serving plate after another—chicken, lamb, pork, beef, followed by rice, white potatoes, sweet potatoes, greens, peas, beans, and more—would be set in front of Father. He'd put a little, a very little, from each plate on his dish, then pass the plate to his left, and thus it would move around the table until its contents were gone. . . .

UPON ARRIVING IN HARLEM

GORDON PARKS SR.

From *A Choice of Weapons* (1965)

In the early 1930s, Gordon Parks (1912–   ) dropped a nickel in the
subway slot, boarded the A train to Harlem, and got off at 145th
Street. In a stream-of-consciousness style, Parks composed the
first impressions of a community he had longed to see. Over the
succeeding years, the versatile artist would wear the community
like a second skin, his photographs capturing its potential and
neglect, as well as the wayward, troubled denizens and the pride-
ful elite as they sauntered the crowded streets or lolled at a
favorite watering hole. A remarkable storyteller, Parks's pen
equaled his all-seeing camera, his words sculpting image after
fascinating image with the same sense of beauty he has continued to express into the autumn of his days.

The problem of hunting for a job hit me when I touched
the street. The sun was higher now, the sky clear, and far
in the distance I could see Manhattan's skyscrapers rising
from the tenements like rows of carved stone. I bought a
newspaper at the corner, and on the front page there was
a photograph of Franklin Delano Roosevelt. His chin was
up, his smile was confident, and his hat brim was raised
to the same angle as his arm as he waved victoriously. It
was March 4, 1933, the day of his inauguration. I walked
east on 145th Street to Lenox Avenue; and when I turned
the corner there was a stand where one could get a hot

dog and root beer for seven cents. I ate two portions while checking the want ads. Someone needed a plumber's helper; the Park Central Hotel needed waiters and dishwashers, and the plumber wanted a white helper. The ads said so. Harlem was fully alive now, but a chill still hung in the air, and the stoops were filling with Negroes, who stood warming in the sun. I walked slowly down the avenue observing them. They were gathered in groups, their eyes sullen against the morning light. Their mood seemed as ugly as their clothing and they looked as if all promise had died inside them.

The sidewalks were filling too, carrying a steady stream of slow-moving people in both directions, and soon I was lost in the stream, closed in by Ethel's Beauty Shoppe and Joe's Burgers and a funeral home and the Church of God in Christ and the church of good hope and small's paradise and a funeral parlor and the harlem bar and harlem lunch and harlem barbers and Saturday night caskets between the black and tan bar and ebony lounge and pilgrims' baptist *shine mister?* and honking taxis doorway johnnies eyeing miss mighty stockings miss fine gams miss good bread all big-breasted and hip-swinging *black bastards who do they think I am?* and the sign of the believer and the sirens and hospital meat wagons FATS WALLER RECORDS COME IN AND LISTEN and undertaking establishment and funeral home *shine mister?* and butcher shops chitterlings collard greens hog maws crackling bread and the sharpie flipping the quarter georgie raft-style and the shiloh baptist and etha mae's beautee shoppe and earl's hot dogs root beer seven cents *give me some skin daddy-o* and the apollo the harlem master tailors jew him down baby jew him down mount zion funeral home and herbs for healing shine mister? ofay cops on every corner looking mean daddy-o looking mean herbs bibles candles pictures of black Jesus marty's pawn shop and jock's place thievin bastards police! Police! Police! SADIE'S BALL GOWNS HALF PRICE DOLLAR DOWN DOLLAR A WEEK the duke's latest hit come in listen the mooche come on in brother it don't cost you nothing and the african methodist episcopal church and chick webb at the Savoy What a friend we have in Jesus! Halt halt halt or I'll shoot and POLICE BRUTALITY CONTINUES IN HARLEM! BOY MURDERED! NEGRO GROUPS SET FOR PROTEST! Get your paper here read all about it brother read all about it ads ads ads white waiter wanted ads ads ads white plumber needed ads ads ads white nurse wanted ads ads white bartender needed Can you use me for any kind of work mister any kind sweeping dishwashing window washing waiter cook any kind mister any kind? And to you, my friends throughout the land, as your president let me assert my firm belief that the only thing we have to fear is fear itself—nameless, unreasoning, unjustified terror . . . we are stricken by no plague of locusts. Plenty is at our doorstep. Shine mister shine? HARLEM SOCIALITES TO ENTERTAIN AT THE SAVOY BALLROOM THIS WEEKEND DRESS FORMAL ads ads ads negro maid that can cook sew clean and care for two-month-old baby. Get your amsterdam news your pittsburgh courier your Chicago defender here read your black papers get the truth. HARLEM SOCIALITE CAUGHT IN LOVE TRIANGLE POLICE BRUTALITY ON THE RISE WAKE UP HARLEM shine mister? MASS RALLY AT 125TH STREET TONIGHT COME ONE COME ALL HELP BURY POLICE BRUTALITY HIGH RENT BAD HOUSING

STARVATION But the cotton club's in harlem so why can't a black man go there? So the moon is cheese daddy-o and why can't you eat it? MASS RALLY COME ONE COME ALL HELP BURY MISTER OFAY TONIGHT AT SEVEN Come in close brothers let me tell you like it is here in harlem let 'em in brothers make way for my people all my black friends who have come to bury the white devil now I'm going to tell you something that nobody else has had the guts to tell you in front of these gun-toting cops standing all around you no no no I ain't scared of none of 'em no matter how big their guns are come closer come closer git around me so you can hear something that's going to help you the white man's day is coming to an end and we my friends are going to push that day along we're gonna run 'em out of harlem as sure as the african is gonna run 'em out of africa mark my word I'm sick of our children being shot down in the streets like dogs by these pasty-face bullies with guns that they make you buy with your own tax money yes brother I said your tax money listen did you hear what I said you pay for those guns with your own tax money for those ofay bandits to shoot your own children down in cold blood how long are you going to let it go on brother how long before you stop praying to god for help and help your selfs he ain't caring nothing about you he's white just like the cops you oughta know that by now so why are you running to these dog-ass churches every night and falling on your knees giving money to a white god who is murdering your children and the same time you are praying to him for mercy and help wake up brothers brothers wake up move in closer let my friends in closer gather around me and hear the truth like it's never been told before mister ofay is all worried now talk-ing about a depression hell man we have been depressed for over three hundred years and they are still depressing us beating us rob-bing us in these filthy rat-gnawed buggy smelly funky firetraps that they charge us more for than they ever charged the whites before they left all this crap behind for us black people o my brothers and sisters I ask you how long are we going to put up with this before we arch our backs and run the jews and all the rest of these white bastards off our doorsteps how long children how long will you allow these ofay bandits to suck your life's blood like leeches where are your so-called black leaders tell me where are they I'll tell you where they are they are out in mister ofay's kitchen begging him for a crust of mangy bread and mister ofay says here nigger now I'm giving you some bread so you keep all the rest of those niggers up in spooksville quiet yassuh mister ofay yassuh mister ofay I tell you my friends you and me are going to have to solve our own problems with our own black hands 'cause our leaders pardon my expression ain't shit no sir they ain't shit now you take walter white he's supposed to be goin' down south passin' for white so he can find out what the white man is planning to do to us negroes hell man who does he think he's foolin' he is white and he's taking your black money and goin' down south to see his relatives and gitting drunk and layin up with the rest of these crackers and laughing like hell 'cause you bunch of stupid niggers yeh that's what he calls you stupid black niggers give him money to help you o my children wake up wake up can't you see what the white man is doin for you can't you see yeh mister ofay said in the papers not so long ago that we had to war against a scarcity of money food and unemployment hell man he oughta make us his generals because we got more experience at fightin' those things than anybody on earth right right right right tell me I'm right brothers and move in closer now there's only one way to fight this battle that's with money and guns the same weapons mister ofay uses against you but first we're gonna need money o yes we gotta have money 'cause mister ofay ain't got nothin' but money so we have got to

fight fire with fire blood with blood so I'm gonna ask all you brothers and sisters to step up and help me start the ball rollin' 'cause
we've got to have lots of things if we are gonna bring mister ofay to
his miserable cotton-pickin' knees yeh you heard me he should have
been pickin' all that cotton your poppy and your mammy has been
pickin' tell me I'm right that's right yell it out hell ain't nobody
gonna hurt you now it's too many of us here tonight let my brothers in closer let my brothers and sisters put something in this can so
I can come back this weekend and keep telling you some more truth
like you never heard before right right I'm tellin' you like it is now
let those good people come in with their money to help advance the
cause thank you brother thank you sister thank you thank you
thank you they talk about communist hell with communist thank
you brother thank you sister hell all we want is something to eat
and a decent place to sleep and some good schools to educate our
children hell brothers and sisters that's all we want right tell me I'm
right ain't nobody going to hurt you say I'm right there's too
many of us tonight they're scared when we're all together like this
thank you thank you brother thank you sister no we don't want
their women we got pretty women of our own just look around you
brothers at those choice brownskins at your sides hell their women
are like bloodless pups in comparison tell me I'm right thank you
pretty little heart let 'em in closer closer don't leave I've got plenty
more to tell . . .

MACBETH IN HARLEM

WENDY SMITH

From *Civilization* magazine (1996)

Wendy Smith's articles on the arts and theater have appeared in numerous publications, including *Newsday*, the *Chicago Sun-Times*, the *Cleveland Plain Dealer*, and *Publishers Weekly*. Smith (1956–) is also a noted authority on the Group Theatre, which her book *Real Life Drama* (1992) surveys in detail between 1931 to 1940.

For days, Harlem residents strolling anywhere between Lexington Avenue and Broadway from 125th to 140th Streets had seen the word MACBETH stenciled in glowing paint at every corner. New York's African-American community had been discussing the new production by the Federal Theater Project's Negro Unit with mingled pride and anxiety for months, and by opening night on April 14, 1936, anticipation had reached a fever pitch. At 6:30 P.M., ten thousand people stood as close as they could come to the Lafayette Theatre on Seventh Avenue near 131st Street, jamming the avenue for ten blocks and halting northbound traffic for more than an hour.

Spotlights swept the crowd as mounted policemen strove to keep the entrance to the theater open for the arriving ticket holders, an integrated group of "Harlemites in ermine, orchids and gardenias, Broadwayites in mufti," as the *New York World-Telegram* noted the next day. Every one of the Lafayette's 1,223 seats was taken; scalpers were getting three dollars for a pair of forty-cent tickets. The lobby was so packed people couldn't get to their seats; the curtain, announced for 8:45, didn't rise until 9:30. When it finally did, on a jungle scene complete with witches and voodoo drums, the frenzied mood outside the theater was matched by that within.

"Excitement . . . fairly rocked the Lafayette Theatre," *The New York Times* commented the next morning. The spectators were enthusiastic and noisy; they vocally encouraged Macbeth's soliloquies and clapped vigorously when the second act opened with more than half of the one-hundred-plus cast massed on stage for his coronation ball, a sea of colorful costumes swaying to the strains of Joseph Lanner waltzes. After the curtain fell on the final grim tableau of the witches holding Macbeth's severed head aloft as Hecate intoned ominously, "The charm's wound up!" cheers and applause filled the auditorium for fifteen minutes. Not bad for a show directed by an actor barely out of his teens with a cast that was 95 percent amateur, and a scenery and costume budget of two thousand dollars.

The "Voodoo *Macbeth*," as this all-black version set in nineteenth-century Haiti came to be called, was notable on several counts. It was one of four Manhattan premieres in the spring of 1936 that solidified the shaky reputation of the Federal Theater Project, the most controversial of the Works Progress Administration's arts programs. (The project had been under fire since its founding in August 1935 for spending taxpayers' money on salaries without actually providing much theater for the public to see.) *Macbeth* launched the meteoric directing career of Orson Welles, not yet twenty-one when it opened, who would go on to astonish New York theatergoers with several more bold stage productions before departing for Hollywood in 1939. It gave African-American performers, usually restricted to dancing and singing for white audiences, a chance to prove they were capable of tackling the classics.

For all its individual brilliance, the Voodoo *Macbeth* was fairly representative of American theater in the 1930s, a decade whose passionate political debates and general sense of a world gone dangerously awry—whether you identified the danger as coming from fascist Germany, communist Russia or the capitalist West—seemed to find their most fulfilling artistic expression in drama. The rambunctious *Macbeth* premiere was one of several electrifying opening nights in the mid-thirties. For *The Cradle Will Rock* (also directed by Welles), an FTP show shuttered at the last minute by nervous WPA officials who found the labor opera's sentiments too radical, the audience followed the cast twenty-one blocks uptown to another theater and roared its approval as the actors (forbidden by their union to appear onstage) sang their parts from the auditorium. The Group Theatre production of Clifford Odets's *Waiting for Lefty*, another working-class drama, prompted the first-night crowd of 1,400 people to leap to their feet and shout, "Strike! Strike!" at its conclusion. Unfortunately for the FTP, its work prompted an equally strong political response from Congress, which in 1939 noisily killed the project.

Macbeth, however, began quietly enough in the fall of 1935 when John Houseman became the head of the FTP's Negro Unit in New York. Hallie Flanagan, the project's feisty national director, wanted an African-American leader, but the black professionals she consulted felt that a white man would give the unit additional prestige and clout. The thirty-three-year-old Houseman had directed the Virgil Thomson–Gertrude Stein opera *Four Saints in Three Acts*, and his work with the show's all-black cast convinced Flanagan that he had the sensitivity and tact required of a white administrator running an African-American company.

Houseman had to skirt some political land mines in selecting material for the Negro Unit. African-American theater was in decline by the 1930s—the victim, ironically, of the smashing success in the twenties of all-black musicals like Noble Sissle and Eubie Blake's *Shuffle Along*, which prompted white investors to get into a business formerly dominated by black theater owners and producers. As a result, resident stock companies like Chicago's Pekin Theatre and New York's Lafayette Players, which had produced plays about African-American life as well as the musicals popular with both blacks and whites, withered. There were serious plays in the 1920s with African-American protagonists, but *The Emperor Jones*, *In Abraham's Bosom* and *Porgy* all had white authors. "The Negro theatre has not really progressed," commented the Baltimore *Afro-American* in 1933. "It has merely been absorbed."

Harlem audiences, Houseman concluded, would be offended by uptown productions of racial dramas written from a white point of view. And in the militant atmosphere of the thirties, the revues and musicals that had gained mainstream acceptance for many black performers "were regarded as 'handkerchief-head' and so, for our purposes, anathema," as he wrote in his memoirs. He solved his immediate problem by launching the Negro Unit with two contemporary plays written by well-known African-Americans. But neither Frank Wilson's earnest, awkward *Walk Together Chillun!* nor Rudolph Fisher's slick *Conjur Man Dies* was the kind of ambitious fare Houseman hoped to present.

Inspired by the example of *Four Saints in Three Acts*, for which he and Virgil Thomson cast black singers as sixteenth-century Spaniards solely on the basis of their voices and physical presence, Houseman decided that one part of the Negro Unit should do classical plays "without concession or reference to color." He knew exactly who he wanted to direct this audacious enterprise: the "monstrous boy" whose performance as Tybalt in Katharine Cornell's *Romeo and Juliet* had overwhelmed him one year earlier, and with whom he had talked throughout the spring of 1935 about creating contemporary versions of Elizabethan drama. This actor's only directing experiences were a high-school production of *Julius Caesar* and a summer festival performance of *Trilby* in Illinois.

Orson Welles had earned a reputation for erratic behavior (including practical jokes and chronic lateness) on the *Romeo and Juliet* tour, and there was no reason to believe he had the maturity to guide a largely inexperienced company through the thickets of Shakespearean verse. But Houseman had absolute faith in Welles's talent and, with the psychological shrewdness that characterized his entire career, sensed that the self-assured, protean actor would rise to the occasion. He offered Welles the job of directing the unit's first classical production and asked him to suggest a play.

Welles's wife, Virginia, came up with the idea of setting *Macbeth* in nineteenth-century Haiti and making the witches voodoo priestesses, and Welles responded with zest. He drastically revised Shakespeare's text to build up the witches' role, and turned Hecate into a male ring-leader of the forces of darkness, which dominated the play and controlled Macbeth from the very beginning. While this interpretation scanted the drama's central theme of a man destroyed by ambition, it allowed for striking visual and sound effects that were at least as important as the acting—a tendency evident in every play and film Welles subsequently directed.

With *Macbeth*, Welles's desire to subordinate the performances to the production's overall concept was actually helpful, since his cast contained only four professional actors. The Federal Theater Project, it should be remembered, was a relief organization whose primary mission was to put people to work; Hallie Flanagan's stated goal was to spend 90 percent of the FTP budget on salaries. Although she also decreed that only those who had previously made their living in the theater could be hired, in practice this conflicted with the bureaucratic requirement that 90 percent of the employees be taken from the relief rolls. Of the 750 people in the Negro Unit, most had done only occasional work as extras or chorus dancers; barely

150 were real professionals, and they included elocution-ists and African drummers as well as experienced actors.

At least the African drummers—a Sierra Leonean group headed by a genuine witch doctor—could be put to good use in *Macbeth*. For his murderous thane, Welles chose Jack Carter, who had made a sensation as Crown in *Porgy* but was also known as difficult and dangerous drunk. Balanc-ing him as Lady Macbeth was Edna Thomas, a seasoned pro from the Lafayette Players who had also worked on Broadway. She had performed only one minor Shake-spearean role, Carter none, but the actor cast as Hecate—Eric Burroughs, a graduate of London's Royal Academy of Dramatic Art—presumably had some background in speaking verse. Canada Lee as a cigarette-smoking Banquo completed the production's professional acting roster.

Rehearsals began with a good deal of tension in the air. The Harlem community was not at all sure what it thought of "Shakespeare in blackface" directed by a white man. Some African-Americans feared the production would make their race look ridiculous. One local zealot, con-vinced that *Macbeth*'s director was deliberately creating a travesty to humiliate blacks, attacked Welles with a razor in the Lafayette Theater lobby, apparently without hurting him. Within the FTP, a memo complained that *Macbeth* was consuming a disproportionate percentage of the Negro Unit's budget and staff time—a comment that seemed borne out by the elaborate costumes and vivid sets taking shape in Nat Karson's designs. (In fact the scenic budget was a mere two thousand dollars, low even in the thirties, though generous by the standards of the FTP.)

The director responded to these pressures by creating a

sense of community among his actors. He brought food and drink to rehearsals, paid for out of his earnings from radio work. That work kept him busy in the evenings, so the company assembled after midnight and rehearsed in nocturnal isolation, which also helped draw them together. Welles knew he had to establish his authority with a cast that quite possibly harbored doubts about his ability and intentions. He quickly won over Edna Thomas, respected by the others for her professionalism and dignity, by treating her with delicate consideration and respect. With the turbulent Jack Carter, he created a camaraderie of hell-raising, joining the actor after rehearsals ended at dawn to prowl through Harlem's nightspots.

Rehearsals were often chaotic; a friend of Nat Karson's attended one and found "absolute pandemonium, with Welles barking orders over the amplification system." The director was volatile and caustic: "Jesus Christ, Jack—learn your lines!" and "What the hell happened to the Virgil Thomson sound effects between acts?" were among the exasperated comments found in his notes. Hallie Flanagan recalled later that "our Negro company . . . was always . . . threatening to murder Orson in spite of their admiration for him." But they were confident that the director's outbursts weren't racially motivated; he reserved his most venomous criticisms for the white lighting designer, Abe Feder. Welles knew how to get results from people, Houseman observed: "He had a shrewd instinctive sense of when to bully or charm, when to be kind or savage—and he was seldom mistaken."

As the production took shape during technical run-throughs, it became clear that Welles had fashioned a dynamic, dazzlingly theatrical version of *Macbeth* that both compensated for his performers' weaknesses and took advantage of their strengths. The actors spoke Shakespeare's verse in a simple, unstudied manner perfectly suited to the production's ferociously direct style. Their untrained voices were supported and given added impressiveness during the most important speeches by Welles's use of drums, percussion and sound effects as underscoring.

The witches' scenes were truly menacing, with the costumes, jungle backdrops and authentic voodoo drumming and chants creating a convincingly supernatural atmosphere. Garry Wills argues in *Witches and Jesuits*, his provocative book on *Macbeth*, that most psychologically oriented modern productions have failed to provide the coherent spiritual framework essential to making Macbeth's downfall understandable; Welles seemed instinctively to grasp that voodoo would substitute nicely for the Elizabethans' belief in witches as servants of the devil. The total effect was of a violent universe ruled by evil. Rewritten by Welles, the ending no longer suggested reconciliation and rebirth; instead, Malcolm seemed likely to be the witches' next victim. Though Welles's interpretation was not overtly political, this nightmare vision had obvious resonance in a world menaced by fascism and the threat of world war.

The critics were a bit bewildered by it all. They couldn't help but respond to the production's swirling excitement and lush imagery (the black-and-white photographs in the Federal Theater Project archives at the Library of Congress, alas, give little sense of the riot of color that exploded on the Lafayette Theatre stage), and most realized that transposing the scene to Haiti gave the witches an effectiveness they seldom had in contemporary presentations. Some critics carped, however, that this radical rethinking of *Macbeth* "wasn't Shakespeare at all" but rather "an experiment in Afro-American showmanship." Percy Hammond of the anti–New Deal *Herald Tribune* went further and called the show "an exhibition of deluxe boondoggling," complaining that the government was squandering taxpayer dollars on a wasteful vanity production no commercial producer would be insane enough to undertake. When Hammond died suddenly a few days later, a rumor circulated among the Negro Unit staff that he was the victim of malevolent spells cast by the enraged voodoo drummers.

The Voodoo *Macbeth* certainly cast a spell over audiences, which did not share the critics' reservations. It ran for ten sold-out weeks at the Lafayette, then moved downtown for a ten-day run at the Adelphi Theatre before going on tour to FTP theaters in Bridgeport, Hartford, Dallas, Indianapolis, Chicago, Detroit, Cleveland and Syracuse. It also inspired Negro units in other cities to adapt the classics: Seattle's did an all-black *Lysistrata*, closed by WPA officials who found Aristophanes' verse "too risque," and when Los Angeles couldn't get the Welles *Macbeth*, the unit produced its own, set in Africa. Cincinnati did not make *Macbeth*'s touring schedule because local authorities said the audience would have to be segregated, which was against FTP policy; at all WPA productions, blacks could sit anywhere, not just in the balcony.

Everywhere it went, *Macbeth* caused an enormous stir. The one thing it did not do was make money. An FTP memo estimated the production's touring costs at nearly

$3,400 a week (including railroad fares and subsistence pay for the company) and noted that the best weekly gross at the Lafayette had been $1,935—this at a time when a modest Broadway hit like the Group Theatre's *Awake and Sing!* was pulling in $10,000 a week. When the tour was over, *Macbeth* had netted $14,000—and spent $97,000.

The Federal Theater Project was not intended to turn a profit. Its aim was twofold: to put people back to work and to provide free or low-cost entertainment to audiences previously unreached because of ticket prices or the lack of live theater in their area. Two-thirds of the FTP's productions were free, and tickets for the rest were cheap. *Macbeth* in Harlem, for example, had a price scale from fifteen to forty cents, while a Broadway show, by comparison, charged one dollar for a balcony and three dollars for the orchestra.

The FTP established companies in regions where people had not seen live performances since the movies killed vaudeville. Extravaganzas like *Macbeth* and sharply political works like the Living Newspaper productions, which grappled with such charged issues as venereal disease and labor activism, got all the press attention. But it was the quiet, day-to-day work of the federally supported local theaters, which presented everything from children's plays to such stock staples as *Up in Mabel's Room*, that most affected average Americans. Beyond the FTP's immediate goals, Hallie Flanagan dreamed of creating a distinctively American national theater, diverse and democratic as the highly centralized state theaters of Europe were not, that would express the country's varied cultural heritage, yet draw people together in shared theatrical experiences.

The FTP, however, did not have as long a professional life as Welles and Houseman. (After departing the project, they went on to stir up New York with the Mercury Theater productions of *Julius Caesar* and *Heartbreak House*—as well as the infamous radio broadcast of *The War of the Worlds*.) Between 1936 and 1939, the FTP presented some 1,200 productions at a cost of approximately $46 million. More than 30 million Americans saw these shows, which took in about $2 million in admissions—more revenue, Flanagan pointed out, than any other WPA project generated. But on June 30, 1939, the FTP was shut down by an act of Congress.

The popularity of big-spending New Deal programs had waned by 1939, and although closing the FTP saved not one cent—its budget was simply distributed among other projects—it gave congressmen who had always disliked the idea of the government funding show business an opportunity to make a political point. Almost all the witnesses invited to testify before the House Committee on Appropriations were opponents of the FTP; the WPA foolishly decided not to permit Flanagan to reply to their charges until it was too late. By then, hostile congressmen had succeeded in depicting the FTP as a hotbed of communism (which it was not) and as a tax-subsidized organization disseminating New Deal propaganda (which it more or less was). The WPA appropriations bill for 1939 specifically stated that none of its funds "shall be available . . . for the operation of any Theatre Project."

Independent African-American companies did not spring up to take the place of the Negro units, and without such institutional support serious black playwrights floundered until galvanized by the civil-rights movement. After 1939, black actors were once again relegated to stereotyped roles in mainstream white shows, and the black technicians trained by the FTP were excluded from every theatrical union in the United States. It would be two decades before the actors and technicians who had gained employment and artistic self-respect on *Macbeth* and the other Federal Theater Project productions would again find sustained work in the theater.

ZORA

LAURENCE HOLDER

From *New Plays for the Black Theatre,*
edited by Woodie King Jr. (1989)

Zora Neale Hurston was often as outrageous as she was talented. Laurence Holder, in his play *Zora*, steps inside Hurston's complex mind and sculpts portions of her dramatic life. And nothing was as bizarre and farfetched as the scene below, when she is on a mission to fulfill a college course assignment.

Barnard [College] turned out to be a new world for me. I met Franz Boas, leading anthropologist, in 1925. He was liberal and wanted to study the Negro. Now, you might be wondering why I was interested in Anthro, but that was because it was the only way I could study the Negro. See, even in those days there were questions about whether the Negro had as large a brain as the Occidental. Boas and his colleagues wanted to find out about the correlation of intelligence and head size. When I heard that, I had to laugh. I mean, I knew all about the Negro, and since I was the only colored at Barnard, I got the bug to prove all I knew to the white man, so I accepted the assignment. But they soon made it clear to me that it wasn't enough to point out history to them, I've got to gather more information. Well, they soon realized that this colored girl was for real because the first thing I did was go over to Harlem and start measuring skulls. Can you imagine this cullud girl standing on 125th street with a pair of calipers measuring the size of folks' heads? But the folk was all interested in this.

HEY! THE WHITE FOLKS SAY WE IS DUMB AND NOT EQUAL TO THEM 'CAUSE OUR HEADS IS SMALL AND OUR BRAINS IS TOO. SO COME ON UP HERE AND LET ME MEASURE YOUR BRAIN, HONEY. YES! AIN'T IT THE TRUTH! WHAT WILL THOSE PEOPLE THINK OF NEXT?

Yes! The colored folks was interested all right. They wanted to know the truth, and they weren't disappointed neither. Them niggers got big bald heads . . .

Of course, that wasn't proof about nothing. See, Papa, that's what I called Boas, had created a criteria of standards that told what a developed society was really like. He said it was based on how people responded. Well, natchally colored folks respond very differently. But Boas just couldn't see that even though he was feeling stupid about asking me about the possibility of a lower intellectual standard for the Negro people because I was burning them, burning them where they stood. Here I was, just a li'l ole country gal from the most rural part of the country, and I dint have no shame. You hear me! They knew I was extraordinary because I knew I was extraordinary. I must've mentioned that too, dint I? Well, you just never can say it enough to yourself. I mean, this ole mole ain't afraid of no coon shine. Yeah!

And it was the time of the Harlem Renaissance. I mean to tell you colored folks were soaring through the air like eagles. There was Claude [McKay], and Countee [Cullen], and Langston [Hughes], and Wallace [Thurman], Du Bois, Garvey, Ethel Waters. I knew them all, and we were all thriving, growing, finding out all about ourselves, on all levels. And all that energy ain't never been matched. Oh, I know what America was and what it is now.

We were grand and used to strut, honey. I was probably the original Darktown Strutter. And the white folks was having a hard time trying to prove that we was inferior and all. And not only were we intelligent, we were beautiful. Langston and Wallace were two incredibly handsome stallions. Pretty, pretty men! And the three of us used to strut. We would walk right into a rent party or some of them white folks' gatherings and just knock them dead. And nothing started until I started telling some of my patented porch lies. "Tell 'em a story 'bout something, Zora." Shucks! I had me enough stories to last a lifetime.

SEE, THERE WAS THIS SLAVE WHO HAD A REPUTA-TION FOR KEEPING OUT OF WORK BECAUSE HE COULD OUTWIT ALL HIS MASTERS. AND BECAUSE OF THAT HE WAS ALWAYS BEING SOLD. WELL, ONE DAY HIS NEW MASTER CALLS HIM OVER AND SAYS TO HIM: "YOU GONNA PICK UP 400 POUNDS OF COTTON TODAY OR I'MA SHOOT YOU. I KNOW ALL ABOUT YOU AND YOUR TRICKS." WELL, THIS SLAVE'S MOUTH JUST FALLS OFF, BUT HE SIDLES UP TO THE MASTER AND LOOKS HIM DEAD IN THE EYE AND SAYS TO

HIM: "IF'N I MAKE YOU LAUGH, YOU'LL LET ME OFF, WON'T YOU?" THE MASTER LOOKS HIM BACK, DEAD IN THE EYE, AND SAYS: "IF'N YOU MAKE ME LAUGH, I'MA GIVE YOU YOUR FREEDOM." NOW, THIS MASTER WAS NOT KNOWN TO LAUGH, EVEN IN BED, BUT THE SLAVE SAYS, RIGHT BACK TO HIM, "BOSS, YOU SURE ARE A FINE-LOOKING YOUNG MAN." THE BOSS SAYS: "SORRY, I CAN'T SAY THE SAME THING ABOUT YOU." AND THE SLAVE SAYS: "OH, YES YOU CAN, IF YOU TOLD A LIE AS BIG AS THE ONE I JUST TOLD YOU." WELL, THE BOSS JUST COULDN'T CONTAIN HIMSELF, AND HE BUSTS OUT LAUGHING, AND THAT OLD DARKY HAD HIS FREEDOM THAT NIGHT.

Oh, it was a good time. Langston, Wallace and me put together an anthology of our work. Langston had his poems, and I had my poems and my award-winning stories, and Wallace was just the grandest editor anybody ever did have. And even without money or too much recognition, we gave the world "FIRE." It was a good time because everything was happening everywhere.

SKIRT BY SKIRT ON EVERY FLIRT. THEY'RE GETTING HIGHER AND HIGHER. DAY BY DAY IN EVERY WAY, THERE IS MORE TO ADMIRE. SOCK BY SOCK AND KNEE BY KNEE, THE MORE THEY SHOW THE MORE WE SEE. THE SKIRT RUN UP, THE SOCK RUN DOWN, JINGLING BELLS RUN ROUND AND ROUND. OH, WEEK BY WEEK AND DAY BY DAY, LET'S HOPE THINGS KEEP ON THIS WAY LET'S KNEEL RIGHT DOWN AND PRAY

It was the Jazz Age. We were exotic and beautiful. And me and Langston quickly realized that. Langston, the Father of the Weary Blues.

Anyway, we realized that Eatonville had a whole lot of potential to it.* Our folktales had been with us without any corruption. And me and him wanted to do a Broadway show, a collaboration. We were going to call it *Mule Bone*. Just him and me. He had just the right touch with some of those ideas. A real genius.

LAURENCE
HOLDER

---

* Eatonville, Florida, was Hurston's birthplace and childhood home.

409 EDGECOMBE, BASEBALL AND MADAME ST. CLAIR

KATHERINE BUTLER JONES

From an unpublished memoir

Jones is a longtime Harlem resident who was in touch with the diversity of the community. Her precise memories of an apartment building in Harlem where a host of notables lived is indicative of her passion and love for a legendary domicile located in a remarkable neighborhood.

Everyone who was anyone in New York City's African-American community knew of "409." Just hail a cab in Harlem and say "409" and the driver would know where to take you. Walter White, W. E. B. Du Bois, Roy Wilkins, Thurgood Marshall, leaders of the NAACP, and other black elite lived at 409 during the 1930s and through World War II.

This thirteen-story red brick apartment house on Edge-combe Avenue dwarfs the other buildings on Sugar Hill that overlook the Harlem Valley. Sited on Coogan's Bluff, high above the Harlem River and Harlem Valley, the E-shaped structure commands a view of the Bronx and lower Manhattan as well as the Palisades of northern New Jersey. Neighbors sit and chat on a series of green slatted wooden benches directly across the street from the entrance to 409. Behind the benches, iron grille work extends ten blocks along an uninterrupted promenade where maple trees shade the avenue. Cool water bubbles up from the pebbly stone fountain where you may quench your thirst after climbing the seemingly endless concrete steps from Eighth Avenue to the Hill.

It was April 1936 when my parents, Meme and Thede Butler, and I rode home to 409 in a cab from nearby Columbia Presbyterian Hospital, where I had been born. My father carried me under the green awning emblazoned with the white numerals "409"; the uniformed doorman tipped his hat and opened the wrought-iron-framed glass door. We ascended the four marble steps into the lobby. White and black rectangular tiles set in a herringbone pattern edged the oriental carpets. The rugs muffled the sound of footsteps as my parents walked the length of the T-shaped lobby to the elevator. The hall man is announcing a visitor on the intercom and directs the guest to one of the elevators that anchor each end of the lobby. . . .

For the first twenty-one years of my life, until I married Hubey Jones and moved to the Boston area, 409 was my home. Then 409 became a second home for our growing family. "I see Ba's house, I see Ba's house," children would chorus from the rear of the station wagon as we motored down the Harlem River Drive to visit my widowed mother. It was in this apartment, which I now own, that I discovered a legacy that my father inadvertently handed down to me—the collection of letters, documents, and photographs he saved in his bookcase. The building still remains an important part of my life. It is a place I connect with my growing-up years and my roots. The apartment was used by most of our eight children when they studied or worked in New York City, and it is the place where I now do some of my research and writing. But 409 means even more to me because in its elegance, its glamour, and the pride reflected by the tenants who lived there, it represents a part of Harlem in its glorious days. Some of the people who were my neighbors when I was growing up still reside in the building today. These neighbors assisted my mother in her advanced years, and they add a sense of continuity to my life.

When Mom arrived from Jamaica, British West Indies, in 1921, she was a self-described bachelor girl. She told me that when my dad proposed, eleven years later, she hesitated and answered demurely, "I'll think about it." But in response to his next question, "Where do you want to go for our honeymoon?" she quickly replied, "Niagara Falls, of course." And so the date was set for August 21, 1932. . . .

I grew up loving baseball, perhaps because we lived within walking distance of the two parks: the Polo Grounds, across the street, and Yankee Stadium, where Joe DiMaggio played, just over the Macombs Dam Bridge that links Manhattan to the Bronx.

The kitchen window overlooked the Polo Grounds, built in the 1890s, home of the New York Giants baseball team before they moved to San Francisco in 1958. The Polo Grounds was also shared with the Cuban Giants of the Negro Leagues until baseball was desegregated in 1947. The stadium was shared with the New York Yankees from the time it was built until 1923, when Yankee Stadium, "the house that Ruth built," was designed to accommodate the increasing number of fans who came to see George Herman Ruth, the Sultan of Swat.

From our apartment I could see the colorful clothing of the fans seated in the leftfield stands and hear the booming sound of the announcer's voice: "Number 15—first baseman—Johnny Mize, at bat."

Sometimes I'd see the white ball rise into the upper deck of the rightfield stands for a home run. The roar from the crowd was almost deafening. I could listen to the games on the radio while watching the Polo Grounds to see the pop-up fly balls. I noticed that the only time large numbers of white people came into our neighborhood was to attend sporting events held at the two ballparks. Finally, when I was eight years old, Dad took me to the Polo Grounds and the Yankee Stadium to watch the games.

Mr. Harold Thomas, occupant of apartment 13E, has lived in 409 for more than sixty years. During his 1931 and 1932 school summer vacations when living at the YMCA (which had moved to 135th Street), he was an elevator operator in the "house" where his aunt, Dr. Beulah Gardner, and cousin Billy lived. Mr. Thomas's older sister, Thelma Wilson, told me, "I was hired in 1927 by Nail and Parker, the successful colored realty firm, to manage the building and collect rents at a time when many apartments were still vacant because of the glut in the market. This was my first job after graduating from Wadleigh High that year, and I was offered an apartment in the house rent-free. The Metropolitan Life Insurance Company owned the building, and John Thornton was the superintendent. It was a pleasure to work there because the tenants and staff were so friendly.

"I remember Madame Stephanie St. Clair breezing through the lobby with her fur coat dramatically flowing behind her. She had a mystical aura about her, and she wore exotic dresses with a colorful turban wrapped around her head. She was always very pleasant to me. When I went to her apartment to collect the rent, she invited me in to see her collection of gold coins embedded in a glass-topped table. l was impressed." I was impressed, too, when I thought about the courage, intelligence, skill, and savvy needed for a woman of the 1920s to control the numbers racket in Harlem—an illegal, lucrative gambling operation. When notorious gangster and bootlegger Dutch Shultz, who controlled the numbers in other areas of the city, attempted to encroach on Madame's territory, she resisted.

Based on her own experience with the police, Madame St. Clair became the self-proclaimed "Queen of Policy," and spokeswoman for the people of Harlem. Promising to organize "my people to work and support the mayor in the coming election," Madame St. Clair writes, "I close my letter with tears in my eyes. . . . I beg of you to please do something to remedy these terrible conditions of mistreatment of the members of my race." But, on the afternoon before New Year's Eve in 1929, Madame St. Clair was picked up by police after leaving her apartment. Number slips allegedly found in her pocketbook gave the officers a reason to escort St. Clair to headquarters. The police booked her and set bail at $2,500. The Queen of Policy, however, presents a different account of her arrest in her January 1930 column:

"On Monday morning I left my home at eleven o'clock. . . . When I reached the corner of 155th Street and Edgecombe Avenue, I met Officer Moore in company with another colored man. I was waiting for the bus, and when it came I got on. . . . When I got off, I felt an enemy following me, and when I entered 177 West 141st Street I was rushed by three policemen, . . . arrested and framed by the bravest and noblest cowards who wear civilian clothes. . . . I will fight them legally to the finish . . . and I will never stop. I am going to dig up everything and expose them more." After serving less time than her two-year sentence on Welfare Island, the fiery numbers woman was released, having accused the district attorney, two judges, and scores of police bondsmen and political fixers of corruption, giving names, dates, and amounts paid as graft. Many of the named were fired from their positions.

This tall, statuesque entrepreneur of French-Caribbean ancestry stated that she was not afraid of Dutch Shultz or any other man. She hired ten controllers and forty runners to protect her business, in addition to retaining a personal henchman. Harold Thomas recalls, "One day during the summer of 1931 when I was operating the elevator, the hall man on duty signaled for me to come to where he stood, as a black limo stopped in front of the house. I saw the four doors open simultaneously and one man got out of each door. They closed the doors in unison, making a single sound. They were very businesslike in their appearance; they about-faced and walked into the building military style. I took them up on the south elevator to Madame St. Clair's floor. They rang for me about twenty minutes later and repeated the routine, by leaving the building the same as when they entered, without saying a word. These men were Madame St. Clair's protectors. My cousin Billy Gardner, who lived on the first floor with his mother, told me that Dutch Shultz sent one of his men up to see Madame St. Clair. She pushed him into a closet, locked the door, and called her men to take care of him," Mr. Thomas reported.

When Dutch Shultz was gunned down by mobsters and taken to the Newark city hospital, he received a telegram from his guileful antagonist. "As ye sow, so shall you reap." it was signed "Madame Queen of Policy." Shultz never recovered from his wounds, and died in the hospital on October 24, 1935.

The following year Madame St. Clair entered a marriage of convenience with Sufi Hamid, the Muslim religious leader of the Universal Holy Temple of Tranquility in Harlem. Equally flamboyant, Hamid also wore turbans and elegant robes. Although he claimed to be an Egyptian, he was in fact Afro-American. Sufi Hamid organized picket lines in front of targeted shops to demonstrate against Harlem retailers who refused to hire black employees, during the hard days of the Depression. Hamid's rallying cry, "Don't Buy Where You Can't Work," guaranteed the popular leader a large following, although he was castigated by the traditional Harlem leadership who disdained this radical form of protest, preferring more conciliatory negotiations. When Reverend Adam Clayton Powell Jr., assistant minister of Abyssinian Baptist Church, the largest black church in Harlem, joined the picket line on 125th Street, both Hamid's and Powell's influence ascended. But the Harlemites's anger over lack of employment even in their own community reached a boiling point on March 19, 1935, when a riot broke out after a teenager was allegedly beaten by a merchant for shoplifting a small item. Windows were smashed and stores looted.

Madame St. Clair's marriage ended when she suspected Sufi Hamid of having an affair with a Madame Futtam. The Queen of Policy took a few potshots at Hamid with a revolver and again landed herself in prison, this time at the New York State Prison for Women at Bedford, New York, where she was sentenced to five to ten years. Although Hamid and Futtam did marry, Madame St. Clair needn't have troubled herself with the attempted murder; Sufi Hamid was killed in an airplane accident in August 1938.

116TH STREET

ANN PETRY

From *The Street* (1946)

Ann Petry (1908–1997) never received the celebrity of her fellow writers of the era such as Richard Wright and Ralph Ellison, but she was a thoughtful and insightful author who mined her journalistic experience to shape novels that were realistic to the core. In *The Street* we follow the travails of Lutie Johnson, a single mother struggling valiantly to raise a child amid the squalor and vice of post–World War II Harlem.

There was always a crowd in front of the Junto Bar and Grill on 116th Street. For in winter the street was cold. The wind blew the snow into great drifts that stayed along the curb for weeks, gradually blackening with soot until it was no longer recognizable as snow, but appeared to be some dark eruption from the street itself.

As one cold day followed swiftly on the heels of another, the surface of the frozen piles became encrusted with bags of garbage, old shoes, newspapers, corset lacings. The frozen debris and the icy wind made the street a desolate place in winter and the people found a certain measure of escape from it by standing in front of the Junto where the light streaming from the windows and the music from the jukebox created an oasis of warmth.

The inside of the Junto was always crowded, too,

because the white bartenders in their immaculate coats greeted the customers graciously. Their courteous friendliness was a heart-warming thing that helped rebuild egos battered and bruised during the course of a day's work.

The Junto represented something entirely different to the women on the street and what it meant to them depended in large measure on their age. Old women plodding past scowled ferociously and jerked the heavy shopping bags they carried until the stalks of celery and the mustard greens within seemed to tremble with rage at the sight of the Junto's doors. Some of the old women paused to mutter their hatred of it, to shake their fists in a sudden excess of passion against it, and the men standing on the sidewalk moved closer to each other, forming a protective island with their shoulders, talking louder, laughing harder so as to shut out the sound and the sight of the old women.

Young women coming home from work—dirty, tired, depressed—looked forward to the moment when they would change their clothes and head toward the gracious spaciousness of the Junto. They dressed hurriedly in their small dark hall bedrooms, so impatient for the soft lights and the music and the fun that awaited them that they fumbled in their haste.

For the young women had an urgent hunger for companionship and the Junto offered men of all sizes and descriptions: sleek, well-dressed men who earned their living as numbers runners; even better-dressed and better-looking men who earned a fatter living supplying women to an eager market; huge, grimy longshoremen who were given to sudden bursts of generosity; Pullman porters in on overnight runs from Washington, Chicago, Boston; and around the first of the month the sailors and soldiers flush with crisp pay-day money.

On the other hand, some of the young women went to the Junto only because they were hungry for the sight and sound of other young people and because the creeping silence that could be heard under the blaring radios, under the drunken quarrels in the hall bedrooms, was no longer bearable.

Lutie Johnson was one of these. For she wasn't going to the Junto to pick up a man or to quench a consuming, constant thirst. She was going there so that she could for a moment capture the illusion of having some of the things that she lacked.

As she hurried toward the Junto, she acknowledged the fact that she couldn't afford a glass of beer there. It would be cheaper to buy a bottle at the delicatessen and take it home and drink it if beer was what she wanted. The beer was incidental and unimportant. It was the other things that the Junto offered that she sought: the sound of laughter, the hum of talk, the sight of people and brilliant lights, the sparkle of the big mirror, the rhythmic music from the jukebox.

Once inside, she hesitated, trying to decide whether she should stand at the crowded bar or sit alone at one of the small tables in the center of the room or in one of the booths at the side. She turned abruptly to the long bar, thinking that she needed people around her tonight, even all these people who were jammed against each other at the bar.

They were here for the same reason that she was—because they couldn't bear to spend an evening alone in some small dark room; because they couldn't bear to look what they could see of the future smack in the face while listening to radios or trying to read an evening paper.

"Beer, please," she said to the bartender.

There were rows of bottles on the shelves on each side of the big mirror in back of the bar. They were reflected in the mirror, and looking at the reflection Lutie saw that they were magnified in size, shining so that they had the appearance of being filled with liquid, molten gold.

She examined herself and the people standing at the bar to see what changes the mirror wrought in them. There was a pleasant gaiety and charm about all of them. She found that she herself looked young, very young and happy in the mirror.

Her eyes wandered over the whole room. It sparkled in the mirror. The people had a kind of buoyancy about them. All except Old Man Junto, who was sitting alone at the table near the back.

She looked at him again and again, for his reflection in the mirror fascinated her. Somehow even at this distance his squat figure managed to dominate the whole room. It was, she decided, due to the bulk of his shoulders which were completely out of proportion to the rest of him.

Whenever she had been in here, he had been sitting at that same table, his hand cupped behind his ear as though he were listening to the sound of the cash register; sitting there alone watching everything—the customers, the bartenders, the waiters. For the barest fraction of a second, his eyes met hers in the mirror and then he looked away.

Then she forgot about him, for the jukebox in the far corner of the room started playing "Swing It, Sister." She hummed as she listened to it, not really aware that she was humming or why, knowing only that she felt free here where there was so much space.

The big mirror in front of her made the Junto an enormous room. It pushed the walls back and back into space. It reflected the lights from the ceiling and the concealed lighting that glowed in the corners of the room. It added a rosy radiance to the men and women standing at the bar; it pushed the world of other people's kitchen sinks back where it belonged and destroyed the existence of dirty streets and small shadowed rooms.

She finished the beer in one long gulp. Its pleasant bitter taste was still in her mouth when the bartender handed her a check for the drink.

"I'll have another one," she said softly.

No matter what it cost them, people had to come to places like the Junto, she thought. They had to replace the haunting silences of rented rooms and little apartments with the murmur of voices, the sound of laughter; they had to empty two or three small glasses of liquid gold so they could believe in themselves again.

She frowned. Two beers and the movies for Bub and the budget she had planned so carefully was ruined. If she did this very often, there wouldn't be much point in having a budget—for she couldn't budget what she didn't have.

For a brief moment she tried to look into the future. She still couldn't see anything—couldn't see anything at all but 116th Street and a job that paid barely enough for food and rent and a handful of clothes. Year after year, like that. She tried to recapture the feeling of self-confidence she had had earlier in the evening, but it refused to return, for she rebelled at the thought of day after day of work and night after night caged in that apartment that no amount of scrubbing would ever get really clean.

She moved the beer glass on the bar. It left a wet ring and she moved it again in an effort to superimpose the rings on each other. It was warm in the Junto, the lights were soft, and the music coming from the jukebox was sweet. She listened intently to the record. It was "Darlin'," and when the voice on the record stopped she started singing: "There's no sun, darlin'. There's no fun, darlin'."

The men and women crowded at the bar stopped drinking to look at her. Her voice had a thin thread of sadness running through it that made the song important, that made it tell a story that wasn't in the words—a story of despair, of loneliness, of frustration. It was a story that all of them knew by heart and had always known because they had learned it soon after they were born and would go on adding to it until the day they died.

Just before the record ended, her voice stopped on a note so low and so long sustained that it was impossible to tell where it left off. There was a moment's silence around the bar, and then glasses were raised, the bartenders started making change and opening long-necked bottles, conversations were resumed.

The bartender handed her another check. She picked it up mechanically and then placed it on top of the first one, held both of them loosely in her hand. That made two glasses and she'd better go before she weakened and bought another one. She put her gloves on slowly, transferring the checks from one hand to the other, wanting to linger here in this big high-ceilinged room where there were no shadowed silences, no dark corners; thinking that she should have made the beer last a long time by careful sipping instead of the greedy gulping that had made it disappear so quickly.

A man's hand closed over hers, gently extracted the two checks. "Let me take 'em," said a voice in her ear.

She looked down at the hand. The nails were clean, filed short. There was a thin coating of colorless polish on them. The skin was smooth. It was the hand of a man who earned his living in some way that didn't call for any wear and tear on his hands. She looked in the mirror and saw that the man who had reached for the checks was directly in back of her.

He was wearing a brown overcoat. It was unfastened so that she caught a glimpse of a brown suit, of a tan-colored shirt. His eyes met hers in the mirror and he said, "Do you sing for a living?"

She was aware that Old Man Junto was studying her in the mirror and she shifted her gaze back to the man standing behind her. He was waiting to find out whether she was going to ignore him or whether she was going to answer him. It would be so simple and so easy if she could say point-blank that all she wanted was a little companionship, someone to laugh with, someone to talk to, someone who would take her to places like the Junto and to the movies without her having to think about how much it cost—just that and no more; and then to explain all at once and quickly that she couldn't get married because she didn't have a divorce, that there wasn't any inducement he could offer that would make her sleep with him.

It was out of the question to say any of those things.

There wasn't any point even in talking to him, for when he found out, which he would eventually, that she wasn't going to sleep with him, he would disappear. It might take a week or a month, but that was how it would end.

No. There wasn't any point in answering him. What she should do was to take the checks out of his hand without replying and go on home. Go home to wash out a pair of stockings for herself, a pair of socks and a shirt for Bub. There had been night after night like that, and as far as she knew the same thing lay ahead in the future. There would be the three rooms with the silence and the walls pressing in. "No, I don't," she said, and turned around and faced him. "I've never thought of trying." And knew as she said it that the walls had beaten her or she had beaten the walls. Whichever way she cared to look at it.

"You could, you know," he said. "How about another drink?"

"Make it beer, please." She hesitated, and then said, "Do you mean that you think I could earn my living singing?"

"Sure. You got the kind of voice that would go over big." He elbowed space for himself beside her at the bar. "Beer for the lady," he said to the bartender. "The usual for me." He leaned nearer to Lutie. "I know what I'm talkin' about. My band plays at the Casino."

"Oh," she said. "You're—"

"Boots Smith." He said it before she could finish her sentence. And his eyes on her face were so knowing, so hard, that she thought instantly of the robins she had seen on the Chandlers' lawn in Lyme, and the cat, lean, stretched out full length, drawing itself along on its belly, intent on its prey. The image flashed across her mind and was gone, for he said, "You want to try out with the band tomorrow night?"

"You mean sing at a dance? Without rehearsing?"

"Come up around ten o'clock and we'll run over some stuff. See how it goes."

She was holding the beer glass so tightly that she could feel the impression of the glass on her fingers and she let go of it for fear it would snap in two. She couldn't seem to stop the excitement that bubbled up in her; couldn't stop the flow of planning that ran through her mind.

A singing job would mean she and Bub could leave 116th Street. She could get an apartment someplace where there were trees and the streets were clean and the rooms would be full of sunlight. There wouldn't be any more worry about rent and gas bills and she could be home when Bub came from school.

He was standing so close to her, watching her so intently, that again she thought of a cat slinking through grass, waiting, going slowly, barely making the grass move, but always getting nearer and nearer.

The only difference in the technique was that he had placed a piece of bait in front of her—succulent, tantalizing bait. He was waiting, watching to see whether she would nibble at it or whether he would have to use a different bait.

She tried to think about it dispassionately. Her voice wasn't any better or any worse than that of the women who sang with the dance bands over the radio. It was just an average good voice and with some coaching it might well be better than average. He had probably tossed out this sudden offer with the hope that she just might nibble at it.

Only she wasn't going to nibble. She was going to swallow it whole and come back for more until she ended up as vocalist with his band. She turned to look at him, to estimate him, to add up her chances.

His face was tough, hard-boiled, unscrupulous. There was a long, thin scar on his left cheek. It was a dark line that stood out sharply against the dark brown of his skin. And she thought that at some time someone had found his lack of scruple unbearable and had in desperation tried to do something about it. His body was lean, broad-shouldered, and as he lounged there, his arm on the bar, his muscles relaxed, she thought again of a cat slinking quietly after its prey.

There was no expression in his eyes, no softness, nothing to indicate that he would ever bother to lift a finger to help anyone but himself. It wouldn't be easy to use him. But what she wanted she wanted so badly that she decided to gamble to get it.

"Come on. Let's get out of here," he suggested. He shoved a crisp ten-dollar bill toward the barkeep and smiled at her while he waited for his change, quite obviously satisfied with whatever he had read in her face. She noticed that though his mouth curved upward when he smiled, his eyes stayed expressionless, and she thought that he had completely lost the knack of really smiling.

He guided her toward the street, his hand under her elbow. "Want to go for a ride?" he asked. "I've got about three hours to kill before I go to work."

"I'd love to," she said.

They turned down 117th Street, and she wondered whether a ride with him meant a taxi or a car of his own. If there was plenty of money floating through the town, then she assumed he must have a car of his own. So when he opened the door of a car drawn in close to the curb, she wasn't over-surprised at its length, its shiny, expensive look. It was about what she had expected from the red leather upholstery to the white-walled tires and the top that could be thrown back when the weather was warm.

She got in, thinking, This is the kind of car you see in the movies, the kind that swings insolently past you on Park Avenue, the kind that pulls up in front of the snooty stores on Fifth Avenue where a doorman all braid and brass buttons opens the door for you. The girls that got out of cars like this had mink coats swung carelessly from their shoulders, wore sable scarves tossed over slim wool suits.

This world was one of great contrasts, she thought, and if the richest part of it was to be fenced off so that people like herself could only look at it with no expectation of ever being able to get inside it, then it would be better to have been born blind so you couldn't see it, born deaf so you couldn't hear it, born with no sense of touch so you couldn't feel it. Better still, born with no brain so that you would be completely unaware of anything, so that you would never know there were places that were filled with sunlight and good food and where children were safe.

Boots started the car and for a moment he leaned so close to her that she could smell the after-shaving lotion that he used and the faint, fruity smell of the bourbon he had been drinking. She didn't draw away from him; she simply stared at him with a cold kind of surprise that made him start fumbling with the clutch. Then the car drew away from the curb.

He headed it uptown. "We got time to get up the Hudson a ways. Okay?"

"Swell. It's been years since I've been up that way."

"Lived in New York long, baby?"

"I was born here." And next he would ask if she was married. She didn't know what her answer would be.

Because this time she wanted something and it made a difference. Ordinarily she knew exactly how it would go—like a pattern repeated over and over or the beginning of a meal. The table set with knife, fork, and spoons, napkin to the left of the fork and a glass filled with water at the tip end of the knife. Only sometimes the glass was a thin delicate one and the napkin, instead of being paper, was thick linen still shining because a hot iron had been used on it when it was wet; and the knife and fork, instead of being red-handled steel from the five-and-ten, was silver.

He had said there was plenty of money in Harlem, so evidently this was one of the thin-glass, thick-napkin, thin-china, polished-silver affairs. But the pattern was just the same. The soup plate would be removed and the main course brought on. She always ducked before the main course was served, but this time she had to figure out how to dawdle with the main course, appear to welcome it, and yet not actually partake of it, and continue trifling and toying with it until she was successfully launched as a singer.

They had left Harlem before she noticed that there was a full moon—pale and remote despite its size. As they went steadily uptown, through the commercial business streets, and then swiftly out of Manhattan, she thought that the streets had a cold, deserted look. The buildings they passed were without lights. Whenever she caught a glimpse of the sky, it was over the tops of the buildings, so that it, too, had a faraway look. The buildings loomed darkly against it.

Then they were on a four-ply concrete road that wound ahead gray-white in the moonlight. They were going faster and faster. And she got the feeling that Boots Smith's relationship to this swiftly moving car was no ordinary one. He wasn't just a black man driving a car at a pell-mell pace. He had lost all sense of time and space as the car plunged forward into the cold, white night.

The act of driving the car made him feel he was a powerful being who could conquer the world. Up over hills, fast down on the other side. It was like playing god and commanding everything within hearing to awaken and listen to him. The people sleeping in the white farmhouses were at the mercy of the sound of his engine roaring past in the night. It brought them half-awake—disturbed, uneasy. The cattle in the barns moved in protest, the chickens stirred on their roosts and before any of them could analyze the sound that had alarmed them, he was gone—on and on into the night.

And she knew, too, that this was the reason white people turned scornfully to look at Negroes who swooped past them on the highways. "Crazy niggers with autos" in the way they looked. Because they sensed that the black men had to roar past them, had for a brief moment to feel equal, feel superior; had to take reckless chances going around curves, passing on hills, so that they would be better able to face a world that took pains to make them feel that they didn't belong, that they were inferior.

Because in that one moment of passing a white man in a car they could feel good and the good feeling would last long enough so that they could hold their heads up the next day and the day after that. And the white people in the cars hated it because—and her mind stumbled over the thought and then went on—because possibly they, too, needed to go on feeling superior. Because if they didn't it upset the delicate balance of the world they moved in when they could see for themselves that a black man in a ratclap car could overtake and pass them on a hill. Because if there was nothing left for them but that business of feeling superior to black people, and that was taken away even for the split second of one car going ahead of another, it left them with nothing.

She stopped staring at the road ahead to look at Boots. He was leaning over the steering wheel, his hands cupped close on the sides of it. Yes, she thought, at this moment he has forgotten he's black. At this moment and in the act of sending this car hurtling through the night, he is making up for a lot of the things that have happened to him to make him what he is. He is proving all kinds of things to himself.

"Are you married, baby?" he asked. His voice was loud above the sound of the engine. He didn't look at her. His eyes were on the road. After he asked the question, he sent the car forward at a faster pace.

"I'm separated from my husband," she said. It was strange when he asked the question, the answer was on the tip of her tongue. It was true and it was the right answer. It put up no barriers to the next step—the removal of the soup plates and the bringing-on of the main course. Neither did it hurry the process.

"I thought you musta been married," he said. "Never saw a good-looking chick yet who didn't belong to somebody."

She saw no point in telling him that she didn't belong to anybody; that she and Jim were as sharply separated as though they had been divorced, and that the separation wasn't the result of some sudden quarrel but a clean-cut break of years standing. She had deliberately omitted all mention of Bub because Boots Smith obviously wasn't the kind of man who would maintain even a passing interest in a woman who was the mother of an eight-year-old child. She felt as though she had pushed Bub out of her life, disowned him, by not telling Boots about him.

He slowed the car down when they went through Poughkeepsie, stopping just long enough to pay the guard at the entrance to the Mid-Hudson Bridge. Once across the river, she became aware of the closeness of the hills, for the moon etched them clearly against the sky. They seemed to go up and up over her head.

"I don't like mountains," she said.

"Why?"

"I get the feeling they're closing in on me. Just a crazy notion," she added hastily, because she was reluctant to have him get the slightest inkling of the trapped feeling she got when there wasn't a lot of unfilled space around her.

"Probably why you sing so well," he said. "You feel things stronger than other folks." And then, "What songs do you know?"

"All the usual ones. 'Night and Day,' 'Darlin',' 'Hurry Up, Sammy,' and 'Let's Go Home.'"

"Have any trouble learnin' 'em?"

"No. I've never really tried to learn them. Just picked them up from hearing them on the radio."

"You'll have to learn some new ones." He steered the

car to the side of the road and parked it where there was an unobstructed view of the river.

The river was very wide at this point and she moved closer to him to get a better look at it. It made no sound, though she could see the direction of its flow between the great hills on either side. It had been flowing quietly along like this for years, she thought. It would go on forever— silent, strong, knowing where it was going and not stopping for storms or bridges or factories. That was what had been wrong with her these last few weeks, she hadn't known where she was going. As a matter of fact, she had probably never known. But if she could work hard at it, study, really get somewhere, it would give direction to her life—she would know where she was going.

"I don't know your name, baby," Boots said softly.

"Lutie Johnson," she said.

"Mrs. Lutie Johnson," he said slowly. "Very nice. Very, very nice."

The soft, satisfied way he said the words made her sharply aware that there wasn't a house in sight, there wasn't a car passing along the road and hadn't been since they parked. She hadn't walked into this situation. She had run headlong into it, snatching greedily at the bait he had dangled in front of her. Because she had reached such a state of despair that she would have clutched at a straw if it appeared to offer the means by which she could get Bub and herself out of that street.

As his tough, unscrupulous face came closer and closer to hers, she reminded herself that all she knew about him was that he had a dance band, that he drove a high-priced car, and that he believed there was plenty of money in

Harlem. And she had gone leaping and running into his car, emitting little cries of joy as she went. It hadn't occurred to her until this moment that from his viewpoint she was a pick-up girl.

When he turned her face toward his, she could feel the hardness of his hands under the suede gloves he wore.

He looked at her for a long moment. "Very, very nice," he repeated, and bent forward and kissed her.

Her mind sought some plausible way of frustrating him without offending him. She couldn't think of anything. He was holding her so tightly and his mouth was so insistent, so brutal, that she twisted out of his arms, not caring what he thought, intent only on escaping from his ruthless hands and mouth.

The dashboard clock said nine-thirty. She wanted to pat it in gratitude.

"You're going to be late," she said, pointing at the clock.

"Damn!" he muttered, and reached for the ignition switch.

LIFE IN BLACK AND WHITE

SIDNEY POITIER

From *The Measure of a Man:*
A Spiritual Autobiography (2000)

**In his second autobiography, Sidney Poitier covers some of the
same ground he did in *This Life*. The only difference is the focus
and how the material is compressed when it is re-encountered.
Here he discusses those years just before he entered the army,
recalling a man who cut a fine figure, sometimes arrayed in a
doeskin suit and a Panama hat.**

My haphazard political education got under way in 1943.
The school in which that education occurred was that district north of Central Park known as Harlem, New York.
Now, the school of hard knocks provided no classes in
political science, but long before I arrived, Harlem residents knew full well that politics was a deck stacked
against them—an invisible force of exclusion expertly
woven into the fabric of everyday life. In the school of
hard knocks, politics was a name for the way white folks
arranged things to their own advantage. Harlem residents
had figured a good many things out. (1) They knew that
for practical economic reasons, there never was a time
when downtown politics didn't embrace Harlem as a
cheap and handy labor pool. (2) In cultural terms, they
knew downtown politics' insistence on a requisite distance being kept once they day's work was done. (3) They

knew that in matters of race, downtown politics had set in place rules and ways to enforce those rules, to ensure that all residents from Harlem were respectful of the "civilized traditions" that had been erected between themselves and the larger community over the preceding two hundred years. (4) They also knew that when need required, downtown politics would bombard Harlem with promises Harlem's residents knew, from experience, would never materialize.

The Harlem that I knew for fourteen years was an amazing place—a fabled destination well known in African-American communities throughout the country. Its dazzling power drew visitors of many races from many places to experience by taste, by smell, by touch its bewitching energies, its mysterious vibrations, and its signature rhythms, each of which was said to be in the very air a visitor breathed. And all of Harlem's visitors were encouraged to believe that each breath they took would also contain spiritual blessings that came flowing out of the soul of its loving people through the gateways of their hearts.

Harlem's attractions beckoned with a wink and a smile. Jazz at Minton's. Vaudeville at the Apollo. Floor shows at Smalls' Paradise. Comedians and torch singers at the Baby Grand. Jitterbuggers at the Savoy and the Renaissance Casino. Soul food at Jennylou's. Elegant late-night dining at Wells. The Palm. Frank's. Sugar Ray Robinson's. The Shalamar. Joe's Barbecue. And after midnight, when the legitimate bars closed, the speakeasies would open. There was gambling at the Rhythm Club twenty-four hours a day. There were pleasure houses offering high-quality interludes at prices that guaranteed satisfaction. And then there was the Theresa Hotel—a symbol of community pride and joy—where visitors of big-time status would hold court. Dignitaries from the Caribbean, Africa, South America, and elsewhere. Showbiz heavyweights like the Duke of Ellington, the Count of Basie. Jimmie Lunceford. Louis Jordan. Billy Eckstine. Dinah Washington. Sarah Vaughan. Ruth Brown. And countless others. But the most memorable characters of all appeared suddenly out of another life, and just as suddenly disappeared again.

Baron Smith, for example, was a tall, large-framed, brown-skinned man of some three hundred or more pounds who never failed to cut a most imposing figure when he entered or exited the lobby of the Theresa Hotel. Perhaps he would be impeccably done up in a white doeskin double-breasted suit, with a boutonniere in his lapel, a Panama hat sitting slightly forward on his head, two-toned black-and-white shoes on his feet, and an emerald-and-diamond ring on his left-hand pinkie finger—an ensemble that, taken together, served as perfect background for an elegant, black, custom-made shirt and the Savile Row necktie that completed the picture. Next day, perhaps an off-white linen suit, with equally arresting accessories. The following day, an entirely new look yet again.

Each summer, this man of substance would return to be eagerly received by the hotel's management and staff, as well as other establishments in Harlem including certain ladies of the evening who had been graced by his presence and his wallet on previous visits.

But Baron Smith's image and presence were a tailor-made fabrication. A performance mounted for a week's run on the stage of Harlem's hot spots, with annual revivals scheduled for as many summers as the traffic would bear.

The real life of the real Baron Smith was set in Nassau, Bahamas. There he was a barkeeper who sold rum to the locals. His barroom was of modest size, and so were his sales. His profit margin had to ignore other obligations in order to cover his seven-day pilgrimage to Harlem each summer. But dream chasers and sacrifices are never strangers for long. My father used to make daily stops at Baron Smith's barroom to sell cigars to the Baron's customers. Life in Nassau was pretty routine and uneventful for Mr. Smith. It didn't boogie. He yearned for a wild-side excitement, but all he could manage was a week of living on the edge in the ideal manner, in the perfect setting, in the flawless background of his dreams. Harlem, New York.

I knew Mr. Smith quite well. When I was twelve or thereabouts, I used to sneak into the local movie house through a small ventilation window at the rear of the theater, behind the screen. The window was too high for me to reach from the outside, so an accomplice was necessary. I would stand on the shoulders of my friend Yorick, and once safely through the window, I would reach back, grab Yorick's wrists, and haul him up and in. We then would slither under a thick curtain hanging over an entranceway that separated the backstage area from the theater itself, slither on under the first few rows of seats, and pop up innocently in the fourth or fifth row. There we would sit, doing our best to look like regular, paying customers. After roughly a dozen or so successes, one day we popped up, took our seats, and—guess what? Standing over us was Mr. Baron Smith. He was the manager of the movie house in those earlier days.

He grabbed us by the back of our collars, lifted us to our feet, and marched us to his office as pictures of reform school flashed through our heads. We knew that if he called the cops, an example would be made of us as a warning to all young males of similar age and reckless persuasion. That would mean six years in the slammer for each of us.

He sat us down in the privacy of his office. "I know your father," he said to me. "What do you think he would say if he knew what you've been doing?"

Yorick and I knew that the question wasn't meant to be answered, so we sat quietly. The lecture was short, but it found its mark.

"Now, get out of here," he said, after letting us stew a few minutes. "If you try something like this again, you'll regret it the rest of your lives. What you did is as bad as stealing. You don't want to grow up to be thieves, do you? Thieves wind up in jail; remember that. Honesty really is the best policy."

We weren't going to wind up as thieves. We were thieves already. But we weren't going to compound our problems by being honest enough to divulge that information. Mr. Smith escorted us out to the street and let us fly away. Free as birds.

Sixty years have passed since Mr. Smith let Yorick and me walk, but the generosity he displayed was a great lesson for me. Likewise, I learned much from Harlem's generosity in welcoming Baron Smith with his image as a man of importance, wealth, generosity, and presence (all fashioned with clothing and pretense) and its generosity in keeping such dreams alive for Baron Smith and dreamers like him from all over the world.

For Baron Smith the dreamer, Harlem was a stage-setting reflecting mere images of reality; but the fact is we the people of Harlem were real. Consequently, Harlem nourished another kind of dreamer to speak to our concerns. As a young man I began to ask myself, Who is speaking for me, and who is speaking to me? And as the saying goes, "When the student is ready, the teacher appears."

From the pages of newspapers, from the radio, from newsreels in the movie houses, and from poems and sermons, teachers—men of vision and courage from all walks of life—began to appear. One by one they spoke to me, and they spoke for me. Paul Robeson, Dr. Ralph Bunche, A. Philip Randolph, Adam Clayton Powell Jr., Roy Wilkins, Mary McLeod Bethune, Walter White, Whitney Young, Langston Hughes. And others. And in the course of time the voices of new-found friends from my generation, including William Garfield Greaves, Harry Belafonte, Leon Bibb, Philip and Dons Rose, William Branch, William Marshall, Julian Mayfield, and others, would be added. Like me, they were young. Unlike me, they were not political greenhorns. These intelligent young people—Harry Belafonte, Leon Bibb, and Philip and Dons Rose most especially—would become and remain invaluable contributors to my political education. By their example and my own intense effort at reading the newspapers, I picked up useful bits of basic information every day.

In 1945, at eighteen years of age and fresh out of the army, I was unaware, for instance, what it meant to be a

"Democrat," a "Republican," a "progressive," a "social-ist," a "communist," an "anarchist," a "northern liberal," a "southern conservative." Nor had I a clue as to how people who earned those labels differed from one another. It took some time before I came to understand who among the spokespeople for these various positions were genuine allies of those who spoke for the men and women of Harlem, and for the youngsters of my generation. But by the age of twenty-one, I had grown familiar with the land-scape and had acquired a general understanding of what was driving each major player philosophically.

HOSTESS OF HARLEM

CLAUDE MCKAY

From *Harlem Glory:*
A Fragment of AfraAmerican Life (1990)

Among the literary lights of the Harlem Renaissance, Claude McKay (1890–1948) perhaps best captured the everyday habits, speech, and dreams of the working class, particularly those immigrants who had come from the West Indies as he did. *Banana Bottom* and *Home to Harlem* are his most celebrated novels, but there were many others, including his last novel, *Harlem Glory*, written in the late 1940s, from which this chapter is taken. Though he is mainly noted as a novelist, his poem "If We Must Die" is widely acclaimed and often anthologized.

Buster's early career had paralleled Millinda's. Both had traveled out of the deep South in quest of a larger life in the North. Their destiny had brought them together in Harlem. But Millinda had covered a more easily romantic road. Her happy marriage had projected her into a position luxurious beyond her wildest imagination. Harlem had no real knowledge of the extent of the wealth which Ned Rose had acquired from the operation of the numbers game. With the spreading of the game far and wide, many new bankers had sprung up who were flashy livers. They spun around Harlem in splendid cars, set the pace in stylish clothes, and were prominent at smart social functions. But Ned Rose preferred to live quietly. His first wife was a West Indian, who was unknown in Harlem society.

He had identified himself with the less spectacular way of life. He gave money to the Colored Orphanage, the Negro Aid Association, and the Negro churches. He also played a leading role in the fraternal lodge. When the lodge was in financial difficulties, Ned undertook its reorganization and finally pulled it up on its feet again.

He established, through the lodge, scholarships for the higher education of impoverished students. Often sneered at as a racketeer by more respectable Harlemites, he nevertheless was extremely charitable. He gave money even to a charitable white institution, which gave aid to poor white intellectuals. Some of his critics called his gifts "atonement money."

However, while Ned lived like a dignified, middle-aged businessman, Millinda was attracted to the smart, pace-making set. She adored dancing and parties. Moving from Harlem-under-the-hill to Sugar Hill, she started entertaining. And as soon as the fast set became aware of Millinda and her command of big money, she was flattered with many invitations. Millinda responded with her own invitations and soon had the satisfaction of having at her house the leading stars of the amusement world and members of the professional elite of Harlem. It was at this time that Buster South came into her life. Buster was the black Beau Brummell of the fast set. He was a splendid dancer and much desired as a partner by the fashionable dames. Millinda became specially interested in him. Perhaps it was because, like herself, he did not legitimately belong to the smart, professional, and educated group of colored folk. Only by the magic of his Aladdin's lamp had he horned his way there, even as she had with her feminine charm and power. Ned Rose gave Millinda his passive support. He was proud of her excelling as Harlem's hostess: it was a new and novel world for him. But he appreciated the modern trends of life. And though Millinda liked to make large social gestures, she was a wise and careful housekeeper.

Most interesting were some white friends of the smart colored set who visited their house. For it was at that time that Harlem was hectic with frequent and huge winnings in the numbers game, and tall tales of its kings and queens, incredible like oriental fantasies, were being circulated, that the quarter attracted a certain coterie of whites. These whites were a different set from the creatures of the underworld who have always patronized colored amusement places. They were members of the ultra-sophisticated literati and the bohemian fringe of New York's intelligentsia. Besides an amazingly wide-open wet area of speakeasies and cabarets, they found that there existed in Harlem an exclusive, extraordinarily highly developed dark bohemia and an aspiring little literati. They also discovered Millinda and Buster.

Mainly it was through Millinda that the white reading world became aware of the numbers game. There were journalists among the white visitors. Excited and delighted by her sumptuously furnished home and her luxurious way of living, they were astounded when they learned that her husband had acquired his wealth through the manipulation of the Harlem lottery. And soon titillating items about the Harlem game began appearing in the national newspapers.

The colored newspapers reproduced such items, and the eyes of the colored journalists were opened to a field that they were daily trampling underfoot and yet never saw. All of colored America looked to the goldmine of Harlem as the numbers game was touted as a million-dollar business.

Hot numbers were peddled on the street corner to the credulous masses by the diviners and interpreters of numbers. Not so crudely and visibly operating were the mysterious tipsters. A couple of shrewd Harlemites had established a connection by which they could obtain knowledge of the Stock Exchange figures in advance of their publication. Through a special clique of players they often played the lucky number, and their winnings were heavy. The clique was organized not to break the numbers bankers, but to obtain a maximum of their heavy profits. The bankers were convinced that there was a leak, but could not trace the tipsters.

There was one week, however, when even the clique was tricked, and the real lucky number was tipped off to the Harlem public. Whisperings ran like rats down the ways of Harlem: "Play number 772." That number was heavily played and it was the winning one. Thousands of dollars had to be paid out. The banks cracked. When the players discovered that the bankers were bankrupt, some bloody battles were staged in Harlem. Enraged, they patrolled the streets, hunting collectors and controllers, savagely beating and even knifing them. One big banker was shot dead in a hallway. Some went into hiding; others took a sea change over to Cuba, Jamaica and Trinidad.

About six big bankers on that wild day had closed their banks, having been warned not to send out their collectors to take numbers. Among them was Ned Rose. With the other banks ruined, the big six reorganized and consolidated the numbers business in their hands.

The publicity given the wild riot of numbers attracted the manipulators of the white underworld business to the game. These buccaneers were already powerful in Harlem as the vast depot of bootleg liquor. They knew of the existence of the numbers game but had contemptuously dismissed it as the "nigger pool," which was unworthy of their attention. But now they realized that thousands of dollars were being made out of those "nigger nickels."

The underworld whites were initiated into the ways of operating the numbers game by some of the ruined colored bankers, who acted in a spirit of revenge and also with the hope of starting in again with white protectors. The white operators established a chain of cigar stores as a front for operating the game. They broadened its scope by establishing banks in other cities, exciting the white population to play. And soon Harlem's numbers game was being played ardently by white and colored in all the great American cities.

Also trouble began shooting between the white bankers and the colored bankers. The white syndicate was determined to bring the entire field of the numbers game under its control. It ordered the colored number kings to join the syndicate; otherwise, they would be driven out of the field. A few of the blacks capitulated, but the big six held out. The whites threatened them and then went into action. One big black banker was kidnapped and held for thousands of dollars ransom. The ransom was paid, but it broke his bank. Another, hounded and pursued, finally had the top of his expensive car blown off by machine-gun. Miraculously he escaped injury. He was warned that on the next occasion it would be sure death. He joined the syndicate. One who would not heed the warnings of the syndicate, not taking them seriously, was hurled down a shaftway.

But Ned Rose refused to join the syndicate. He and Millinda put their heads together and it was decided that Ned should take a sea change and visit the West Indies. After Ned's departure, Millinda gave up entertaining to concentrate upon holding the intricate threads of the numbers business together and beating the white syndicate. She used her woman's wits. Headstrong Ned was bitter against the white competitors, denouncing them for entering the circumscribed field of black racketeering and had vowed that he would never join them in exploiting his people in that game.

But Millinda thought differently. She shared Ned's resentment. She also hated "white trash." But the white people she had known in the South were a little different in many ways from those that Ned had known in the West Indies, and that made a difference in determining their respective attitudes, even though they were emotionally united in their feeling of hostility. Millinda's background was dominated by individuals of the colored group who were protected by influential white people, and it did not matter that the white people referred to them as "good niggers" and the resentful colored people as "white folks' niggers." That protection was a real concrete thing.

There were two groups of the white underworld disputing the Harlem field: one was Italian, the other Jewish. Millinda's bootlegger was an Italian. He introduced her to the Italian group. She negotiated with them and sold out some of her business, with the understanding that she was to obtain protection for herself. When she had the transaction completed and everything settled, she brought Ned back from the West Indies.

By that time municipal and federal investigators were aroused and hot on the heels of Harlem; for the marvelous tales of its brazen bootleg and magical numbers manner of existence had penetrated to the sanctums of law and order. Accompanied by nationwide publicity, there began an official investigation of the numbers game. The police found it expedient at last to pick up scores of collectors with slips, acting as if they were not all along acquainted with all such persons and their business.

The collectors laughed and said that the police played the numbers regularly, like everybody else in Harlem. Nevertheless hundreds of collectors, controllers, and other numbers game officials were arrested and brought to trial, but most of them were eventually released.

The large bank accounts of the bankers were uncovered. But Ned Rose's was not. For when he was abroad, Millinda had drawn out their money from different banks and placed it in one bank, where no government investigators imagined a Negro would have an account. Meanwhile Ned was still hiding in Harlem. He and Millinda agreed to depart secretly for Europe and remain there until the noise about the numbers had died down. On the eve of sailing Ned visited the Submarine Speakeasy, whose owner was his friend. It was rather early and there were few customers besides the waiters. Ned stood at the bar talking to the proprietor. A man walked up to him and cried: "You can't get away with everything," and pumped bullets into his guts.

Millinda cremated Ned. And she resolved to take that vacation in Europe as they had planned. She had lost interest in the numbers business and sold out what was left of it.

A TOAST TO HARLEM

LANGSTON HUGHES

From *The Best of Simple* (1961)

No writer personified Harlem's literary legacy like Langston Hughes (1902–1967). In his poetry, plays, lyrics, and essays, Harlem was a constant metaphor, a resourceful image he could exploit with elegance and wit. Jesse B. Semple was a sort of fictional alter ego for Hughes, allowed to say many things the writer only thought.

Quiet can seem unduly loud at times. Since nobody at the bar was saying a word during a lull in the bright blues-blare of the Wishing Well's unusually overworked juke box, I addressed my friend Simple. "Since you told me last night you are an Indian, explain to me how it is you find yourself living in a furnished room in Harlem, my brave buck, instead of on a reservation?"

"I am a colored Indian," said Simple.

"In other words, a Negro."

"A Black Foot Indian, daddy-o, not a red one. Anyhow, Harlem is the place I always did want to be. And if it wasn't for the landladies, I would be happy. That's a fact! I love Harlem."

"What is it you love about Harlem?"

"It's so full of Negroes," said Simple. "I feel like I got protection."

"From what?"

"From white folks," said Simple. "Furthermore, I like Harlem because it belongs to me."

"Harlem does not belong to you. You don't own the houses in Harlem. They belong to white folks."

"I might not own 'em," said Simple, "but I live in 'em. It would take an atom bomb to get me out."

"Or a depression," I said.

"I would not move for no depression. No, I would not go back down South, not even to Baltimore. I am in Harlem to stay! You say the houses ain't mine. Well, the sidewalk is—and don't nobody push me off. The cops don't even say, 'Move on,' hardly no more. They learned something from them Harlem riots. They used to beat your head right in public but now they beat it after they get you down to the station house. And they don't beat it then if they think you know a colored congressman."

"Harlem has a few Negro leaders," I said.

"Elected by my own vote," said Simple. "Here I ain't scared to vote—that's another thing I like about Harlem. I also like it because we've got subways and it does not take all day to get downtown, neither are you Jim Crowed on the way. Why, Negroes is running some of these subway trains. This morning I rode the A Train down to 34th Street. There were a Negro driving it, making ninety miles a hour. That cat were really driving that train. Every time he flew by one of them local stations looks like he was saying, 'Look at me! This train is mine!' That cat were gone, ole man.

"Which is another reason why I like Harlem! Sometimes I run into Ellington on 125th Street and I say, 'What you know there, Duke?' Duke says, 'Solid, ole man.' He does not know me from Adam, but he speaks. One day I saw Lena Horne coming out of the Hotel Theresa and I said 'Hubba! Hubba!' Lena smiled. Folks is friendly in Harlem. I feel like I got the world in a jug and the stopper in my hand! So drink a toast to Harlem!"

Simple lifted his glass of beer:

"Here's to Harlem!
They say Heaven is Paradise.
If Harlem ain't Heaven,
Then a mouse ain't mice!"

"Heaven is a state of mind," I commented.

"It sure is mine," said Simple, draining his glass. "From Central Park to 179th, from river to river, Harlem is mine! Lots of white folks is scared to come up here, too, after dark."

"That is nothing to be proud of," I said.

"I am sorry white folks is scared to come to Harlem, but I am scared to go around some of them. Why, for instance, in my home town once before I came North to live, I was walking down the street when a white woman jumped out of her door and said, 'Boy, get away from here because I'm scared of you.' I said, 'Why?' She said, 'Because you are black.' I said, 'Lady, I am scared of you because you are white.' I went on down the street, but I kept wishing I was blacker—so I could of scared that lady to death. So help me, I did. Imagine somebody talking about they is scared of me because I am black! I got more reason to be scared of white folks than they have of me."

"Right," I said.

"The white race drug me over here from Africa, slaved me, freed me, lynched me, starved me during the depression, Jim Crowed me during war—then they come talking about they is scared of me! Which is why I am glad I have got one spot to call my own where I hold sway—Harlem. Harlem, where I can thumb my nose at the world!"

"You talk just like a Negro nationalist," I said.

"What's that?"

"Someone who wants Negroes to be on top."

"When everybody else keeps me on the bottom, I don't see why I shouldn't want to be on top. I will, too, someday."

"That's the spirit that causes wars," I said.

"I would not mind a war if I could win it. White folks fight, lynch, and enjoy themselves."

"There you go," I said. "That old *race-against-race* jargon. There'll never be peace that way. The world tomorrow ought to be a world where everybody gets along together. The least we can do is extend a friendly hand."

"Every time I extend my hand I get put back in my place. You know poetries about the black cat that tried to be friendly with the white:

> "*The black cat said to the white cat,*
> *'Let's sport around the town.'*
> *The white cat said to the black cat,*
> *'You better set your black self down!'*"

"Unfriendliness of that nature should not exist," I said. "Folks ought to live like neighbors."

"You're talking about what ought to be. But as long as

what is is—and Georgia is Georgia—I will take Harlem for mine. At least, if trouble comes, I will have my own window to shoot from."

"I refuse to argue with you any more," I said. "What Harlem ought to hold out to the world from its windows is a friendly hand, not a belligerent tirade."

"It will not be my attitude I will have out my window," said Simple.

"That Joyce," said Simple, "is not a drinking woman—for which I love. But if she wasn't my girl friend, I swear she would make me madder than she do sometimes."

"What's come off between you and Joyce now?" I asked.

"She has upset me," said Simple.

"How?"

"One night last week when we come out of the subway, it was sleeting too hard to walk and we could not get a cab for love nor money. So Joyce condescends to stop in the Whistle and Rest with me and have a beer. If I had known what was in there, I would of kept on to Paddy's, where they don't have nothing but a juke box."

"What was in there?"

"A trio," said Simple. "They was humming and strumming up a breeze with the bass just a-thumping, piano trilling, and electric guitar vibrating every string overcharged. They was playing off-bop. Now, I do not care much for music, and Joyce does not care much for beer. So after I had done had from four to six and she had had two, I said, 'Let's go.' Joyce said, 'Baby! I want to stay awhile more.' Now that were the first time I have ever heard Joyce say she wants to set in a bar.

"I said, 'What ails you?'

"Joyce said, 'I love his piano playing.'

"I said, 'You sure it ain't the piano player you love?' He were a slick-headed cat that looked like a shmoo and had a part in his teeth.

"Joyce said, 'Don't insinuate.'

"I said, 'Before you sin, you better wait. It looks like to me that piano player is eyeing you mighty hard. He'd best keep his eyes on them keys, else I will close one and black the other, also be-bop his chops.'

"Joyce says, 'Huh! It is about time you got a little jealous of me. Sometimes I think you take me for granted. But I do like that man's music.'

"'Are you sure it's his music you like?' I says. 'As flirtatious as you is this evening, your middle name ought to be Frisky.'

"'Don't put me in no class with Zarita,' says Joyce right out of the clear skies. 'I am no bar-stool hussy'—which kinder took me back because I did not know Joyce had any information about Zarita. A man can't do nothing even once without Harlem and his brother knowing it. Somebody has been talking, or else Joyce is getting too well acquainted with some of my friends—like you."

"I never mention your personal affairs to anyone," I said, "least of all to Joyce, whom I scarcely know except through your introduction."

"Well, anyhow," said Simple, "I did not wish to argue. I says to her, 'I ignore that remark.'"

"Joyce says, 'I ignore you.' And turned her back to me and cupped her ear to the music. "'Don't rile me, woman,' I says. 'Come out of here and lemme take you home. You know we have to work in the morning.'

"'Work does not cross your mind,' says Joyce, turning around, 'when you're setting up drinking beer all by yourself—so you say—at Paddy's. I do not see why you have to mention work to me when I am enjoying myself. The way that man plays "Stardust" sends me. I swear it do. Sends me ! Sends me!'

"'Be yourself, Joyce,' I said. 'Put your coat around your shoulder. Are you high? We are going home.'

"I took Joyce out of there. And by Saturday, to tell the truth, I had forgot all about it. Come the weekend, I says, 'Let's walk a little, honey. Which movie do you want to see?'

"Joyce says, 'I do not want to see a picture, daddy. They are all alike. Let's go to the Whistle and Rest Bar.'

"'O.K.,' I said, because I knowed every Friday they change the music behind that bar. They had done switched to a great big old corn-fed man who looked like Ingagi, hollered like a mountain-jack, and almost tore a guitar apart. He were singing:

> Where you goin', Mr. Spider,
> Walking up the wall?
> Spider said, I'm goin'
> To get my ashes hauled.

"The joint were jumping—rocking, rolling, whooping, hollering, stomping. It was a far cry from 'Stardust' to that spider walking up the wall.

"When I took Joyce in and she did not see her light-dark shmoo conked crown curved over the piano smearing riffs, she said, 'Is this same place we was at last time?'

"I said, 'Sure baby! What's the matter? Don't you like the blues?'

"Joyce said, 'You know I never did like the blues. I am from the North.'

"'North what?' I said. 'Carolina?'

"'I thought this was a refined cocktail lounge,' say Joyce, turning up her nose. 'But I see I was in error. It's a low dive. Let's go on downtown and catch John Garfield after all.'

"'No, no, no. No after all for me,' I said. 'Here we are— and here we stay right in this bar till I get ready to go . . . Waiter a beer! . . . Anyhow, I do not see why you would want to see John Garfield. Garfield does not conk his hair. Neither is he black. Neither does he play "Stardust."'

"'You are acting just like a Negro,' says Joyce.

"'It's my Indian blood,' I admitted."

IF YOU AIN'T GOT HEART, YOU AIN'T GOT NADA

PIRI THOMAS

From *Down These Mean Streets* (1967)

After a rather troubled adolescence and early youth, Piri
Thomas (1928–   ) was reborn in the prison system of New York
State, developing a writing style and focus that quickly earned
him accolades from the nation's most notable authors. His
book *Down These Mean Streets* established Thomas as a leading
Hispanic voice, and it was a voice that resonated with passion
and conviction.

We were moving—our new pad was back in Spanish
Harlem—to 104th Street between Lex and Park Avenue.

Moving into a new block is a big jump for a Harlem kid.
You're torn up from your hard-won turf and brought into
an "I don't know you" block where every kid is some kind
of enemy. Even when the block belongs to your own
people, you are still an outsider who has to prove himself
a down stud with heart.

As the moving van rolled to a stop in front of our new
building, number 109, we were all standing there, waiting
for it, Momma, Poppa, Sis, Paulie, James, Josh, and
myself. I made out like I didn't notice the cats looking us
over, especially me—I was gang age. I read their faces and
found no trust, plenty of suspicion, and a glint of rising
hate. I said to myself, These cats don't mean nothin'.

They're just nosy. But I remembered what had happened to me in my old block, and that it had ended with me in the hospital.

This was a tough-looking block. That was good, that was cool; but my old turf had been tough, too. I'm tough, a voice within said. I hope I'm tough enough. I am tough enough. I've got mucho corazón, I'm king wherever I go. I'm a killer to my heart. I not only can live, I will live, no dunk out, no die out, walk bad; be down, cool breeze, smooth. My mind raced, and thoughts crashed against each other, trying to reassemble themselves into a pattern of rep. I turned slowly and with eyelids half-closed I looked at the rulers of this new world and with a cool shrug of my shoulders I followed the movers into the hallway of number 109 and dismissed the coming war from my mind.

The next morning I went to my new school, called Patrick Henry, and strange, mean eyes followed me.

"Say, pops," said a voice belonging to a guy I later came to know as Waneko, "where's your territory?"

In the same tone of voice Waneko had used, I answered, "I'm on it, dad, what's shaking?"

"Bad, huh?" He half-smiled.

"No, not all the way. Good when I'm cool breeze and bad when I'm down."

"What's your name, kid?"

"That depends. 'Piri' when I'm smooth and 'Johnny Gringo' when stomping time's around."

"What's your name now?" he pushed.

"You name me, man," I answered, playing my role like a champ.

He looked around, and with no kind of words, his boys

cruised in. Guys I would come to know, to fight, to hate, to love, to take care of. Little Red, Waneko, Little Louie, Indio, Carlito, Alfredo, Crip, and plenty more. I stiffened and said to myself, Stomping time, Piri boy, go with heart.

I fingered the garbage-can handle in my pocket—my homemade brass knuckles. They were great for breaking down large odds into small, chopped-up ones.

Waneko, secure in his grandstand, said, "We'll name you later, panin."

I didn't answer. Scared, yeah, but wooden-faced to the end, I thought, Chevere, panin.

It wasn't long in coming. Three days later, at about 6 P.M., Waneko and his boys were sitting around the stoop at number 115. I was cut off from my number 109. For an instant I thought, Make a break for it down the basement steps and through the back yards get away in one piece! Then I thought, Caramba! Live punk, dead hero. I'm no punk kid. I'm not copping any pleas. I kept walking, hell's a-burning, hell's a-churning, rolling with cheer. Walk on, baby man, roll on without fear. What's he going to call?

"Whatta ya say, Mr. Johnny Gringo?" drawled Waneko.

Think, man, I told myself, think your way out of a stomping. Make it good. "I hear you 104th Street coolies are supposed to have heart," I said. "I don't know this for sure. You know there's a lot of streets where a whole 'click' is made out of punks who can't fight one guy unless they all jump him for the stomp." I hoped this would push Waneko into giving me a fair one. His expression didn't change.

"Maybe we don't look at it that way."

Crazy, man. I cheer inwardly, the cabron is falling into

my setup. We'll see who gets messed up first, baby! "I wasn't talking to you," I said. "Where I come from, the pres is president 'cause he got heart when it comes to dealing."

Waneko was starting to look uneasy. He had bit on my worm and felt like a sucker fish. His boys were now light on me. They were no longer so much interested in stomping me as in seeing the outcome between Waneko and me. "Yeah," was his reply.

I smiled at him. "You trying to dig where I'm at and now you got me interested in you. I'd like to see where you're at."

Waneko hesitated a tiny little second before replying, "Yeah."

I knew I'd won. Sure, I'd have to fight; but one guy, not ten or fifteen. If I lost I might still get stomped, and if I won I might get stomped. I took care of this with my next sentence. "I don't know you or your boys," I said, "but they look cool to me. They don't feature as punks."

I had left him out purposely when I said "they." Now his boys were in a separate class. I had cut him off. He would have to fight me on his own, to prove his heart to himself, to his boys, and most important, to his turf. He got away from the stoop and asked, "Fair one, Gringo?"

"Uh-uh," I said, "roll all the way—anything goes." I thought, I've got to beat him bad and yet not bad enough to take his prestige all away. He had corazón. He came on me. Let him draw first blood, I thought, it's his block. Smish, my nose began to bleed. His boys cheered, his heart cheered, his turf cheered. "Waste this chump," somebody shouted.

Okay, baby, now it's my turn. He swung. I grabbed innocently, and my forehead smashed into his nose. His eyes crossed. His fingernails went for my eye and landed in my mouth—crunch, I bit hard. I punched him in the mouth as he pulled away from me, and he slammed his foot into my chest.

We broke, my nose running red, my chest throbbing, his finger—well, that was his worry. I tied him up with body punching and slugging. We rolled onto the street. I wrestled for acceptance, he for rejection or, worse yet, acceptance on his terms. It was time to start peace talks. I smiled at him. "You got heart, baby," I said.

He answered with a punch to my head. I grunted and hit back, harder now. I had to back up my overtures of peace with strength. I hit him in the ribs, I rubbed my knuckles in his ear as we clinched. I tried again. "You deal good," I said.

"You too," he muttered, pressuring out. And just like that, the fight was over. No more words. We just separated, hands half up, half down. My heart pumped out, You've established your red. Move over, 104th Street. Lift your wings, I'm one of your baby chicks now.

Five seconds later my spurs were given to me in the form of introductions to streetdom's elite. There were no looks of blankness now; I was accepted by heart.

"What's your other name, Johnny Gringo?"

"Piri."

"Okay, Pete, you wanna join my fellows?"

"Sure, why not?"

But I knew I had first joined their gang when I cool-looked them on moving day. I was cool, man, I thought. I could've wasted Waneko any time. I'm good, I'm damned good, pure corazón. Viva me! Shit, I had been scared, but that was over. I was in; it was my block now.

Not that I could relax. In Harlem you always lived on the edge of losing rep. All it takes is a one-time loss of heart.

Sometimes, the shit ran smooth until something just had to happen. Then we busted out. Like the time I was leaning against the banister of my stoop, together with Little Louie, Waneko, Indio, and the rest of the guys, and little Crip, small, dark and crippled from birth, came tearing down the block. Crip never ran if he could walk, so we knew there was some kind of trouble. We had been bragging about our greatness in rumbles and love, half truths, half lies. We stopped short and waited cool-like for little Crip to set us straight on what was happening.

"Oh, them lousy motherfuckers, they almost keeled me," he whined.

"Cool it, man," Waneko said, "what happened?"

"I wasn't doin' nothing, just walking through the fuckin' Jolly Rogers' territory," Crip said. "I met a couple of their broads, so friendly-like, I felt one's culo and asked, 'How about a lay?' Imagine, just for that she started yelling for her boys." Crip acted out his narrow escape. We nodded in unimpressed sympathy because there wasn't a mark on him. A stomping don't leave you in walking condition, much less able to run. But he was one of our boys and hadda be backed up. We all looked to Waneko, who was our president. "How about it, war counselor?" he asked me.

We were ready to fight. "We're down," I said softly, "an' the shit's on."

That night we set a meet with the Jolly Rogers. We put on our jackets with our club name, "TNT's." Waneko and I met Picao, Macho, and Cuchee of the Jolly Rogers under the Park Avenue bridge at 104th Street. This was the line between their block and ours. They were Puerto Ricans just like we were, but this didn't mean shit, under our need to keep our reps.

"How's it going to be?" I asked Macho.

Picao, who I dug as no heart, squawked out, "Sticks, shanks, zips—you call it."

I looked at him shiftily and said, "Yeah, like I figured, you ain't got no heart for dealing on fists alone."

Macho, their president, jumped stink and said, "Time man, we got heart, we deal with our manos. Wanna meet here at ten tomorrow night?"

"Ten guys each is okay?"

"That's cool," Macho said and turned away with his boys. The next night we got our boys together. They were all there with one exception—Crip. He sent word that he couldn't make our little 10 P.M. get-together. His sister, skinny Lena, was having a birthday party. We took turns sounding his mother for giving birth to a maricón like him.

Our strategy was simple. We'd meet in the Park Avenue tunnel and each gang would fight with its back to its own block to kill any chance of getting sapped from behind. Our debs sat on the stoops watching for the fuzz or for any wrong shit from the Jolly Rogers.

It got to 10 P.M. and we dug the Jolly Rogers coming under the Park Avenue tunnel. We walked that way too. Macho had heart; he didn't wait for us in the tunnel; he came with his boys right into our block. My guts got tight, as always before a rumble, and I felt my breath come in short spurts. I had wrapped handkerchiefs around each hand to keep my knuckles from getting cut on any Jolly Roger's teeth. We began to pair off. I saw Giant, a big, ugly Jolly Roger, looking me over.

"Deal, motherfucker," I screamed at him.

He was willing like mad. I felt his fist fuck up my shoulder. I was glad 'cause it cooled away my tight guts. I side-slipped and banged my fist in his guts and missed getting my jaw busted by an inch. I came back with two shots to his guts and got shook up by a blast on the side of my head that set my eyeballs afire. I closed on him and held on, hearing the noise of pains and punches. Some sounded like slaps, others hurt dully. I pushed my head into Giant's jaw. He blinked and swung hard, catching my nose. I felt it running. I didn't have a cold, so it had to be blood. I sniffed back hard and drove rights and lefts and busted Giant's lip open. Now he was bleeding too. Chevere.

Everybody was dealing hard. Somebody got in between me and Giant. It was Waneko, and he began dealing with Giant. I took over with the Jolly Roger he'd been punching it out with. It was Picao. He had been fighting all along— not too hard, I suspected. I got most happy. I'd been aching to chill that maricón. He didn't back down and we just stood there and threw punches at each other. I felt hurt a couple of times, but I wanted to put him out so bad, I didn't give a fuck about getting hurt. And then it happened—I caught Picao on his chin with an uppercut and he went sliding on his ass and just lay there.

I felt king-shit high and I wanted to fight anybody. I had the fever. I started for Giant, who was getting wasted by

Waneko, when one of our debs opened up her mouth like an air-raid siren. "Look out, ya gonna get japped," she shouted.

We saw more Rogers coming from Madison Avenue. They were yelling their asses off and waving stickball bats.

"Make it," Waneko shouted. "Them cabrones wanna make a massacre!"

Everybody stopped fighting and both gangs looked at that wasting party tearing up the street toward us. We started cutting out and some of the Rogers tried grabbing on to some of us. Waneko pulled out a blade and started slashing out at any J.R. he could get to. I tore my hand into my back pocket and came out with my garbage-can-handle brass knucks and hit out at a cat who was holding on to one of my boys. He grabbed at a broken nose and went wailing through the tunnel.

We split, everybody making it up some building. I felt bad those cabrones had made us split, but I kept running. I made it to number 109 and loped up the stairs. "Adios, motherfuckers," I yelled over my shoulder. "You cabrones ain't got no heart!" I crashed through my apartment door with thanks that Momma had left it open, 'cause two or three Jolly Rogers were beating the air inches behind me with stickball bats.

"Qué pasa?" yelled Momma.

The Jolly Rogers outside were beating their stickball bats on the door for me to come out if I had any heart. I hollered to them, "I'm coming out right now, you motherfuckers, with my fucking piece!" I didn't have one, but I felt good-o satisfaction at hearing the cattle stampede down the stairs.

"What happened, muchacho?" Momma asked, in a shookup voice.

I laughed. "Nothing, Moms, we was just playing ring-a-livio."

"What about your nose, it got blood on it," said Sis.

I looked bad at her. "Bumped it," I said, then turning to Momma, I asked, "Say, Moms, what's for dinner? Je-sus, I'm starvin'."

PIRI
THOMAS

189

HOMEGIRLS ON ST. NICHOLAS AVENUE

SONIA SANCHEZ

From *Wounded in the House of a Friend* (1995)

If there is a poet laureate of the Black Liberation struggle, an uncompromising voice for the dispossessed, it belongs to Sonia Sanchez. Back in the day, as the youth like to say now, of the turbulent sixties and sizzling seventies, Sanchez could sanctify a rally or a conference with a single stanza of her always remarkably passionate and politically relevant poetry. The brief sketch here captures a portion of her coming of age on the streets of Harlem and her remembrance of Malcolm X, who continues to be an untarnished icon for the poet. Lecturing widely and teaching at Temple University, Sanchez (1934–   ) produces books almost as fast as her often rapid-fire delivery, including *Wounded in the House of a Friend*, from which this vignette is taken. "The poetry of Sonia Sanchez is full of power and yet always clean and uncluttered," wrote the great African novelist Chinua Achebe. "It makes you wish you had thought those thoughts, felt those emotions, and, above all, expressed them so effortlessly and so well." *I've Been a Woman* (1978), *Homegirls and Handgrenades* (1984), *Under a Soprano Sky* (1987), and *Shake Loose My Skin* (1999) are among her other books of poetry and prose.

We were the homegirls on St. Nicholas Avenue in Harlem. Grace, Silvia, and I were the good ones who didn't play around or screw the brothers in the gangs. Just casual kisses. Flirtations that led to the front door of an apartment, and nothing else. We were the girls who stood on the stoops and styled our black ballerina shoes and skirts while Bubba and the other brothers looked and laughed and taunted us for our young vanity. And we waited.

We were the homegirls who smiled and danced and kept our dresses down because everybody knew we were going to make something of our lives. And the people on our block waited for their deliverance. The young and the old, the believers and the nonbelievers, waited for us to deliver them from some unspoken curse.

Silvia was the prettiest homegirl on our block. Silvia the singer who looked like Lena Horne. Her voice was small, sparrow-like, but she was beautiful in an angular fashion. Silvia walked her crinoline walk down St. Nicholas Avenue with her long model strides. And we, the shorter ones, followed her strides, imitating her angular pace. Silvia who eloped at seventeen and had four babies in four years. Silvia who fell in love with a man as beautiful as she and stopped waiting.

Grace and I went to college. We went our separate homegirl ways. She went South to school, graduated magna cum laude, married a wealthy businessman who carried her off to Europe for their honeymoon. Grace who tripped the light European fantastic each year, a world traveler who wiped her hands on overseas towels and left her footprints behind.

I lived at home during college, walked inside stained-glass Hunter College doors and exited in a four-year flush of females. I borrowed the seasons and fell silent as I set out each day at dawn trying to catch my voice and returned home each night trying to understand my words. The body stayed cold so I packed up my eyes and left.

Where to go when you've been educated not to hear

your own echo? Where to go when your soul has lost its beat?

Between sleep and waking I lived. I crowned myself Queen of the Palladium. Remember, O dancers, if you would, the Palladium sitting on Broadway where we mamboed, merengued, and calypsoed till the night fell silent with our rhythms.

It was another of those rallies. New York CORE had planned this rally for weeks. The day was cloudy and grey and wet. As we stood in front of the Hotel Theresa, he ascended the platform. A tall red man. Big Red they used to call him. Now he was Malcolm X. A man I had seen on two other occasions. A man whose eyes made you restless. I turned towards the CORE office. I didn't want to hear him. His words made my head hurt. I was content to picket Woolworth and downtown TV stations. Why did he bring his hand-grenade words into my space?

He stood up and the martial music sounded. I crouched in fear. But I listened on this rainy day and I saw Sundiata and Chaka walking all the way from Africa, spears in their hands. And I saw Bubba running to greet them on our Harlem streets. And the day was like no other.

Malcolm's voice shook the ground. He demanded, "Do you know who you are? Who do you really think you are? Have you looked in a mirror recently brother and sister and seen your Blackness for what it is? Do you know what your Blackness means?"

And something began to stir inside me. Something that I had misplaced a long time ago in the classrooms of America. On that cold wet afternoon, I became warm again. What time of day it was I do not know. What time of year it was I do not remember. All I know is that I began to hear voices—tenants of a long ago past leaped out at me as Malcolm spoke.

And his voice was many voices. And his face became many faces as he spoke. And my skin began to sweat away the years. And the dead skin shook loose and new skin appeared, darker than before. Black in its beauty.

And the day was like no other when he said:

When the people create a program, you get action.

And the years became shorter when he spoke:

We are living in a time when image making has become a science.

They say that Malcolm man don't live here no mo'. They say when a Motswana doctor throws his bones and when they tell him of a loss so terrible he says:

> Se iling se ile
> Se ile mosimeng, motlbaela-thupa
> Lesilo Ke moeelatedi.*

I say Malcolm lives in the eyes of the homegirls who wait no longer.

---

* What is gone is gone / It has gone down the hole, the unreachable-by-a-rod /
  The irrational is he who follows it.

HARLEM BACKGROUND

HAROLD CRUSE

From *The Crisis of the Negro Intellectual* (1984)

With the publication of one book, Harold Cruse (1916–   ) leaped to the forefront of commentators on black social and political thought. When *The Crisis of the Negro Intellectual* appeared in 1967, it shook up the entire intellectual firmament with its critical assessments of such significant thinkers as Paul Robeson, Lorraine Hansberry, John Henrik Clarke, and John Oliver Killens. Cruse spared few in his indictment, with a particularly pointed analysis for those activists, scholars, and intellectuals of Harlem who, in his view, had failed in their leadership tasks and responsibilities. Central to their failure was an integrationist tendency that subverted the importance of black power and self-determination, he concluded.

Harlem has, in this century, become the most strategically important community of Black America. Harlem is still the pivot of the Black world's quest for identity and salvation. The way Harlem goes (or does not go) so goes all Black America. Harlem is the Black world's key community for historical, political, economic, cultural, and/or ethnic reasons. The trouble is that Harlem has never been adequately analyzed in such terms. The demand often heard—'Break up the Harlem ghetto!' (as a hated symbol of segregation)—represents nothing but a romantic and empty wail of politically insolvent integrationists, who fear ghetto riots only more than they fear the responsibilities of political and economic power that lie in the Harlem potential. Caring little or nothing for the ethnic solvency of the Negro group, the integrationists maintain that since Harlem was created by segregation the only solution is to desegregate it by abolishing it. But this is fallacious logic that refuses to admit the class nature of the American social dynamic that permits social mobility only upwards into the middle class.

On the other hand, a forced abolition of a ghetto composed primarily of unemployed and unskilled non-whites would be tantamount to resettlement by decree with all its "undemocratic" implications. Thus, it has not been understood that with all the evils and deprivations of the Harlem ghetto, this community still represents the Negro's strongest bastion in America from which to launch whatever group effort he is able to mobilize for political power, economic rehabilitation and cultural re-identification. Hence, for the Negro to lose his population control of the Harlem area means an uprooting from his strongest base in the American social structure. It is these considerations which reveal the incompetence of much Northern integrationist philosophy, which when carried to its characteristic extremes, sees integration as solving everything. Since integrationists see very little in group economic power, or black political power, to say nothing of cultural identity, they ultimately mislead many Negroes on the bottom of the social scale whose fundamental ethnic group problems the integrationists evade and cannot solve. It must be said that these are the causes behind ghetto uprisings. These glaring defects in the social analysis of Negro ghettoes are what lend that quality of unreality to much of what integrationists say and do.

As long as the Negro's cultural identity is in question, or open to self-doubts, then there can be no positive identification with the real demands of his political and economic existence. Further than that, without a cultural identity that adequately defines himself, the Negro cannot even identify with the American nation as a whole. He is left in the limbo of social marginality, alienated and directionless on the landscape of America, in a variegated nation of whites who have not yet decided on their own identity. The fact of the matter is that American whites, as a whole, are just as much in doubt about their nationality, their cultural identity, as are Negroes. Thus the problem of Negro cultural identity is an unsolved problem within the context of an American nation that is still in process of formation.

It is the Negro movement's impact that brings such historical questions to the fore. It forces the whole nation to look into itself, which it has never wanted to do. Historically, the American psychology has been conditioned by the overriding economic motivation of plundering the continent for the wealth of its natural resources. Every aspect of America's national morality is predicated on that materialistic ethos. With no traditional love for the land he adopted, the American has remained to this day a stranger in the land of his birth: ill-at-ease with his power, uncertain about his nationality, an extroverted pragmatist for whom every exposure of the social immorality of his inner life becomes a scandal. A racial integration movement that does not care to look first into the internal disorder of its own house, is also blind to the fact that ghetto pathologies cannot be treated by attacking them from the other side of the racial fence, by way of integration. A social critique of the Negro's position in America that does not perceive the pivotal characteristics of Harlem as a community, fails as a positive critique and throws the entire Negro movement into a disordered melee of conflicting, and often directionless, methods. These pragmatic protest methods, as a result, become so institutionalized that they can no longer be guided, altered, and channeled away from the pursuit of the integrationist mirage, which in the North, recedes farther away after every protest demonstration. The result has been that the northern civil rights movement, in recent years, has created a legion of zealots for whom integration has been hypostatized into a religion rather than a socially scientific method based on clearly understood principles. It is perhaps cruel to have to say so, but we have to face many truths: In the North, the civil rights movement has produced a crackpot trend marked by a zealous commitment without understanding that borders on anarchism; there has in fact been considerable verbal exposition of the desire for the "revolution of chaos," rather than what could be called "mainstream social change." This anarchistic development has its roots in the accumulated history of incompetent methods.

In Negro life the cultural spheres appear to many as being rather remote, intangible and hardly related to what is called the more practical aspect of race relations. However, the truth is that the more practical sides of the Negro problem in America are bogged down organizationally and methodologically precisely because of cultural confusion and disorientation on the part of most Negroes. Thus it is only through a cultural analysis of the Negro approach to group "politics" that the errors, weaknesses and goal failures can cogently be analyzed and positively worked out.

The years between the day I entered the army, and the war's end in 1945, marked the end of an era for Harlem. For myself, at that time, it merely meant the disappearance of that special adolescent flavor that attaches to a certain locale. Beyond that, it took a while to understand that World War II represented a very abrupt break, a switch over in the continuity of Harlem traditions. New migrations from the South (as in World War I), the creation of a new middle-class stratum on the crest of the war boom, the war veteran's psychology, etc., all served to hide prewar Harlem behind the mask of a transitional kind of postwar personality. If one tried to be nostalgic about the Harlem flavor that was gone forever, such sentiments were quickly dissipated in the urgencies of adjustment to postwar problems—and they were many.

But after a few years, it became apparent that the very abruptness of that break in the continuity of Harlem traditions served to confound and aggravate the community's postwar problems. Harlem was trying to push forward, it seemed, by cutting itself off from every vestige of its past in that strangely distant time before the war. Intellectually, this attitude proved, in time, to be unworkable. Eventually, one had to go back into the 1930s, the 1920s, and even before World War I, in order to understand the Harlem saga—where it had come from, where it had been, and where it might be going.

LORRAINE HANSBERRY: ON TIME!

JOHN OLIVER KILLENS

From *Freedomways Reader,*
edited by Esther Cooper Jackson (2000)

John Oliver Killens (1916–1987) and Lorraine Hansberry (1930–1965) were comrades of the pen. They shared common artistic and ideological perspectives, and both achieved popular fame and were honored in radical political circles during their active lifetimes. Harlem was also a favorite haunt for them, and Killens, whose books include *And Then We Heard the Thunder*, recalls with gusto his notable constituent.

At a writers' conference at Howard University sponsored by the Institute for the Arts and the Humanities in April of 1976, Sister Toni Cade Bambara said, "The responsibility of a writer representing an oppressed people is to make revolution irresistible." Several decades before, the great Paul Robeson had said, "An artist must elect to fight for freedom or for slavery. . . . I have made my choice. I had no alternative." To immodestly quote myself from a book of essays entitled *Black Man's Burden*, I wrote: "Every time I sit down to the typewriter, every line I put on paper, I'm out to change the world, to capture reality, to melt it down and forge it into something entirely different."

How does one evaluate the life of the late Lorraine Hansberry, as a Black person, as a Black woman, as a human being? How is she to be evaluated literarily, politically, historically?

Did Lorraine Hansberry take upon herself the responsibility "to make revolution irresistible"? Did she recognize the battle lines, freedom or slavery? Did she choose sides?

To me, Lorraine Hansberry was a one-woman literary warrior for change—qualitative and fundamental change. She was, moreover, a Pan-Africanist. In her plays *A Raisin in the Sun* and *Les Blancs*, she expressed, through character development and dramatic situations, a oneness with the African peoples and their struggles for liberation. This is certainly the meaning of Asagai, the young, articulate African student in *Raisin*. And it is the entire meaning of *Les Blancs*, which endorses change and revolution. Lest there be any misunderstanding, however, it should be emphasized that Lorraine was a consummate artist. Her writing is not agit-prop. Her characters are flesh and blood people who possess all the flaws and fears and foibles and aspirations and courage that lie restive in human beings. The situations she placed them in are believable and recognizable. She knew that the Western notion of "art for art's sake" is an unadulterated myth, and that art can be a weapon to liberate the people.

I remember Lorraine Hansberry when she first came to New York from her native Chicago. I remember her as a brilliant young woman when she worked with Louis Burnham for Paul Robeson's newspaper, *Freedom*. We engaged in many dialogues and shared many concerns about the world, about its movement in the direction of fundamental change and how the change would affect Black people. The question that would always come up was what role should the artist play in bringing this change about? Those days were a profound learning experience for all of us Youngbloods, a time when I was working with Dr. Alphaeus Hunton and Mr. Robeson and Dr. W. E. B. Du Bois in an organization known as the Council on African Affairs. Our offices were in the same building the *Freedom* office was in on 125th Street in Harlem.

We had many lively discussions about the state of the world and the nation, and especially about the condition of the Afro-American people. It was a time of great excitement, when we took our convictions into the streets, a time of boycotts, of demonstrations and mass meetings at Rockland Palace and the Golden Gate Ballroom, of street meetings on the corner of 125th Street and Seventh Avenue in front of Michaux's bookstore, which boasted of containing "A Hundred Thousand Facts About the Negro." We were part of all that along with Paul Robeson, Adam Powell, Benjamin Davis! It was time when so many of us young warriors matriculated in the University of the Streets. Robeson was an inspiration to us all. By his example, he taught us the true meaning of manhood and womanhood and, especially, of commitment. In the arts, he was our patron saint. Who was Lorraine Hansberry?

One could safely say, in retrospect, that Lorraine Hansberry was a Pan-Africanist with a socialist perspective. Let me be even bolder. In my view, Lorraine was a Black nationalist with a socialist perspective. Her world view combined a commitment to Black liberation with an equally fierce commitment to the demise of capitalism. I think she knew that the contradiction was more apparent than real. As an artist, she saw the paradox and irony of every human being's sojourn on this earth, especially where Black Americans are concerned. The ancestors of most Americans came to these shores seeking freedom, while most of our ancestors came in chains. There is the terrible paradox, the national contradiction. I think she saw contradictions as the very spice of life, and dialectics as the method one uses to go about resolving the contradictions.

A Black nationalist with a socialist perspective? Have not all revolutions of the twentieth century been about national liberation? Haven't they all been socialist revolutions—Russia, China, Vietnam?

Her double commitment was explicit and implicit in everything she wrote, in every lecture and every statement. As with Robeson and Malcolm, her nationalism had an internationalist context that is reflected in a statement by one of her African characters in *Les Blancs*. Tshembe tells the white man, Charlie Morris:

> I shall be honest with you, Mr. Morris. I do not "hate" all white men—but I desperately wish I did. It would make everything infinitely easier! But I am afraid that, among other things, I have seen the slums of Liverpool and Dublin and the caves of Naples. I have seen Dachau and Anne Frank's attic in Amsterdam. I have seen too many raw-knuckled Frenchmen coming out of the Metro at dawn and too many pop-eyed Italian children to believe that those who raided Africa for three centuries ever "loved" the white race either.

Lorraine believed that the road to socialism is through national liberation, just as the literary road to universality is through local identity. Many critics said of *Raisin* that it is "universal," that it isn't specifically about Blacks. "It is about people. It could be about anybody." But a play that could be about anybody would most probably be about nobody at all. Lorraine was very clear on this point when she said in an interview:

> One of the most sound ideas in dramatic writing is that in order to create the universal, you must pay very great attention to the specific. . . . In other words, I have told people that not only is this a Negro family . . . it is specifically South Side Chicago. . . . So I would say it is definitely a Negro play before it is anything else.

One of the most important qualities of Lorraine Hansberry was that she cared. She cared about the whole damn human race. Her caring is expressed eloquently in *The Sign in Sidney Brustein's Window*, when her protagonist says:

> Is that all you can ever say? Who cares, who cares? Let the damn bomb fall, if somebody wants to drop it, 'tis the last days of Rome, so rejoice ye Romans and swill ye these last sick hours away! Well, I admit it. I care! I care about it all. It takes too much energy not to care. Yesterday I counted twenty-six grey hairs in the top of my head—all from trying not to care.

Lorraine unquestionably identified herself with the aspirations of the people of the so-called Third World (which I prefer to call the First World, since even racist anthropologists grudgingly concede that civilization first began in Africa and Asia). She was always there with Fanon's "wretched of the earth," her anti-fascist vision of liberation embracing all of the oppressed regardless of race, color or ethnicity. Ahead of her time? I think not. As Sister Betty Shabazz once said of her husband, Malcolm, Lorraine was not ahead of her time—she was on time. Too many of the rest of us were lagging far behind the times.

In a historic Town Hall forum entitled "The Black Liberation Movement and the White Blacklash," she called for "a basic change of society" and called upon the white liberal to "stop being a liberal and become an American radical." She also said she'd never heard of Negroes booing the name of John Brown and noted that "the vantage point of Negroes is entirely different [from the rest of the nation]."

Lorraine Hansberry was an extraordinarily articulate young Black woman, committed to the struggle and very fast on the draw. Indeed, literarily and intellectually, she was one of the fastest guns in the East—and her gun was for revolution and for change. She was a humanist; she was anti-slavery (meaning she was anti-capitalist). The pity of it, and the loss to us, is that she was with us for so terribly short a period. Who knows to what heights this courageous falcon might have soared!

FIFTH AVENUE UPTOWN: A LETTER FROM HARLEM

JAMES BALDWIN

From *Nobody Knows My Name* (1954)

If there is a prophetic and preeminent voice from Harlem, a witness that embodies its plight and plea, it's James Baldwin (1924–1987). This native son rose from the teeming community to become an international literary figure. But no matter where he roamed and the subjects of his many books, Harlem was always a special place for him, and he never evoked it better than in this memorable essay. Whether on the mountain, in the valley, or in the deep recesses of the human soul, Baldwin was an intimate communicator.

There is a housing project standing now where the house in which we grew up once stood, and one of those stunted city trees is snarling where our doorway used to be. This is on the rehabilitated side of the avenue. The other side of the avenue—for progress takes time—has not been rehabilitated yet and it looks exactly as it looked in the days when we sat with our noses pressed against the windowpane, longing to be allowed to go "across the street." The grocery store which gave us credit is still there, and there can be no doubt that it is still giving credit. The people in the project certainly need it—far more, indeed, than they ever needed the project. The last time I passed by, the Jewish proprietor was still standing among its shelves, looking sadder and heavier but scarcely older. Farther down the block stands the shoe-repair store in which our shoes were repaired until reparation became impossible and in which, then, we bought all our "new" ones. The Negro proprietor is still in the window, head down, working at the leather. These two, I imagine, could tell a long tale if they would (perhaps they would be glad to if they could), having watched so many, for so long, struggling in the fishhooks, the barbed wire, of this avenue.

The avenue is elsewhere the renowned and elegant Fifth. The area I am describing, which, in today's gang parlance, would be called "the turf," is bounded by Lenox Avenue on the west, the Harlem River on the east, 135th Street on the north, and 130th Street on the south. We never lived beyond these boundaries; this is where we grew up. Walking along 145th Street—for example—familiar as it is, and similar, does not have the same impact because I do not know any of the people on the block. But when I turn east on 131st Street and Lenox Avenue, there is first a soda-pop joint, then a shoeshine "parlor," then a grocery store, then a dry cleaner's, then the houses. All along the street there are people who watched me grow up, people who grew up with me, people I watched grow up along with my brothers and sisters; and, sometimes in my arms, sometimes underfoot, sometimes at my shoulder—or on it—their children, a riot, a forest of children, who include my nieces and nephews.

When we reach the end of this long block, we find ourselves on wide, filthy, hostile Fifth Avenue, facing that project which hangs over the avenue like a monument to the folly, and the cowardice, of good intentions. All along the block, for anyone who knows it, are immense human gaps, like craters. These gaps are not created merely by those who have moved away, inevitably into some other ghetto; or by those who have risen, almost always into a greater capacity for self-loathing and self-delusion; or yet by those who, by whatever means—World War II, the Korean war, a policeman's gun or billy, a gang war, a brawl, madness, an overdose of heroin, or, simply, unnatural exhaustion—are dead. I am talking about those who are left, and I am talking principally about the young. What are they doing? Well, some, a minority, are fanatical churchgoers, members of the more extreme of the Holy Roller sects. Many, many more are "moslems," by affiliation or sympathy, that is to say that they are united by nothing more—and nothing less—than a hatred of the white world and all its works. They are present, for example, at every Buy Black street-corner meeting— meetings in which the speaker urges his hearers to cease trading with white men and establish a separate economy. Neither the speaker nor his hearers can possibly do this, of course, since Negroes do not own General Motors or RCA or the A&P, nor, indeed, do they own more than a wholly insufficient fraction of anything else in Harlem (those who do own anything are more interested in their profits than in their fellows). But these meetings nevertheless keep alive in the participators a certain pride of bitterness without which, however futile this bitterness may be, they could scarcely remain alive at all. Many have given up. They stay home and watch the TV screen, living on the earnings of their parents, cousins, brothers, or uncles, and only leave the house to go to the movies or to the nearest bar. "How're you making it?" one may ask,

JAMES
BALDWIN

207

running into them along the block, or in the bar. "Oh, I'm TV-ing it"; with the saddest, sweetest, most shamefaced of smiles, and from a great distance. This distance one is compelled to respect; anyone who has traveled so far will not easily be dragged again into the world. There are further retreats, of course, than the TV screen or the bar. There are those who are simply sitting on their stoops, "stoned," animated for a moment only, and hideously, by the approach of someone who may lend them the money for a "fix." Or by the approach of someone from whom they can purchase it, one of the shrewd ones, on the way to prison or just coming out.

And the others, who have avoided all of these deaths, get up in the morning and go downtown to meet "the man." They work in the white man's world all day and come home in the evening to this fetid block. They struggle to instill in their children some private sense of honor or dignity which will help the child to survive. This means, of course, that they must struggle, stolidly, incessantly, to keep this sense alive in themselves, in spite of the insults, the indifference, and the cruelty they are certain to encounter in their working day. They patiently browbeat the landlord into fixing the heat, the plaster, the plumbing; this demands prodigious patience; nor is patience usually enough. In trying to make their hovels habitable, they are perpetually throwing good money after bad. Such frustration, so long endured, is driving many strong, admirable men and women whose only crime is color to the very gates of paranoia. One remembers them from another time—playing handball in the playground, going to church, wondering if they were going to be promoted at school. One remembers them going off to war—gladly, to escape this block. One remembers their return. Perhaps one remembers their wedding day. And one sees where the girl is now—vainly looking for salvation from some other embittered, trussed, and struggling boy—and sees the all-but-abandoned children in the streets.

Now I am perfectly aware that there are other slums in which white men are fighting for their lives, and mainly losing. I know that blood is also flowing through those streets and that the human damage there is incalculable. People are continually pointing out to me the wretchedness of white people in order to console me for the wretchedness of blacks. But an itemized account of the American failure does not console me and it should not console anyone else. That hundreds of thousands of white people are living, in effect, no better than the "niggers" is not a fact to be regarded with complacency. The social and moral bankruptcy suggested by this fact is of the bitterest, most terrifying kind.

The people, however, who believe that this democratic anguish has some consoling value are always pointing out that So-and-So, white, and So-and-So, black, rose from the slums into the big time. The existence—the public existence—of, say, Frank Sinatra and Sammy Davis Jr. proves to them that America is still the land of opportunity and that inequalities vanish before the determined will. It proves nothing of the sort. The determined will is rare at the moment, in this country, it is unspeakably rare—and the inequalities suffered by the many are in no way justified by the rise of a few. A few have always risen—in every country, every era, and in the teeth of regimes which can by no stretch of the imagination be thought of as free. Not all of these people, it is worth remembering, left the world better than they found it. The determined will is rare, but it is not invariably benevolent. Furthermore, the American equation of success with the big time reveals an awful disrespect for human life and human achievement. This equation has placed our cities among the most dangerous in the world and has placed our youth among the most empty and most bewildered. The situation of our youth is not mysterious. Children have never been very good at listening to their elders, but they have never failed to imitate them. They must, they have no other models. That is exactly what our children are doing. They are imitating our immorality, our disrespect for the pain of others.

All other slum dwellers, when the bank account permits it, can move out of the slum and vanish altogether from the eye of persecution. No Negro in this country has ever made that much money and it will be a long time before any Negro does. The Negroes in Harlem, who have no money, spend what they have on such gimcracks as they are sold. These include "wider" TV screens, more "faithful" hi-fi sets, more "powerful" cars, all of which, of course, are obsolete long before they are paid for. Anyone who has ever struggled with poverty knows how extremely expensive it is to be poor; and if one is a member of a captive population, economically speaking, one's feet have simply been placed on the treadmill forever. One is victimized, economically, in a thousand ways— rent, for example, or car insurance. Go shopping one day in Harlem—for anything—and compare Harlem prices and quality with those downtown.

The people who have managed to get off this block have only got as far as a more respectable ghetto. This respectable ghetto does not even have the advantages of the disreputable one—friends, neighbors, a familiar church, and friendly tradesmen—and it is not, moreover, in the nature of any ghetto to remain respectable long. Every Sunday, people who have left the block take the lonely ride back, dragging their increasingly discontented children with them. They spend the day talking, not always with words, about the trouble they've seen and the trouble—one must watch their eyes as they watch their children—they are only too likely to see. For children do not like ghettos. It takes them nearly no time to discover exactly why they are there.

The projects in Harlem are hated. They are hated almost as much as policemen, and this is saying a great deal. And they are hated for the same reason: both reveal, unbearably, the real attitude of the white world, no matter how many liberal speeches are made, no matter how many lofty editorials are written, no matter how many civil-rights commissions are set up.

The projects are hideous, of course, there being a law, apparently respected throughout the world, that popular housing shall be as cheerless as a prison. They are lumped all over Harlem, colorless, bleak, high, and revolting. The wide windows look out on Harlem's invincible and indescribable squalor: the Park Avenue railroad tracks, around which, about forty years ago, the present dark community began; the unrehabilitated houses, bowed down, it would seem, under the great weight of frustration and bitterness they contain; the dark, ominous schoolhouses from which the child may emerge maimed, blinded, hooked, or enraged for life; and the churches, churches, block upon block of churches, niched in the walls like cannon in the walls of a fortress. Even if the administration of the projects were not so insanely humiliating (for example: one must report raises in salary to the management, which will then eat up the profit by raising one's rent; the management has the right to know who is staying in your apartment; the management can ask you to leave, at their discretion), the projects would still be hated because they are an insult to the meanest intelligence.

Harlem got its first private project, Riverton*—which is now, naturally, a slum—about twelve years ago because at that time Negroes were not allowed to live in Stuyvesant Town. Harlem watched Riverton go up, therefore, in the most violent bitterness of spirit, and hated it long before the builders arrived. They began hating it at about the time people began moving out of their condemned houses to make room for this additional proof of how thoroughly the white world despised them. And they had scarcely moved in, naturally, before they began smashing win-

---

* The Inhabitants of Riverton were much embittered by this description; they have, apparently, forgotten how their project came into being; and have repeatedly informed me that I cannot possibly be referring to Riverton, but to another housing project which is directly across the street. It is quite clear, I think, that I have no interest in accusing any individuals or families of the depredations herein described: but neither can I deny the evidence of my own eyes. Nor do I blame anyone in Harlem for making the best of a dreadful bargain. But anyone who lives in Harlem and imagines that he has not struck this bargain, or that what he takes to be his status (in whose eyes?) protects him against the common pain, demoralization, and danger, is simply self-deluded.

dows, defacing walls, urinating in the elevators, and forni-
cating in the playgrounds. Liberals, both white and black,
were appalled at the spectacle. I was appalled by the liberal
innocence—or cynicism, which comes out in practice as
much the same thing. Other people were delighted to be
able to point to proof positive that nothing could be done
to better the lot of the colored people. They were, and are,
right in one respect: that nothing can be done as long as
they are treated like colored people. The people in Harlem
know they are living there because white people do not
think they are good enough to live anywhere else. No
amount of "improvement" can sweeten this fact. Whatever money is now being earmarked to improve this, or
any other ghetto, might as well be burnt. A ghetto can be
improved in one way only: out of existence.

Similarly, the only way to police a ghetto is to be oppres-
sive. None of the Police Commissioner's men, even with
the best will in the world, have any way of understanding
the lives led by the people they swagger about in twos and
threes controlling. Their very presence is an insult, and it
would be, even if they spent their entire day feeding gum-
drops to children. They represent the force of the white
world, and that world's real intentions are, simply, for that
world's criminal profit and ease, to keep the black man
corraled up here, in his place. The badge, the gun in the
holster, and the swinging club make vivid what will happen should his rebellion become overt. Rare, indeed, is the
Harlem citizen, from the most circumspect church member to the most shiftless adolescent, who does not have a
long tale to tell of police incompetence, injustice, or brutality. I myself have witnessed and endured it more than

once. The businessmen and racketeers also have a story. And so do the prostitutes. (And this is not, perhaps, the place to discuss Harlem's very complex attitude toward black policemen, nor the reasons, according to Harlem, that they are nearly all downtown.)

It is hard, on the other hand, to blame the policeman, blank, good-natured, thoughtless, and insuperably innocent, for being such a perfect representative of the people he serves. He, too, believes in good intentions and is astounded and offended when they are not taken for the deed. He has never, himself, done anything for which to be hated—which of us has?—and yet he is facing, daily and nightly, people who would gladly see him dead, and he knows it. There is no way for him not to know it: there are few things under heaven more unnerving than the silent, accumulating contempt and hatred of a people. He moves through Harlem, therefore, like an occupying soldier in a bitterly hostile country; which is precisely what, and where, he is, and is the reason he walks in twos and threes. And he is not the only one who knows why he is always in company: the people who are watching him know why, too. Any street meeting, sacred or secular, which he and his colleagues uneasily cover has as its explicit or implicit burden the cruelty and injustice of the white domination. And these days, of course, in terms increasingly vivid and jubilant, it speaks of the end of that domination. The white policeman standing on a Harlem street corner finds himself at the very center of the revolution now occurring in the world. He is not prepared for it—naturally, nobody is—and, what is possibly much more to the point, he is exposed, as few white people are, to the anguish of the black people around him. Even if he is gifted with the merest mustard grain of imagination, something must seep in. He cannot avoid observing that some of the children, in spite of their color, remind him of children he has known and loved, perhaps even of his own children. He knows that he certainly does not want his children living this way. He can retreat from his uneasiness in only one direction: into a callousness which very shortly becomes second nature. He becomes more callous, the population becomes more hostile, the situation grows more tense, and the police force is increased. One day, to everyone's astonishment, someone drops a match in the powder keg and everything blows up. Before the dust has settled or the blood congealed, editorials, speeches, and civil-rights commissions are loud in the land, demanding to know what happened. What happened is that Negroes want to be treated like men.

Negroes want to be treated like men: a perfectly straightforward statement, containing only seven words. People who have mastered Kant, Hegel, Shakespeare, Marx, Freud, and the Bible find this statement utterly impenetrable. The idea seems to threaten profound, barely conscious assumptions. A kind of panic paralyzes their features, as though they found themselves trapped on the edge of a steep place. I once tried to describe to a very well-known American intellectual the conditions among Negroes in the South. My recital disturbed him and made him indignant; and he asked me in perfect innocence, "Why don't all the Negroes in the South move north?" I tried to explain what has happened, unfailingly, whenever a significant body of Negroes move north. They do not escape Jim Crow: they merely encounter another, not-less-deadly variety. They do not move to Chicago, they move to the South Side; they do not move to New York, they move to Harlem. The pressure within the ghetto causes the ghetto walls to expand, and this expansion is always violent. White people hold the line as long as they can, and in as many ways as they can, from verbal intimidation to physical violence. But inevitably the border which has divided the ghetto from the rest of the world falls into the hands of the ghetto. The white people fall back bitterly before the black horde; the landlords make a tidy profit by raising the rent, chopping up the rooms, and all but dispensing with the upkeep; and what has once been a neighborhood turns into a "turf." This is precisely what happened when the Puerto Ricans arrived in their thousands—and the bitterness thus caused is, as I write, being fought out all up and down those streets.

Northerners indulge in an extremely dangerous luxury. They seem to feel that because they fought on the right side during the Civil War, and won, they have earned the right merely to deplore what is going on in the South, without taking any responsibility for it; and that they can ignore what is happening in Northern cities because what is happening in Little Rock or Birmingham is worse. Well, in the first place, it is not possible for anyone who has not endured both to know which is "worse." I know Negroes who prefer the South and white Southerners, because "at least there, you haven't got to play any guessing games!" The guessing games referred to have driven more than one Negro into the narcotics ward, the madhouse, or the river. I know another Negro, a man very dear to me, who says, with conviction and with truth, "The spirit of the South is the spirit of America." He was born in the North and did his military training in the South. He did not, as far as I can gather, find the South "worse"; he found it, if anything, all too familiar. In the second place, though, even if Birmingham is worse, no doubt Johannesburg, South Africa, beats it by several miles, and Buchenwald was one of the worst things that ever happened in the entire history of the world. The world has never lacked for horrifying examples; but I do not believe that these examples are meant to be used as justification for our own crimes. This perpetual justification empties the heart of all human feeling. The emptier our hearts become, the greater will be our crimes. Thirdly, the South is not merely an embarrassingly backward region, but a part of this country, and what happens there concerns every one of us.

As far as the color problem is concerned, there is but one great difference between the Southern white and the Northerner: the Southerner remembers, historically and in his own psyche, a kind of Eden in which he loved black people and they loved him. Historically, the flaming sword laid across this Eden is the Civil War. Personally, it is the Southerner's sexual coming of age, when, without any warning, unbreakable taboos are set up between himself and his past. Everything, thereafter, is permitted him except the love he remembers and has never ceased to need. The resulting, indescribable torment affects every Southern mind and is the basis of the Southern hysteria.

None of this is true for the Northerner. Negroes represent nothing to him personally, except, perhaps, the dangers of carnality. He never sees Negroes. Southerners see them all the time. Northerners never think about them whereas Southerners are never really thinking of anything else. Negroes are, therefore, ignored in the North and are under surveillance in the South, and suffer hideously in both places. Neither the Southerner nor the Northerner is able to look on the Negro simply as a man. It seems to be indispensable to the national self-esteem that the Negro be considered either as a kind of ward (in which case we are told how many Negroes, comparatively, bought Cadillacs last year and how few, comparatively, were lynched), or as a victim (in which case we are promised that he will never vote in our assemblies or go to school with our kids). They are two sides of the same coin and the South will not change—cannot change—until the North changes. The country will not change until it reexamines itself and discovers what it really means by freedom. In the meantime, generations keep being born, bitterness is increased by incompetence, pride, and folly, and the world shrinks around us.

It is a terrible, an inexorable, law that one cannot deny the humanity of another without diminishing one's own: in the face of one's victim, one sees oneself. Walk through the streets of Harlem and see what we, this nation, have become.

MINISTER MALCOLM X

MALCOLM X

From *The Autobiography of Malcolm X* (1965)

Malcolm X, born Malcolm Little and died with the name El Hajj Malik El-Shabazz, led such a rich and adventurous life that no matter what chapter or excerpt you select from his autobiography (ably assisted by Alex Haley) it will be rewarding and exciting. Shortly after his marriage, Malcolm was embroiled in a major incident involving police brutality in Harlem. This incident, on April 14, 1957, would be among several to convey Malcolm's power and charisma that would establish him as one of the most potent black leaders of the twentieth century. Two years later, after Malcolm granted an interview to reporter Mike Wallace, now of the TV news magazine *60 Minutes*, the Nation of Islam gained additional notoriety, and Malcolm's reputation reached beyond Harlem, providing him a national and international platform.

Two white policemen, breaking up a street scuffle between some Negroes, ordered other Negro passers-by to "Move on!" Of these bystanders, two happened to be Muslim brother Johnson Hinton and another brother of Temple Seven. They didn't scatter and run the way the white cops wanted. Brother Hinton was attacked with night sticks. His scalp was split open, and a police car came and he was taken to a nearby precinct. The second brother telephoned our restaurant. And with some telephone calls, in less than half an hour about fifty of Temple Seven's men of the Fruit of Islam were standing in ranks-formation outside the police precinct house. Other Negroes, curious, came running, and gathered in excitement behind the Muslims. The police, coming to the station house front door, and looking out of the windows, couldn't believe what they saw. I went in, as the minister of Temple Seven, and demanded to see our brother. The police first said he wasn't there. Then they admitted he was, but said I couldn't see him. I said that until he was seen, and we were sure he received proper medical attention, the Muslims would remain where they were.

They were nervous and scared of the gathering crowd outside. When I saw our Brother Hinton, it was all I could do to contain myself. He was only semiconscious. Blood had bathed his head and face and shoulder. I hope I never again to have to withstand seeing another case of sheer police brutality like that. I told the lieutenant in charge, "That man belongs in the hospital." They called an ambulance. When it came and Brother Hinton was taken to Harlem Hospital, we Muslims followed, in loose formations, for about fifteen blocks along Lenox Avenue, probably the busiest thoroughfare in Harlem. Negroes who never had seen anything like this were coming out of stores and restaurants and bars and enlarging the crowd following us.

The crowd was big, and angry, behind the Muslims in front of Harlem Hospital. Harlem's black people were long since sick and tired of police brutality. And they never had seen any organization of black men take a firm stand as we were.

A high police official came up to me, saying, "Get those people out of there." I told him that our brothers were standing peacefully, disciplined perfectly, and harming no one. He told me those others, behind them, weren't disciplined. I politely told him those others were his problem.

When doctors assured us that Brother Hinton was receiving the best of care, I gave the order and the Muslims slipped away. The other Negroes' mood was ugly, but they dispersed also when we left. We wouldn't learn until later that a steel plate would have to be put into Brother Hinton's skull. (After that operation, the Nation of Islam helped him to sue; a jury awarded him over $70,000, the largest police brutality judgment New York City has ever paid.)

For New York City's millions of readers of the downtown papers, it was, at that time, another one of the periodic "Racial Unrest in Harlem" stories. It was not played up, because of what had happened. But the police department, to be sure, pulled out and carefully studied the files on the Nation of Islam, and appraised us with new eyes. Most important, in Harlem, the world's most heavily populated black ghetto, the *Amsterdam News* made the whole story headline news, and for the first time the black man, woman, and child in the streets was discussing "those Muslims."

CASTRO IN HARLEM

MAYA ANGELOU

From *The Heart of a Woman* (1981)

Since she emerged on the political and cultural scene more than a generation ago, Maya Angelou (1928–   ) has written herself into the annals of American history. If she had written only the inaugural poem "On the Pulse of Morning" for President Clinton in 1993, her place in the literary pantheon would be secure. But she has produced book after book, each one representing a notable slice of her fantastic career. This excerpt is exemplary of her movement and activities in the late fifties and early sixties.

The Harlem Writers Guild meeting at Sarah Wright's house was ending. As we were saying goodbye, Sarah's phone rang. She motioned us to wait and answered it. When she hung up, she said excitedly that the Cuban delegation to the United Nations, led by President Castro, had been turned out of a midtown hotel. The group was accused of having brought live chickens to their rooms, where they were to use them in voodoo rites. The entire delegation had been invited to the Theresa Hotel in Harlem.

We all shouted. Those few writers and would-be writers who were not members of Fair Play for Cuba nonetheless took delight in Fidel Castro's plucky resistance to the United States.

In moments, we were on the street in the rain, finding cabs or private cars or heading for subways. We were going to welcome the Cubans to Harlem.

To our amazement, at eleven o'clock on a Monday evening, we were unable to get close to the hotel. Thousands of people filled the sidewalks and intersections, and police had cordoned off the main and side streets. I hovered with my friends on the edges of the crowd, enjoying the Spanish songs, the screams of "Viva Castro," and the sounds of conga drums being played nearby in the damp night air.

It was an olé and hallelujah time for the people of Harlem.

Two days later, Khrushchev came to visit Castro at the Theresa. The police, white and nervous, still guarded the intersection of 125th Street and Seventh Avenue, which even in normal times was accepted as the most popular and possibly most dangerous crossroad in black America.

Hazel, Millie and I walked down a block from the office, pushing through the jubilant crowd. We watched as Castro and Khrushchev embraced on 125th Street, as the Cubans applauded and the Russians smiled broadly, showing metal teeth. Black people joined the applause. Some white folks weren't bad at all. The Russians were O.K. Of course, Castro never had called himself white, so he was O.K. from the git. Anyhow, America hated Russians, and as black people often said, "Wasn't no Communist country that put my grandpappa in slavery. Wasn't no Communist lynched my poppa or raped my mamma."

"Hey, Khrushchev. Go on, with your bad self."

Guy left school, without permission, to come to Harlem with a passel of his schoolmates.

They trooped into the SCLC office after the Russian and Cuban delegations had left the neighborhood for the United Nations building.

Millie called and told me my son was in the back, stamping envelopes.

Surprise and a lack of sensitivity made me confront him before his friends.

"What are you doing here? You're supposed to be in school."

He dropped the papers and said in a voice cold and despising, "Do you want to speak to me privately, Mother?"

Why couldn't I know the moment before I had spoken what I knew as soon as my question hit the air. I turned without apology and he followed.

We stopped and faced each other in the hallway.

"Mother, I guess you'll never understand. To me, a black man, the meeting of Cuba and the Soviet Union in Harlem is the most important thing that could happen. It means that, in my time, I am seeing powerful forces get together to oppose capitalism. I don't know how it was in your time, the olden days, but in modern America this was something I had to see. It will influence my future."

I looked at him and found nothing to say. He had an uncanny sense of himself. When I was young I often wondered how I appeared to people around me, but I never thought to see myself in relation to the entire world. I nodded and walked past him back to my office.

Abbey, Rosa and I decided what was needed was one more organization. A group of talented black women who would make themselves available to all the other groups. We would be on call to perform, give fashion shows, read poetry, sing, write for any organization from the SCLC to the Urban League that wanted to put on a fund-raising affair.

MAYA
ANGELOU

HARLEM

HENRY DUMAS

From *Goodbye Sweetwater:*
New and Selected Stories (1988)

What most Harlemites remember of Henry Dumas (1934–1968)
is the mystery that shrouds his death in 1968 when he was shot
by a policeman in a Harlem subway. The official police report
labeled it a case of mistaken identity. It was a tragedy that cut
short the life of a gifted and still-evolving young writer and is
eerily prefigured in the opening of this short story.

The Lenox Avenue subway shot through the tunnel, shaking the tracks and debris. A hot blast of air leaped from the subway cavity, as if the train had screamed. It roared into the station, stopped, recharged itself, and waited. Harold Kane, sitting with his head down and his eyes closed, suddenly looked up. Peered through the standing people, and pushed his way off the train. Just as Harold was half out, the doors began to close. His leg caught; the train hissed, the doors reopened, and Harold stumbled off the train. He looked around, went through the turnstile, and slowly made his way up the steps, brushing often against people, as ants do in a moving line. Harold was tall and muscular. He looked older than twenty-two. As he came up out of the subway and onto the street, the sunless haze over Harlem showed his skin to be dark and tinged with redness, as if the blood were going to suddenly break through. His eyes were very large and watered a lot, and even though he moved along the street in a glide, a slow, aimless flow, there was a latent quickness about his walk. At the corner, he did not wait for the light as some other pedestrians, but weaved behind a passing car, around another, alongside another, and then with his head held dreamlike he stepped upon the sidewalk on the other side of the street. There he stood beside a fire hydrant and looked up at the skeletal remains of the Islamic Temple.

High over the ruins a flock of pigeons circled, arcing off, and then swooping up again, playing in the wind. Harold squinted closely at the building. A man came and stood by him. They both looked up. People passed. A woman stopped at the corner newsstand and bought a paper. The man was young and neatly dressed. He looked at Harold, who continued to examine the wreckage without acknowledging the other.

"Well, Broh," the young man finally said, "I see you anxious to know when the mosque will be rebuilt." Harold rubbed the fire hydrant with his right hand. He looked at the bundle of newspapers under the young man's arms. "Paper?" The young Brother was handing him one. Harold paid for it and tucked it under his arm. The other moved away and began to hustle off the papers to passers-by. The wreckage was strewn all over the sidewalk—bits of burnt wood, debris, and broken glass. The police had erected a barricade around the burnt-out stores. There were several beside the temple, which stood right in the center. On one side were a beauty parlor, dress shop, bakery, and drugstore. On the other were a tavern, barbershop, poolroom, and pawnshop. All these had been completely burned down. But the temple was the hardest hit. A bomb had leveled the walls and pillars. Harold watched the scene with a curious familiarity. While the young Brother was selling papers, he kept a close eye on Harold. Soon he and another Brother had their heads together. They had seen him gazing every day now for the last week. At a certain time Harold emerged from the subway like a man in a trance, and stared at the wreckage for a long time. His expression, twisted up with some concealed misery, kept the astute young Brothers from questioning him. They expected him, any day now, to break out in tears.

A bus roared past. Harold leaned his head against the newsstand. He slowly brought his right hand around and touched the top as if he were feeling for something very small. Then he looked at his smudged fingers. He put his head down on his arms again. For ten minutes he leaned up against the rear of the newsstand, not moving except for the shaking and shuddering of his body like spasms of pain. The subway roared beneath him. The street was loud and noisy. People darted here and there. Many stood and looked at him. Most of them thought that he was about to vomit. Perhaps he was. But the heaving of his body was far deeper than his stomach. Suddenly he raised his head and walked off toward Seventh Avenue and Harlem Square.

A group of kids was running toward Harold, and behind them was a man in an apron, waving a stick. People stopped to look. There were shouts, but the kids soon disappeared, zipping across the street in the middle of traffic. Several cars screeched to a halt. In front of a record store where the music was pouring onto the street like syrup, four teen-age girls and two boys were dancing, and one of the boys was beating out a rhythm on the showcase window with his fist. Harold moved through the crowd. An elderly woman dressed in a long cloak and with a big gold cross around her neck was weaving through the throng, handing out pamphlets. She put one in Harold's hands, but he put it in his pocket automatically, without even looking. A siren sounded blocks away, and a few people ran off in the direction of the siren. A wino was stopping people up the block near Seventh Avenue. He was holding out his hand and leaning forward. When he came to Harold he assumed a different posture, straightening himself up a bit and wiping the dribble from his mouth with his sleeve. Instead of holding his hand out to Harold, he grabbed him by the elbow.

Harold was dressed in a worn suit coat and a pair of khaki pants. His blue sport shirt had sweat and dirt stains overlapping the collar, and his shoes were runover and unshined. The beggar appeared no better off, but he looked Harold over carefully and probably surmised, Here comes a good one. "Please sir," he said—a slight affectation slurring his words—"could you help me get a sandwich?" He showed his hand. "I just need a dime . . ." He was pulling on Harold's coat. Harold dug into his pocket, brought out the newspaper, searched around, brought out cigarettes, then a quarter, and gave it to the man without looking at him. The man, speechless for a split second, thanked him in a low voice and backed off, inspecting the quarter, squeezing it, and then looking around the crowd. He looked as if he were trying to find out who saw him. Then he moved on down the street and began to beg again, adopting the same pose he had taken before he had tapped Harold.

A cop stood in the midst of a group of young toughs across the street. Another cop was crossing the street to them, holding his hand up to stop traffic. The cop on the sidewalk was tongue-lashing the toughs, who taunted him loudly and then scattered. Later, the two cops stood waving them away. The toughs, moving through the crowd, suddenly began to run, and a bottle crashed against the sidewalk. The cops took off, chasing them. They all disappeared around the corner of Lenox Avenue. Harold went on toward Seventh.

At Harlem Square the crowds were gathering. Traffic moved slowly, and all along Seventh Avenue people were sitting on boxes, in chairs, on rails, on the ramp in the middle of the avenue, and even on the roofs. High over the city heads sprouted, leaning over the roofs, making it look as if the building was boiling over. And the street received the crowds, who found that the heat and the boredom were too much to fight alone in the musty roach-ruled tenements. Men, women, children, old and young, poured into the streets. Gangs perched on roofs like vultures waiting for something to happen below. A small parade ensemble made loud music in one block, and the music carried up and down the avenue. Conga drums, timbals, cowbells, guitars, gourds, and flutes harmonized raucously and shook the streets. Even small children were infected by the strange malady of hate and boredom. They had formed little squadrons, and went about with sticks and toy rifles, pistols and cap guns, firing and ambushing unseen enemies. They often aimed at the targets on the roofs, and they ducked down into the basements or into alleyways behind garbage cans for protection and concealment.

Harold stood across from the bookstore. At the corner was Goodman's Jewelry Store, with its huge multicolored diamond flashing on and off overhead. Harold looked up at it, squinting his eyes. He rubbed his head and leaned back against the wall. Closing his eyes briefly, he wavered on his feet. Then he crossed the street with the green light amidst a crowd of people who moved along like ants on a march. When Harold reached the other side he stood by a fire hydrant and watched the sojourn of the American flag as it moved from the door of the bookstore to the center of a crowd standing around a platform under the diamond.

Elder Dawud was preparing to deliver his evening message to the people. He walked behind a man carrying the flag. Another man was setting up a ladder for the Elder, and every once in a while somebody shouted a greeting at Elder Dawud. The people knew him. He was one of the many sidewalk prophets who—more than once—had indirectly caused the people to react in concert over some issue of concern to Harlemites. He was a short, dark man, about forty years old, but his thinness gave him the appearance of youth. He was clean-shaven, but his hair—thick and woolly on the sides, but balding on top—stuck out from the sides of his head. After carefully cleaning his spectacles, he folded some papers, put them in his small briefcase, and handed the case to one of his aides. They stood around the ladder like a cordon. He shook hands with several people, looked at his watch, and mounted the ladder.

When the people saw him, a hush flowed over them. The only noise was the whine of the siren in the distance, the honk and flow of traffic, and the unidentifiable roar that emerged from all of the streets of Harlem.

Harold Kane began to cough. He bent over, holding his sides, and coughed into the gutter.

"Many of you out there . . ." began Elder Dawud, his voice slow and liquid, as if it were being oiled for something. From his throat came a slight rattle, and it gave the impression of motion and force. ". . . want to know just how is it that a black man can live in the middle of the richest country on earth and be starving like a sharecropper. Heh? Many of you want to know about that. Now, again, many of you out there . . ." and he paused to smile and point at the people, ". . . and I ought to know because I lived with a lot of you out there . . ." and there was a slight stir amongst the crowd.

Harold moved in closer. He was shaking.

"Many of you want to know what to tell your children when they ask you why you let the policeman hit you, heh? Now, I am not one to advocate anarchy, no. Brothers, I am the most law-abiding citizen. But I'm talking about conditions that require careful examination; do you hear me?" and he looked at the people for a long time, then he repeated his question, looking around the crowd. "Careful examination, a close look, a breaking of things down into component parts, eh?"

The crowd roared its approval.

"Many of you think you know a lot about the plight of our people in this racist society. You think you know, so you dont try to find out anything new. You are what we call complacent, satisfied, pacified. But you're still feeling the boot of the white man. He kicks you up wherever he wants you to go or sit to be his Uncle and to do his Tomming for him, and when he gets tired of your weakness, he kicks you down. Am I right or wrong?" The crowd roared its approval. "So, you see, the white man doesnt like an Uncle Tom Negro, either. Down South he uses the Toms and lynches bad niggers. Am I right or wrong?" "Right!" the people exclaimed. "So dont think you know all things about this situation until you have done a little investigation. How many of you have done some honest investigation, eh? How many of you out there have looked into the inequities of the system? Huh?" There was a small show of hands. "Good. I can see that there are some seekers after the truth out there."

Harold did not raise his hand. He stood staring at the speaker, but his eyes seemed far away.

The speaker went on. He began a long indictment of Negro leaders, then of the white city officials, then of the rich merchants who made their living off of the Negro ghetto, then he castigated the disunity amongst the Negro groups, particularly the interger factions. He called them whiteminded, brainwashed, whitewashed Toms. Then he brought his argument back to the point of knowing something more important about the trouble Negroes were having. He brought it back to unity, and the knowledge of the coming future . . .

"Many of you out there are going to participate in Jihad, is that right or wrong?" All hands went up, except Harold's. Many turned and looked at him. Some grumbled and murmured. Harold wavered on his feet. His eyes seemed fixed on some point in the sky directly over the head of Elder Dawud.

Soon after Elder Dawud had asked for more hands on various matters, he began to concentrate a lot of attention in the direction of Harold. Not once had Harold raised his hand.

". . . and just as there are wolves amongst the sheep, there are spies and Toms among you. Why, I can spot them a mile away," and he was looking directly at Harold, "and you mark this, Brothers, they run as straight to the Man as if he were God Almighty, and give our precious plans away. That's why whenever we plan anything, there's the white press and police there ahead of us, waiting. Now, aint that a shame? The black man is not the master of his own destiny. I tell you, you are still slaves! Brothers, I know it as well as you do, so dont get mad at me for telling you. You've got spies amongst you. Get rid of them.

"Now, the point of this meeting, Brothers, is to tell you where you can learn something about yourselves. Without a knowledge of yourself, you cant go anywhere. Why, you cant even integrate with the white man right if you dont know anything about yourself. That's if you want to integrate. Example. Not that I am advocating the program of the Internigs! No. But just to show you that the lack of self-knowledge wont help you to even do the wrong thing! Here you have so-called Negroes running around Harlem wearing bleaching creams and trying to make their hair look like Marilyn Monroe's. Is that the truth? Dont deny it!" There were several women and girls in the crowd, which was growing every minute.

"Listen, Brothers and Sisters, the norm by which a

people live doesnt change without some kind of action and force on that norm. The standard you have been taught all your lives is the blond, blue-eye standard. Am I right or wrong? This has been a sin and a shame to a nation of twenty million black children growing up. Children, black as night, walking around with little blond dolls! It is the joke of nations. Other countries do not look twice at an American Negro, because they know he is hooked on trying to be like his conqueror.

"I want you to tell me what is right. You have a nation of twenty million blacks who childishly think they can erase their blackness, the blackness that God gave them in honor of their beauty and strength, trying to bleach it out so that they can look like Roy Rogers and Dale Evans. To me this is a shame. What is it to you! It is nothing short of criminal. I think the people responsible for this crime should be punished . . ."

Elder Dawud had worked himself up into a sweat by now; the crowd was with him all the way. He began to point out other things he disliked. The people approved. Harold began to shudder a bit, and his face was wet with sweat and tears.

All of a sudden, a man leaped forward, his fist open and his face contorted. He glared at Elder Dawud. Quickly he was seized by the cordon.

"We hear you, we hear you, we hear you!" he shouted. "When are we going to stop hearing you and the rest? We hear you, Brother, we hear! Tell us what to do! Tell us! I want to do something! I am tired of hearing and listening, I'm tired and tired and tired," and he folded in the arms of two men. They carried him out of the crowd. Elder Dawud continued, seeming not to notice the disturbance. The man quickly stood on his feet and tried to brush the strong black hands away, but they took him inside the bookstore, sat him down, and gave him water.

"We know you," said one of the men.

Harold made his way through the crowd and stood outside the bookstore showcase. They had the man seated on a box.

A crowd began to gather inside the store. Elder Dawud's voice was driving into a high pitch. The rattle was changing into pistons, and he was fanning the hearts of the people as if he was fanning a fire that had gone out in the night.

"Forgive me, Brother," the man blurted, his eyes darting wildly from man to man, "I didnt mean to disturb the Elder, but I want . . ." He suddenly put his hands over his face and began to sob softly. The Brothers had a huddle together amongst themselves and then—as Harold watched from the doorway—took the man, stumbling, behind a great green curtain that hung at the end of the bookstore. A man stood beside the curtain as if he were a guard. But he opened the curtain for them. Then he resumed his pose in front.

Down the street a man had a portable swimming pool built on the back of a truck. He was charging the kids twenty-five cents for ten minutes. A loudspeaker sent carnival music out with the announcement of the swim truck. A man was loading kids on the truck. There were squeals and shouting. The man was West Indian. His heavy accent could be heard all over the block: "Y'all haf de money reddy, now. I tell you, chil'ren, haf de money in de 'and."

Elder Dawud directed his attention to the swim truck a block away. "Now, you all familiar with Tango's swim truck, eh? If you aint, you kids is. Well, Tango is a black man from the Islands, and he is serving a need of the people. Am I right or wrong? What would you think of running that good black man out of business in order to let a few Internigs go to the white man's pool, eh?

"Let me tell you something, folks, my friends, and this is what my message is tonight to you all. There is a conspiracy going on to deprive you black people of everything you dont have. Did you get what I said? Everything that you dont have! We're strivin for something now, eh?

"Not integration. No. The poor Negro doesnt have enough knowledge of himself to integrate right with the Man. Oh, you think the Man doesnt want you to have his daughter. Ha! Wake up, men. He'll sacrifice his mother, now. He can see the writing on the wall. But this poor Negro still thinks he can be like the Man. Why, the white man would more quickly integrate with the African than the poor American Negro! Why? Why? Because the Negro is a caste man. He doesnt know his total self. He functions in a self-imposed prison, the prison of his narrow vision. He sees himself as the white man defines him. Whatever the white man calls him, the Negro agrees; witness this, Brothers: He calls you Sam, you say 'yes, sir'; he calls you nigger, you argue and fight amongst yourselves and wind up cursin each other out by calling each other nigger! Right or wrong? He tries to be respectable and calls you Nigrah or Negro, and you smile and nod. You repeat it. He rules you. He is your maker. He is your god. You are trying to be like him. Whatever you worship, you try to imitate. Negroes worship Jesus, right? They try to be like him. Now, I see Negroes trying to be like the white man, to me it means they think he is God.

"Justice, eh. But I know for a fact there's forces at work to take it away from you." The people murmured. "That's right. Let me break it down for you. Harlem is the only place on the Earth where so many black people live so close together, and yet are ruled, governed, and manipulated by somebody else, namely the white man. The only place on the planet Earth. I dont know about Mars or Venus, because I havent got there yet. They tell me that the white scientists are planning on getting a man to walk around up there soon and bring us back a piece of the land. Well, if things dont straighten out down here on Earth, then when they get up there they're going to find the place already inhabited, and the only way to get through and take the land is walk over the inhabitants of that land. I guarantee you that if the black man cant get justice on the planet Earth, he damn well aint gonna let a blue-eyed whitey run over him in his own new land, eh? What do you say about it, Brothers?" There was a round of applause. "Now what I want to say is, and mind this carefully, the conspiracy is on. But first, the Afro-American population has got to go and find out something. He has got to do some investigation. He has got to go back into his soul, Brothers, and I know you all know what that is. The black man in this country has first got to look deep into his own soul, and then he has got to travel a road back there and straighten out the mess the white man has made. Do you understand my meaning? Listen, the black man has got to clear out the funk in his own soul. Let's face the truth. The white man has maligned us so much, has stripped us so thoroughly, has whitewashed our minds and ambitions that all we know is what he tells us on his TV and on his radio and at his movie and in his newspapers (we do have a few black papers now, thank you, Brothers) and in his school system. The truth is that the journey is not so easy. It is not easy because no man knows where to start, or which way to go when he starts, or the end thereof . . ."

And he paused, looking at Harold for a long time. Some of the men in the crowd looked Harold up and down. There was a slight movement and a rumbling. The buildings where the bookstore was located seemed to echo the sound of drums and thundering feet. The police siren came nearer, and across the street two cars collided. Elder Dawud, sweating profusely, stepped up one more peg on the ladder and seemed to wind himself up, tighter and tighter . . .

"There is one who knows the way . . ." He paused. ". . . I come in his name and bear witness that he doesnt let a black man down. He is the One. There is no other whereby you can be saved. He has told me that the white man is doomed, and he who follows the evil ways of the white man is likewise doomed. He has sent us Brothers out amongst you to bring you the message of the truth, the Black truth. So long you have heard the white truth. Now you can hear for the first time the Black truth! He who wants to find out his soul must have a map, you got to have a guide, Brothers, if you gonna travel in a region so long uninhabited. The soul of the Negro is an unexplored territory. The map. The master has the key of knowledge, and he will show us how to find out the truth . . . Here is the . . . If you want to learn your way around Harlem, baby, you got to get to know the people. Is that right or wrong? If you want to know what the black man is like, then you got to get to know the black man's soul. If you want to know what goes on in Harlem, then you got to understand what goes on in the mind of the black people who live in Harlem. Is that right or wrong?" And the crowd applauded him.

Harold Kane continued to listen with hypnotized attention.

"Am I right or wrong! I say you would gain integration much faster if you stopped trying to imitate the white man and stand on your own feet and become a man of destiny. A black man of the world! The white man is intelligent, and he would respect you for being what God made you. He wouldnt love you, of course, but he would respect you. Right now he neither loves nor respects you. But the Internigs dont know this. They think if they become the exact carbon copy of their white master, then he will let them in the back door. Ha! Whoever heard of a carbon copy being of any value as long as the original is around. Why, it is a shame, running around trying to be the shadow of another man. Hell, the white man doesnt care about shadows. He cares about men. Not flunkies."

A Brother was circulating around the crowd, passing out a piece of paper. Harold looked anxiously at the man, and when he came near, Harold reached out and received his eagerly. But he only glanced at it, frowned, and put it away . . .

"Why, I would be ashamed of myself if I didnt have something to be proud of. The white man boasts of his wars and his great civilization. He writes histories and books, and teaches you to bow down and worship his white Jesus on the cross, while all the time he has you working for him, and he is paying you to help make his lifestyle into law. The black man in this country has got to learn one thing: how to use the key to his soul, for the soul of the black man is an unexplored region . . . Who has the map of Harlem? Listen, Harlem has it. Harlem has it. And I speak in the name of One who wants to see Harlem keep it."

Across the street the police were trying to break up a restless crowd that had gathered at the scene of the car accident. There was a bitter argument with several belligerent men. The cops were trying to disperse the people. But the people all stared at the white cops (politely ignoring the three Negro policemen) with a bitter hatred. They called out, "Butchers!" "Klux Klaners!" "Beasts!" "Devils!" "White dogs!" "Mad murderers!" The police retaliated by swinging billy-clubs and cracking a few of the slow people on the legs. A bottle thrown from the crowd struck a policeman on the head. He drew his revolver, staggering with one hand on the ground, and fired into the crowd. A youth clutched his belly in a loud scream. The crowd roared and fell back.

A brick struck one of the police cars.

Across the street, Elder Dawud's crowd joined the melee.

Quickly, word spread that the police had killed a black youth.

The police ordered Elder Dawud to close his meeting. Bottles began to fly. The police riot-squad siren started to wail its eerie whine, and the streets around Harlem Square began to clear and alternately fill up as waves of people fell back and then angrily rushed forward, moblike, pursuing the wind with anything they could get their hands on. The police arrived more and more, and soon arrests were being made . . . Harold had moved a block away, watching the disturbance.

Soon he turned his head and headed uptown, walking close to the wall and looking in at the shops and stores of Harlem, as if he were watching the reflections that moved to and fro in the glass, fading and fleeing like ghosts.

MEMORIES OF A SIXTIES GIRLHOOD: THE HARLEM I LOVE

MICHELE WALLACE

From *Invisibility Blues* (1990)

Like her mother, the esteemed artist Faith Ringgold, Michele Wallace (1952–   ) is an intrepid soul not afraid of the heat of controversy. Her ability to provoke is her hallmark, and she has done it remarkably in her books and essays, particularly the oft-cited *Black Macho and the Myth of the Superwoman*. She is a bona fide Harlemite, which she proudly proclaims here.

All my life I've dreaded being labeled 'one of dem niggas what claims to be somethin' dey ain't.' So lets get this straight from the git, as even those of us on the fringe say uptown. I live in Harlem and have always lived there. My mother was born and raised in Harlem, and my grandmother's family migrated there from Jacksonville, Florida, when she was in her early teens (like many Harlemites my line is best traced through the women). But I've never seen a rat outside of a cage. My mother was never a domestic nor was any other woman in my family since slavery (they claim they were too "proud"). I've never been raped behind the stairs, never been evicted, never played much in the streets, except one month in the spring of '63 before the fun we were having was discovered and my sister and I were shuttled off to the tiresome safety of

Oaks Bluff (the Harlem of Martha's Vineyard). I've never worn a door key around my neck, never seen my father hit my mother, was twenty when I ate my first pig foot, and I never went to what my mother contemptuously refers to as 'P.S. 2.'"

So, ecstatic fans of *Harlem on My Mind* and *Down These Mean Streets*, you may not get what you expected! But then Harlem isn't what you think it is anyway. Harlem is mink coats and two-car families, the pathetic humor of the *Amsterdam News* society column and junior executives with Playboy Club keys, as well as no hot water and welfare checks. Harlem is generations old, as well as just off the boat and just up from down south. Harlem is not merely one seething ghetto but a place where people, black people of all different sorts, actually live and choose to live.

When I was a little girl, I was terrified of Harlem, of the incredible poverty that would spring out at me all at once as I turned some unknown corner, of the other girls my own age who, it seemed, were always twice my size, their socks held up by rubber bands, their braids sticking out every which way, just waiting to catch my eye on one of those rare occasions when I raised them: "What you lookin' at girl?"

There simply wasn't any right answer, just the personal matter of which I considered more humiliating: being pushed down in the snow or having my blouse torn over my nonexistent bosom in front of everybody in a fight that the neighborhood boys would be giggling about for weeks. But I reserved my most violent trembling for getting lost on the subway, getting off at the wrong stop,

THE
HARLEM
READER

244

116th and Lenox, for example, wandering through what I never then doubted were the devil's own angels, the world's maddest men and women of all ages just standing in the streets, some of them slobbering drunk, some of them junkies, their bodies bent so low in a nod, their noses almost touching the ground, some of them screaming and fighting, any one of them likely to flash a razor at a moment's notice.

Other fears of my early youth included the possibility of being beaten beyond recognition for my grocery money, of being held down while someone forced a needle into my arm—instant junkie. And then there was the constant threat of somehow ending up with ten babies on relief with rats as big as fire hydrants for front room boarders, of ending up a whore out on the street trying to eke out a living for me and my man. These are the kinds of things I spent a considerable amount of time speculating about when I was a kid. After all, I was looking in the neighborhood pimp's face every day on my way home from school. He was right across the street and anytime I wanted to sign up . . .

However, none of these things ever happened. My childhood was sheltered, eventless, like most American childhoods. On crisp Sunday mornings we would walk down Seventh Avenue (now renamed Adam Clayton Powell Jr. Boulevard) with my grandmother. All along our way to the opulence of Abyssinian Baptist Church, the old men would tip their hats and old women in mink stoles and smart black suits would stop to say hello. We lived on Edgecombe Avenue when I was very little. It was a quiet and clean residential street where gossipy neighbors posted themselves on the benches of the parkside keeping tabs on everyone's comings and goings. When I was a bit older we moved to the big, new apartment house on 145th Street with doormen, two bathrooms, and the safest stairwells in town. There we met our two best friends, sisters like us. We all shared a cab to school in the mornings: they were going to Eton, we to New Lincoln. They later told us they hated us because we were always talking about our trip to Europe. We hated them because they got five dollars allowance apiece, every day.

At some point or another it seemed as though everyone was coming out—our two cousins, our two rich friends whose parents owned a chain of beauty parlors, every female I knew who was old enough to wear sheer stockings and heels. I was missing out on it all—the clubs and societies Jack and Jill, and Hansel and Gretel, the cotillions, the gauzy white dresses, the visits to the beauty parlor, the boys in tuxedos, cameras flashing, a mention in the *Amsterdam News*. I finally asked my mother why.

"You're already out," she said. "A woman once asked me if you could join Jack and Jill but when she told me what they did—give parties and teas—I told her no." The first washcloth I ever had was designed to look like a book. My mother subscribed to the school of thought that said that anything that didn't have an educational value didn't have any value at all. So, my sister and I saw the Uffizi, the Louvre, the Metropolitan, and the Guggenheim, but we missed the cotillions, the social clubs, the afternoon teas, the dancing lessons, and the Sunday school graduations.

Meanwhile, dope addiction reached epidemic proportions in Harlem in the sixties, and the clean sunlit streets of Harlem's Sugar Hill (as opposed to the valley—all of us hill dwellers knew that the valley was the real ghetto) were becoming more treacherous.

From what I can gather, when my grandmother was coming up, Harlem used to be a much safer and a more congenial place to live. "If it was hot, you could lay out on the roof all night long, and nobody'd bother you," she tells me. They had the Savoy with two bands playing every night: the Renaissance, the Lafayette Theatre with plays "as good as downtown. Nobody had any money so people just had to stick together." If someone got a relief package, the contents were shared with next-door neighbors. "If your feet were about to fall clean off—you didn't go nowhere you couldn't walk—you didn't take a bus. Adam Clayton Powell said, "Not till they get a black driver." The entire family went to the dances, not because the girls needed chaperons, but because, my grandmother says, "young people didn't have anything to hide from older people like they do now." A whole gang of them would go roller skating on Sundays after church—Bradhurst was the avenue. Zoom! right down the center of it. The cars used some other street until Monday.

In my mother's youth, Nipsey Russell, Pigmeat Markham, and Redd Foxx played Harlem clubs. Duke Ellington lived right around the corner, and so did Max Roach. People would beg Harry Belafonte not to bring his guitar to parties, and Sonny Rollins drove the neighbors crazy practicing his scales. The world's best music was a short walk and a drink away at the Club Baron, the Baby Grand,

Minton's, Count Basie's. Of course, your life might depend on your being able to remember how the territory was divided, what gang's turf you were on now—the Lords? the Comanches? the Royals? And my mother tells me they meant something entirely different when they talked about crashing a party. It meant the party got turned out, there was a fight, someone might die.

Jail was somewhere you never admitted anyone you knew had gone, especially not anyone in your family. History books report that the Great Depression ended in the forties but in Harlem it continued right through the fifties. Money was something people in the movies had. My mother, an art student, and my father, a musician, both unemployed most of the time, tell me they lived very comfortably on fifteen dollars a week when they were first starting out.

Harlem today is something else again, although some things never change, like corrupt politicians and leaders, like the never-ending quest for "what the figure is today," like mile-long Cadillacs double-parked in front of tenements. There are the innumerable funeral parlors, always the most sumptuous structures in the community, the churches on every block, and the bars on every corner. There's Eighth Avenue, the likes of which I have never seen anywhere in the world. If Eighth Avenue were emptied, you would think no one had lived there in years but, as it is, the streets are extremely crowded twenty-four hours per day with young men, very few women, standing around a fire made in a garbage can, waiting for what I'm not entirely sure. For those who think blacks are really going places, these are the backs they rode on.

But there are also the limousines outside the Lenox Terrace waiting to drive our various public officials to work. There are the doctors, lawyers, and various Indian chiefs, all in Brooks Brothers uniforms, who wear the leather thin on the stools at Jock's (Seventh Avenue) talking money and the pros and cons of black power. There are the neighborhood merchants, mostly black, who never sell rotten meat but who sell for outrageous prices, who know you by name, who discuss the weather and the foolishness of youth as though they were proprietors of general stores in Wisconsin.

But Harlem has changed drastically in my own lifetime, and that's been due to two things which may or may not be related: the prevalence of dope addiction and the fact that Harlemites are no longer victimized only by "The Man" but also by a complicated network of crooks, hustlers, politicians, and "leaders" who come from their own ranks.

Dope addiction has meant that the streets are now much more dangerous—that's true for all of New York. Old people never leave their homes at night. Most businesses close around six. By seven any commercial street is completely deserted, and has donned its nighttime mask—impenetrable fortress of gates, metal walls, and padded locks. An able-bodied adult male without dependence on dope, wine, or hustling flesh or drugs is a rare sight in certain sections of Harlem.

The higher visibility of the black oppressor has meant that the squalor and poverty is that much more senseless and maddening, that there is a greater sense of hopelessness and despair among impoverished Harlemites, and that self-hatred has returned, feeding upon the unkept promises of the sixties with roots thicker and deeper than before.

With very little encouragement, anyone who lives in Harlem is likely to get highly emotional on the subject simply because our solutions seem so close at hand, so obvious, so easy, and yet so confoundingly unattainable. Harlem's story is a difficult dose to swallow—the people who could do something won't and if they did they wouldn't be the people who could do something anymore.

COTTON COMES TO HARLEM

CHESTER HIMES

From *Cotton Comes to Harlem* (1964)

The detective story was a genre that Chester Himes worked to perfection, and to navigate this literary terrain he fashioned two unforgettable characters, Grave Digger Jones and Coffin Ed Johnson. *Cotton Comes to Harlem* is a splendid romp, freighted with Himes's usual fare of local color, violence, and absurdity. In this excerpt, Himes's brutally graphic style provides a telling portrait of post–World War II Harlem with an ensemble of compelling Harlemites. The community and its famous landmarks are also vividly summoned, and his fiction is poignantly interlaced with fact. Himes, born in Jefferson City, Missouri, on July 29, 1909, spent his formative years in Cleveland, Ohio. After dismissal from Ohio State University, he began an odyssey of petty crime, and by the time he was nineteen he was serving a twenty-year sentence for burglary. During his seven years in prison, Himes developed as a writer, and within a few years of being paroled he published his first novel, *If He Hollers Let Him Go* (1945). Between this novel and *Cotton Comes to Harlem* (1965), Himes was extremely productive, churning out more than a dozen books, including the violence-riddled detective novels that earned him the highest literary honors in France. Before his death in 1984 from Parkinson's disease, Himes had written two volumes of autobiography, *The Quality of Hurt* (1972) and *My Life of Absurdity* (1976). *Plan B*, a novel he was completing in Spain when he died, was published posthumously in 1995.

When Grave Digger and Coffin Ed arrived at the lot where the Back-to-Africa rally had taken place, they found it closed off by a police cordon and the desolate black people, surrounded by policemen, standing helpless in the rain.

The police cruiser was still smoking in the barbecue pit and the white cops in their wet black slickers looked mean and dangerous. Coffin Ed's acid-burned face developed a tic and Grave Digger's neck began swelling with rage.

The dead body of the young recruiting agent lay face up in the rain, waiting for the medical examiner to come and pronounce it dead so the men from Homicide could begin their investigation. But the men from Homicide had not arrived, and nothing had been done.

Grave Digger and Coffin Ed stood over the body and looked down at all that was left of the young black face which a few short minutes ago had been so alive with hope. At that moment they felt the same as all the other helpless black people standing in the rain.

"Too bad O'Malley didn't get it instead of this young boy," Grave Digger said, rain dripping from his black slouch hat over his wrinkled black suit.

"This is what happens when cops get soft on hoodlums," Coffin Ed said.

"Yeah, we know O'Malley got him killed, but our job is to find out who pulled the trigger."

They walked over to the herded people and Grave Digger asked, "Who's in charge here?"

The other young recruiting agent came forward. He was hatless and his solemn black face was shining in the rain. "I guess I am; the others have gone."

They walked him over to one side and got the story of what had happened as he saw it. It wasn't much help.

"We were the whole organization," the young man said. "Reverend O'Malley, the two secretaries and me and

John Hill who was killed. There were volunteers but we were the staff."

"How about the guards?"

"The two guards with the armored truck? Why, they were sent with the truck from the bank."

"What bank?"

"The African Bank in Washington, D.C."

The detectives exchanged glances but didn't comment.

"What's your name, son?" Grave Digger asked.

"Bill Davis."

"How far did you get in school?"

"I went to college, sir. In Greensboro, North Carolina."

"And you still believe in the devil?" Coffin Ed asked.

"Let him alone," Grave Digger said. "He's telling us all he knows." Turning to Bill, he asked, "And these two colored detectives from the D.A.'s office. Did you know them?"

"I never saw them before. I was suspicious of them from the first. But Reverend O'Malley didn't seem perturbed and he made the decisions."

"Didn't seem perturbed," Grave Digger echoed. "Did you suspect it might be a plant?"

"Sir?"

"Did it occur to you they might have been in cahoots with O'Malley to help him get away with the money?"

At first the young man didn't understand. Then he was shocked. "How could you think that, sir? Reverend O'Malley is absolutely honest. He is very dedicated, sir."

Coffin Ed sighed.

"Did you ever see the ships which were supposed to take you people back to Africa?" Grave Digger asked.

"No, but all of us have seen the correspondence with the steamship company—The Afro-Asian Line—verifying the year's lease he had negotiated."

"How much did he pay?"

"It was on a per head basis; he was going to pay one hundred dollars per person. I don't believe they are really as large as they look in these pictures, but we were going to fill them to capacity."

"How much money had you collected?"

"Eighty-seven thousand dollars from the . . . er . . . subscribers, but we had taken in quite a bit from other things, church socials and this barbecue deal, for instance."

"And these four white men in the delivery truck got all of it?"

"Well, just the eighty-seven thousand dollars we had taken in tonight. But there were five of them. One stayed inside the truck behind a barricade all the time."

The detectives became suddenly alert. "What kind of barricade?" Grave Digger asked.

"I don't know exactly. I couldn't see inside the truck very well. But it looked like some kind of a box covered with burlap."

"What provision company supplied your meat?" Coffin Ed asked.

"I don't know, sir. That wasn't part of my duties. You'll have to ask the chef."

They sent for the chef and he came wet and bedraggled, his white cap hanging over one ear like a rag. He was mad at everything—the bandits, the rain, and the police cruiser that had fallen into his barbecue pit. His eyes were bright red and he took it as a personal insult when they asked about the provision company.

"I don't know where the ribs come from after they left the hog," he said angrily. "I was just hired to superintend the cooking. I ain't had nothing to do with them white folks and I don't know how many they was—'cept too many."

"Leave this soul-brother go," Coffin Ed said. "Pretty soon he wouldn't have been here."

Grave Digger wrote down O'Malley's official address, which he already knew, then as a last question asked, "What was your connection with the original Back-to-Africa movement, the one headed by Mr. Michaux?"

"None at all. Reverend O'Malley didn't have anything at all to do with Mr. Michaux's group. In fact he didn't even like Lewis Michaux; I don't think he ever spoke to him."

"Did it ever occur to you that Mr. Michaux might not have had anything to do with Reverend O'Malley? Did you ever think that he might have known something about O'Malley that made him distrust O'Malley?"

"I don't think it was anything like that," Bill contended. "What reason could he have to distrust O'Malley? I just think he was envious, that's all. Reverend O'Malley thought he was too slow; he didn't see any reason for waiting any longer; we've waited long enough."

"And you were intending to go back to Africa too?"

"Yes, sir, still intend to—as soon as we get the money back. You'll get the money back for us, won't you?"

"Son, if we don't, we're gonna raise so much hell they're gonna send us all back to Africa."

"And for free, too," Coffin Ed added grimly.

The young man thanked them and went back to stand with the others in the rain.

"Well, Ed, what do you think about it?" Grave Digger asked.

"One thing is for sure, it wasn't the syndicate pulled this caper—not the crime syndicate, anyway."

"What other kinds of syndicates are there?"

"Don't ask me, I ain't the F.B.I."

They were silent for a moment with the rain pouring over them, thinking of these eighty-seven families who had put down their thousand-dollar grubstakes on a dream.

They knew that these families had come by their money the hard way. To many, it represented the savings of a life-time. To most it represented long hours of hard work at menial jobs. None could afford to lose it.

They didn't consider these victims as squares or suck-ers. They understood them. These people were seeking a home—just the same as the Pilgrim Fathers. Harlem is a city of the homeless. These people had deserted the South because it could never be considered their home. Many had been sent north by the white southerners in revenge for the desegregation ruling. Others had fled, thinking the North was better. But they had not found a home in the North. They had not found a home in America. So they looked across the sea to Africa, where other black people were both the ruled and the rulers. Africa to them was a big free land which they could proudly call home, for there were buried the bones of their ancestors, there lay the roots of their families, and it was inhabited by the descendants of those same ancestors which made them related by both blood and race. Everyone has to believe in something; and the white people of America had left them nothing to believe in. But that didn't make a black man any less criminal than a white; and they had to find the criminals who hijacked the money, black or white.

"Anyway, the first thing is to find Deke," Grave Digger put voice to their thoughts. "If he ain't responsible for this caper he'll sure as hell know who is."

"He had better know," Coffin Ed said grimly.

But Deke didn't know any more than they did. He had worked a long time to set up his movement and it had been expensive. At first he had turned to the church to hide from the syndicate. He had figured if he set himself up as a preacher and used his reward money for civil improvement, the syndicate would hesitate about rubbing him out.

But the syndicate hadn't shown any interest in him. That had worried him until he figured out that the syndicate simply didn't want to get involved in the race issue; he had already done all the harm he could do, so they left him to the soul-brothers.

Then he'd gotten the idea for his Back-to-Africa movement from reading a biography of Marcus Garvey, the Negro who had organized the first Back-to-Africa movement. It was said that Garvey had collected over a million dollars. He had been sent to prison, but most of his followers had contended that he was innocent and had still believed in him. Whether he had been innocent or not was not the question; what appealed to him was the fact his followers had still believed in him. That was the con-man's real genius, to keep the suckers always believing.

So he had started his own Back-to-Africa movement, the only difference being when he had got his million, he was going to cut out—he might go back to Africa, himself. He'd heard that people with money could live good in certain places there. The way he had planned it he would use two goons impersonating detectives to impound the money as he collected it; in that way he wouldn't have to bank it and could always keep it on hand.

He didn't know where these white hijackers fitted in. At the first glimpse he thought they were guns from the syndicate. That was why he had hidden beneath the table. But when he discovered they'd just come to grab the money, he had known it was something else again. So he had decided to chase them down and get the money back.

But when they had finally caught up with the meat delivery truck, the white men had disappeared. Perhaps it was just as well; by then he was outgunned anyway. Neither of his guards had been seriously hurt, but he'd lost one of his detectives. The wrecked truck hadn't told him anything and the driver of the truck that had run into them kept getting in the way.

He hadn't had much time so he had ordered them to split and assemble again every morning at 3:00 A.M. in the back room of a pool hall on Eighth Avenue and he would contact his other detective himself.

"I've got to see which way this mother-raping cat is jumping," he said.

He had enough money on him to operate, over five

hundred dollars. And he had a five-grand bank account under an alias in an all-night bank in midtown for his getaway money in case of an emergency. But he didn't know yet where to start looking for his eighty-seven grand. Some kind of lead would come. This was Harlem, where all black folks were against the whites, and somebody would tell him something. What worried him most was how much information the police had. He knew that in any event they'd be rough on him because of his record; and he knew he'd better keep away from them if he wanted to get his money back.

First, however, he had to get into his house. He needed his pistol; and there were certain documents hidden there—the forged leases from the steamship line and the forged credentials of the Back-to-Africa movement—that would send him back to prison.

He walked down Seventh Avenue to Smalls' bar, on the pretense of going to call the police, and got into a taxi without attracting any attention. He had the driver take him over to Saint Mark's Church, paid the fare and walked up the stairs. The church door was closed and locked, as he had expected, but he could stand in the shadowed recess and watch the entrance to the Dorrence Brooks apartment house across the street where he lived.

He stood there for a long time casing the building. It was a V-shaped building at the corner of 138th Street and St. Nicholas Avenue and he could see the entrance and the streets on both sides. He didn't see any strange cars parked nearby, no police cruisers, no gangster-type limousines. He didn't see any strange people, nothing and no one who looked suspicious. He could see through the glass doors into the front hall and there was not a soul about. The only thing was it was too damn empty.

He circled the church and entered the park on the west side of St. Nicholas Avenue and approached the building from across the street. He hid in the park beside a tool shed from which he had a full view of the windows of his fourth-floor apartment. Light showed in the windows of the living room and dining room. He watched for a long time. But not once did a shadow pass before one of the lighted windows. He got dripping wet in the rain.

His sixth sense told him to telephone, and from some phone booth in the street where the call couldn't be traced. So he walked up to 145th Street and phoned from the box on the corner.

"Hellooo," she answered. He thought she sounded strange.

"Iris," he whispered.

Standing beside her, Grave Digger's hand tightened warningly on her arm. He had already briefed her what to say when O'Malley called and the pressure meant he wasn't playing.

"Oh, Betty," she cried. "The police are here looking for—"

Grave Digger slapped her with such sudden violence she caromed off the center table and went sprawling on her hands and knees; her dress hiked up showing black lace pants above the creamy yellow skin of her thighs.

Coffin Ed came up and stood over her, the skin of his face jumping like a snake's belly over fire. "You're so god-damn cute—"

Grave Digger was speaking urgently into the telephone: "O'Malley, we just want some information, that's—" but the line had gone dead.

His neck swelled as he jiggled the hook to get the precinct station.

At the same moment Iris came up from the floor with the smooth vicious motion of a cat and slapped Coffin Ed across the face, thinking he was Grave Digger in her blinding fury.

She was a hard-bodied high-yellow woman with a perfect figure. She never wore a girdle and her jiggling buttocks gave all men amorous ideas. She had a heart-shaped face with the high cheekbones, big wide red painted mouth, and long-lashed speckled brown eyes of a sexpot and she was thirty-three years old, which gave her the experience. But she was strong as an ox and it was a solid pop she laid on Coffin Ed's cheek.

With pure reflex action he reached out and caught her around the throat with his two huge hands and bent her body backward.

"Easy, man, easy!" Grave Digger shouted, realizing instantly that Coffin Ed was sealed in such a fury he couldn't hear. He dropped the telephone and wheeled, hitting Coffin Ed across the back of the neck with the edge of his hand just a fraction of a second before he'd have crushed her windpipe.

Coffin Ed slumped forward, carrying Iris down with

him, beneath him, and his hands slackened from her throat. Grave Digger picked him up by the armpits and propped him on the sofa, then he picked up Iris and dropped her into a chair. Her eyes were huge and limpid with fear and her throat was going black and blue.

Grave Digger stood looking down at them, listening to the phone click frantically, thinking, Now we're in for it; then thinking bitterly, These half-white bitches. Then he turned back to the telephone and answered the precinct station and asked for the telephone call to be traced. Before he could hang up, Lieutenant Anderson was on the wire.

"Jones, you and Johnson get over to 137th Street and Seventh Avenue. Both trucks are smashed up and everyone gone, but there are two bodies DOA and there might be a lead." He paused for a moment, then asked, "How's it going?"

Grave Digger looked from the slumped figure of Coffin Ed into the now blazing eyes of Iris and said, "Cool, Lieutenant, everything's cool."

"I'm sending over a man to keep her on ice. He ought to be there any moment."

"Right."

"And remember my warning—no force. We don't want anyone hurt if we can help it."

"Don't worry, Lieutenant, we're like shepherds with newborn lambs."

The lieutenant hung up.

Coffin Ed had come around and he looked at Grave Digger with a sheepish expression. No one spoke.

Then Iris said in a thick, throat-hurting voice, "I'm going to get you coppers fired if it's the last thing I do."

Coffin Ed looked as though he was going to reply, but Grave Digger spoke first: "You weren't very smart, but neither were we. So we'd better call it quits and start all over."

"Start over shit," she flared. "You break into my house without a search warrant, hold me prisoner, attack me physically, and say let's call it quits. You must think I'm a moron. Even if I'm guilty of a murder, you can't get away with that shit."

"Eighty-seven colored families—like you and me—"

"Not like me!"

"—have lost their life's savings in this caper."

"So what? You two are going to lose your mother-raping jobs."

"So if you cooperate and help us get it back you'll get a ten-percent reward—eight thousand seven hundred dollars."

"You chickenshit cop, what can I do with that chicken feed? Deke is worth ten times that much to me."

"Not anymore. His number's up and you'd better get on the winning side."

She gave a short, harsh laugh. "'That ain't your side, big and ugly."

Then she got up and went and stood directly in front of Coffin Ed where he sat on the sofa. Suddenly her fist flew out and hit him squarely on the nose. His eyes filled with tears as blood spurted from his nostrils. But he didn't move.

"That makes us even," he said and reached for his handkerchief.

Someone rapped on the door and Grave Digger let in the white detective who had come to take over. Neither of them spoke; they kept the record straight.

"Come on, Ed," Grave Digger said.

Coffin Ed stood up and the two of them walked to the door, Coffin Ed holding the bloodstained handkerchief to his nose. Just before they went out, Grave Digger turned and said, "Chances go around, baby."

MY HARLEM

TONYA BOLDEN

Few African-American authors are as prolific as Bolden (1959–   ),
who relates here the story of her formative years in Harlem.
And unlike so many writers, she has managed to balance her
impressive production between children/teenagers and adult
books. Among her most recent books are *Tell All the Children Our
Story*, *Strong Men Keep Coming*, and *The Book of African American Women*. She has also worked with Mother Love, Eartha Kitt,
and Johnnetta Cole, lending her writing skills in the completion
of their memoirs. These endeavors should serve her well when
one day she delivers her own magnificent story to the world.
Until then, here's a portion of it.

"So, why did he bring them here?"

This was, remembered my mother, my rapid response
when she began explaining why her brother had dropped
by with some Finnish acquaintances: they had wanted "to
see where some poor people live."

This was during a 1960s summer, during my wonder
years, when time did not fly and a fruity twin-pop could
be had for a nickel, a slice of pizza for twenty cents, and
grown-ups taught us children what a "case quarter" was.

Home was an eighth-floor, two-bedroom apartment
on 108th Street, in one of the twenty-story buildings of

Franklin Plaza, a Mitchell-Lama development. Never had I thought of myself as *poor*.

Or *culturally deprived*.

Or *underprivileged*.

And I was not permitted to be what folks today call "ghetto."

Like so many in my world, I was a child of that curious class for which there is no tidy label: working class with middle-class sensibilities, strivings.

My Harlem was certainly no paradise. There were bad boys and mean streets, sirens in the middle of the night, and sightings of a him or a her deep-hard in a heroin nod. There were brothers giving gangster leans in Electra 225s, and white-shoed, pinky-ringed Sals and An-toneys who swaggered through street-level black doors on which I knew not ever to knock.

Not far from Franklin Plaza were projects where elevators smelled of urine, sometimes. Across the street from my building were tenements teeming—with rats and roaches? I, frankly, do not know. But I know they housed lots of blacks, Eye-talians, and Ricans. I know there were some women who yelled at their children a lot. And crying babies. And window guards. And the Supremes, Tito Puente, and O-Solo-Mio music streaming from windows, sometimes at the same time. And there were women who thought nothing of sitting on a stoop in a house dress, sipping a can of Rheingold.

I had moments of fear. There was the blackout of 1965, when I feared my father would not reach home safe (he did). The summer before that was the riot: from our window that faced Second Avenue, I witnessed in the distance people heavy-laden running down Third Avenue, and the words "loot," "looters," "looting" entered my vocabulary. After the rage receded, my family drove to 125th Street, site of some of the worst devastation. It was a purposeful sojourn, I sensed, but the precise why of it escaped me. What I knew was that we had not come to gawk, to ooh-and-aah. It was a somber moment; I remember I almost cried. It feels to me now as if we were doing something akin to paying our respects.

Times of tears were hardly my norm in Harlem. There was ample space and grace for me to be a child, to be free for fun: from roller skating, bike riding, ring-a-levio, scullies, a variety of tags, Double Dutch (and Orange) and other jump-rope games. There was heat relief from sprinklers, evening concerts, and a lone, after-dark steel drummer whose sounds sometimes soothed me to sleep. All this from my wonderland of a play-park, which some of our windows overlooked (my mother had selected the apartment precisely because it did). The playground—huge, of course, to my young eyes—offered basketball courts, handball courts, an amphitheater, and several mini-parks with monkey bars, swings, and concrete animals for play safaris and waves of adventures. There came a time, too, when I had the marvel of some "bigger kids" sporting Afros and Dashikis and talking about being black and proud as part of their hanging out. Oddly, when it comes to wintertime in my Harlem, the images that most readily spring to mind are of a blizzard and of a sanitation strike (after a blizzard) and of Mayor Lindsay on TV (during a blizzard?), and of myself going to school on freezing cold days all bundled up and with pants on beneath my dress or skirt because in those days girls could wear pants to school but not in school. And of myself in my room reading a book or by our living-room window that overlooked the play-park, imagining up a poem or story. And of my mother snapping stringbeans. And of being forbidden to watch *Peyton Place*.

Regardless of the season, the play-park was quite empty on Sundays. For most everyone Sunday was for church followed by family time. For the Boldens, that after-church family time was often dinner with relatives who lived in the same complex or elsewhere in Harlem (or elsewhere in NYC). Since my family was Southern-rooted, it was a Southern-style dinner with a multiplicity of dishes, many made from scratch, and of course with fatback and other things we sophisticates must now shun.

Sometimes, when the weather was fine, after-church family time was Ma, Daddy, my sister, and me at La Famille, on 125th and Fifth Avenue, with its real tablecloths and real waiters ("Are you ready to order?" versus "Whakena-getchu?"). To my child's mind it was the fanciest restaurant in the world. And it had a special place in our lives. As did one of the once ubiquitous hazy-hot, grease-pot fish-and-chip joints. As did the hole-in-the-wall Chinese spot on 106th. As did chicken-and-waffles Wells, where I confess to a wisp of a thrill at the slicks who darted in—darted out hustling any- and everything, from a pants suit to a jar of Dixie Peach.

Following a Sunday treat of La Famille, sometimes (at my urging) we took a long way home that allowed for a cruise up and down the Strivers' Row blocks, where I had been told black doctors and lawyers and other black professionals—people rich relative to my family—lived. I was not a masochist: seeing those stately brownstone and limestone townhouses and knowing of their inhabitants seeded in me no envy, nor made me feel poor, but inspired an awe that anchored, a pride.

Most Monday mornings, by the time I awoke Daddy had already headed to work. Ma had breakfast close to ready, and she was ready to ensure that my sister and I left for school clean and neat (often in an outfit she had made.)

The public school I attended was of a class long since abolished: More Effective Schools. At M.E.S. 146, we had relatively small classes. We had eager teachers who cheered those of us blessed with a love for learning, kept at the slackers, and stayed alert for those who were beyond slackers—candidates for a dreaded 600 school. The fact that it was not uncommon for children to be skipped a grade is further evidence that low expectations did not reign supreme at what is today plain ole P.S. 146.

I lived in Harlem from age four to age eleven, and then again, for four years in the 1980s, in an apartment on a Strivers' Row block where, thanks to black flight, few were "rich." So in a way it is rather odd that to this day I regard myself as a Harlemite. But I do.

"Harlem leaves a definite stamp on her children," observed a friend, poet Judy Simmons, during a smorgasbord of a telephone conversation. I cannot recall what sparked her remark, only that it was in the context of talk about identity and sense of self.

If Judy's assertion is true, I had no sense as a child that I was being "marked."

Although I remember, most vividly, my enchantment

with Strivers' Row, as a child I did not know Harlem's history. I did not know the significance of 409 Edgecombe (I don't think Sugar Hill was in my vocabulary). Neither did I know of Harlem's crown as the "capital of Black America," nor that Malcolm X preferred one particular booth when dining at 22 West. I only have a vague memory of my friend-of-the-Finns uncle making sure I understood that 20 East 127th Street was home to Langston Hughes. Yet, somehow, void of all the facts, I grew up with the feeling that Harlem was something special. In retrospect, I know that in Harlem it felt so good to be black. But am I crediting Harlem with things that should rightly be credited to my family?

Turns out I'd been too quick with the lip in response to my mother's "to see where some poor people live." We had not been the Finns' destination, just a pit stop on the journey.

RETURNING TO A HARLEM
I NEVER LEFT

EDDY HARRIS

From *Still Life in Harlem* (1996)

Eddy Harris is a traveling man. Whether down the Mississippi in a kayak, peering into Africa's heart of darkness, or merely sailing comfortably on the flight of his imagination, he is a great storyteller, a fine imagist and chronicler. Harlem, as he relates, is a place that is always with us, even if you've never been there before.

I left on a Saturday afternoon. I was ten years old. My family had recently moved to the suburbs. And on this Saturday I was sent to get a haircut. I left the house, took a right turn, or perhaps a wrong turn, I may never know which, and left Harlem. In leaving this place, I was leaving behind a world that was all black. I never really went back there. I never even looked back—until now. Suddenly Harlem began to whisper in the ear of imaginings. Harlem began to sing to me, to speak to me, to call me home. So I returned to Harlem, even though I had never lived there—came back for the first time a little over two years ago, came back although in truth I had never been there before, came back although in a certain sense I had never been away. Harlem is like that. For blackamericans there is in a way no escaping it, no leaving this place. Even if you have never been here before, you have always been here. As Ralph Ellison once said, "Harlem goes where black folks go," and try as one might to get out from under it, the shadow of Harlem falls over us all. For Harlem is the alabaster vessel that holds the blackamerican heart, that holds the history and hope of black America, that holds as well its frustrations and its desperation, so much of the poverty of spirit, the bitter pain and isolation of being black, and so much too of the energy, vitality, and exuberance. Harlem carries on its back the psychological freight of a entire nation as well.

Harlem is music in the soul of people and perhaps a rhapsody, a torch song, a love song, a child's incantation. Harlem is a lullaby whispered in the long long night, a blues song repeated endlessly and coming from a place so deep in the blackamerican soul and psyche that the words and the music are somehow known long before you have heard them for the first time, and quite impossible to forget. They are ingrained in the blackamerican subconscious and part of the blackamerican idiom. Harlem is the metaphor for black America.

I decided that Saturday afternoon not to go to the barbershop where my father and brother always went, where the barbers were black and the old men who sat and laughed at my father's antics were black and so were the little boys who waited patiently for their turn and never spoke a word. Their legs dangled over the edges of chairs too high for their feet to touch the floor. In an effort to be like the big boys and like the men, they slouched and tried hard to keep at least a toe tipping the ground. They watched in silence as the older men joked or talked about events in the news or in the neighborhood. The little boys kept still. They were watching carefully and listening and learning how to be black men.

I wasn't so interested in being a black man, just a man. I had watched and had been scarred the previous year by the doings of three black men, Johnny Cannon and his partner and the man they both stabbed, and if this was part of what it meant to be a black man, then a black man was not the kind of man I wanted to be.

I went that day to the barbershop where there was no gaiety in getting a haircut. There was just a stern white barber and a few quiet white men reading old magazines, no loud talking, no boasting or bragging, no laughter until I walked in and quickly out again.

"We don't cut black hair in here," the white man said.

I had no idea what he meant. I was just a little boy.

"Mister," I said. "My hair is brown."

Probably they are laughing still, but the world they had inherited, the world they then adopted, adapted, and made their own before passing it on to their heirs, is now no laughing matter. The trickle has turned into a stream turned into a river turned into Niagara Falls. The men in that barbershop could not see or would not see what I, even as a ten-year-old, could see.

I knew their world was not the one I could entirely embrace either. I was and would for a long time be lost somewhere in the middle.

I cannot honestly say that I made up my mind right there and then about anything. I hated haircuts and had not wanted one in the first place. I'm sure it had been my mother's idea. Now I had an excuse and left that barbershop rather gleeful, if slightly confused. Certainly I did not feel humiliated; perhaps I should have. There were no defiant gestures; perhaps there should have been. I did not shout back, made no threats, never once pledged aloud or to myself, "As God is my witness . . . ," or any such thing. Instead I went to play.

But even as I was out playing, I was refusing to be swept to the margins and off the page completely. Or better still, I was deciding, inasmuch as it is at all possible, to make my own tableau, give my tapestry its own design, shape, and texture. All the rest would be background and border.

Such notions sneak rather than spring into the minds of ten-year-old boys. Somehow in the intervening years, however, I woke up to discover I was clinging so hard to the center that I had separated from the margins, the way meringue not firmly held against the sides of the pie pan will pull away from the edges. It makes for an ugly lemon meringue pie, but it's still a pie.

A person, though, can think he or she is something altogether new, an island, perhaps, wholly apart from the exotic lands just off its shore but always in sight. But beneath the sea the lands are one. There is no escaping it.

HARLEM HAIKU: A SCRAPBOOK

JABARI ASIM

From *In the Tradition,*
edited by Kevin Powell and Ras Baraka (1992)

In the "new word order," as many term the current phase of literary development, Jabari Asim moves at warp speed, editing books, reciting his poetry, working on his short stories, and plotting that big novel. His base of operations in St. Louis does not mean he's unaware of the scene in Harlem, as is readily apparent in this selection.

(For Ira B. Jones)

I

morning brought strong rain;
the warm drops reached out to us
with welcoming hands.

we wandered between
Lenox and Liberation
looking for light in

Langston's lair, learning
the language of streets as fast
as New York voices

that spit swift words like
secret music much too rich
for our flat, slow tongues.

2

Harlem, Sweet Harlem
where Renaissance writers wrote
words that breathe fire.

3
Harlem, Sweet Harlem
where brave Marcus and Malcolm
faced down angry Fate.

4
Harlem, Sweet Harlem
where noble ghosts watch and wait
for the rising time.

5
Harlem, Sweet Harlem
what deep secrets sleep beneath
your smouldering breast?

6
dusk brought long shadows;
the last light skipped and danced down
the darkening streets.

we stalked Harlem's haunts
like souls in search of something
to enchant the rhymes.

some kind of power
that makes the brownstones glow and
give off good magic
to make words dance and
solve the riddle of themselves
in perfect stanzas.

7
Sylvia's soul food
seduced our hearts and bellies
while we talked and dreamed.

Recall the waitress
who claimed us with her beauty,
think of her smile as

I offer a toast
to hallowed, holy Harlem,
home away from home.

PASSING STRIVERS' ROW

GRACE EDWARDS

From *Do or Die* (2001)

Grace Edwards has written several novels that take place in
Harlem. Though most of them are based on the investigations
and diligent work of a former police officer, Mali Anderson,
hardly a scene goes by that doesn't in some way touch on the
history of Harlem, particularly the businesses and residential
sections. Here Mali makes one of her typical treks through a
community she knows intimately.

I breathed deeply and offered no comment as we turned
into 139th Street, between Adam Clayton Powell Boulevard and Frederick Douglass Boulevard, Strivers' Row, as
folks called it, a block of three- and four-story neo-
Italianate and Colonial Revival row houses adorned with
wrought-iron balconies and French windows that were
now closed against the humid night air and, hopefully,
the sound of Dad's anger. We walked past 221, home
of Vertner Tandy, the African American architect who
designed St. Phillips Episcopal Church and Madame C. J.
Walker's mansion in Irvington-on-the-Hudson. I counted
the doors until we passed 228, where Fletcher Hender-
son, the bandleader, once lived. While living here he was
able to walk to his gigs at the jazz clubs just as Dad does
now when he doesn't feel like calling a limo.

Exhaustion hit me like a brick. Suddenly, seven days of tapping my foot to the beat of Aretha, Lou Rawls, Branford Marsalis, and Ruth Brown, and lounging in deck chairs until my skin was fried two shades past midnight, and each night wrapped in Tad's arms and rolling to his private and indescribable rhythm, and then rising to jog around the deck with him in a 5:00 A.M. fog, all had finally caught up with me. My eyelids felt like a sandpit. I was ready to tell Dad but he was still swimming in a current of anger.

"The last thing Ozzie said when we left the ship was 'See you tonight. Starr'll be there. I really appreciate what you doin' for her.' And neither one of 'em bothered to show. What the hell is that about? At this stage of the game, I damn sure don't need no half-steppers!"

I knew how Dad felt. If he was able to drag himself out of the house, then everyone else should've done it also. Or at least call. Luckily, a jazz pianist from Brooklyn was in the audience and was more than happy to sit in. And he was damn good. I listened and wondered how a musician—who had never played or practiced with a particular group—could simply walk on, take a seat, and blend so seamlessly with the rhythm, strike the notes as cleanly as if he'd gigged with the band for years.

I heard the ringing above Ruffin's bark as I put the key in the door.

"Maybe it's Alvin," I said. "You know we promised to call as soon as we got back."

"Or could be Ozzie," Dad said as he propped his bass against the sofa and rushed to the phone before the machine kicked in. "If it is, he better have a damn good—"

A second later, I watched the annoyance drain away and

his face change to blank surprise. His hand shook violently and he tried twice before finally hitting the speakerphone button.

Ozzie's voice cracked through the silence like an electric charge. "Bad news, man. Bad, bad. Starr's dead. My baby's been murdered . . ."

REFLECTIONS ON THE METRO NORTH, WINTER, 1990

WILLIE PERDOMO

From *Where a Nickel Costs a Dime* (1996)

Very few poets have managed to blend the street and the academy without losing the essence of both. But the images Willie Perdomo invokes are often stark, dripping with urgency and violence, often mirroring the poet's turbulent clash against reality. These few stanzas are taken from a long, impressionistic poem that reads like an iridescent travelogue.

. . . 110th Street
History of El Barrio, Spanish Harlem
salsa street legends
manteca bombs
many a bad muthafucka
done laughed and cried
ran and died
in the swollen arms
of this street
of life and death
Boricuas in Nueva York
celebrate with this song
forever
para siempre, mami,
para siempre
116th Street

la marqueta is glittering
I don't need books
My culture
My history
is in the aisles
of bacalaito
ajecito
sofrito
pulpo
mi pana
I stretch my neck
to see
If I see
mi panas
Carlito y Marc
walking toward Madison Avenue
to buy a bag
half-n-half
for the rest of the night
awwwright!
A dripping leak-leaky bag
of Purple Rain
so that we can tranquilize
our souls
time
confusion
heartbreak
and get blind
is that me
I see?

looking for a familiar dance
to a warm hip-hop boogie
writing a mad poem
to a sad beat
because the guns we play with
don't squirt water
or make that simulated machine gun rattle

Tanisa is sleeping now
she might be dreaming
about happy we gonna be
if it wasn't for
my girl
my woman
my wifey
my main flame
my baby
always and forever
with a kiss
from Harlem
moreno Harlem
same beat
like my Barrio
soul y salsa
if it wasn't for her
I would be standing on the corner
thinking about the world
drinking blackberry brandy
keeping a cold hustler company
with stories from back in the days

"Damn, Papo. Things ain't like they use to be . . .

125th Street
Harlem, USA
I'm ready to jump off
before the doors close
have a nice day;
and if this poem is too long
I really don't give a fuck
Because my heart is beating
and I'm alive
You know what I'm sayin'?
Can you hear my muses, Tanisa?

Shhhh . . .
I could tell her that I got some business to take care of
but she'll look at me with those sleepy eyes and that
soft voice and she'll say:
         "I am your business, Will."
And that's it—
Apollo Theater to the West
Willis Avenue Bridge to the East
A river waiting at each end of the boulevard
Poets and dead gangsters
chillin' at the bottoms
Nothing for me to do but jump
or turn back
cuz it ain't my time yet

I close my eyes and clench my teeth
I ask my grandmother's spirit for the strength to say no

I kiss Tanisa
careful not to shake her awake from her dreams

Doors close
steam whispers
a slow drag
away
I'm running away
with my woman
and I can't turn back
the El Barrio
Harlem night
is no longer mine . . .

MAKING HARLEM MY BUSINESS

DOROTHY PITMAN HUGHES

From *Wake Up and Smell the Dollars* (2000)

Among Harlem's endangered species is the black woman as a proprietor. And in this shrinking category Dorothy Pitman Hughes seems determined to hang on, using a combination of ingenuity and spunk to stay afloat. Harlem has been her bedrock, and upon it she has built an office supply business that still flourishes despite the spiraling rent along 125th Street.

I've learned so much from experiencing ownership in Harlem. Mostly I have gained knowledge of how the blueprint for gentrification can be drawn with the participation of the victims. I challenge that if we know how to serve personally, we are obligated to bring others along with us. When I speak of Harlem, I tell my story. Your story is probably very similar in your city (especially if it's an inner city or an Empowerment Zone) anywhere in the United States. I moved to 138th Street in Harlem in 1972. At that point I was fully involved in child advocacy and community activism—a role that would continue for the next ten years. During that time I taught at Columbia University, the College of New Rochelle, and City College, and spent three years touring as a speaker with Gloria Steinem, whom I met in 1972 when she interviewed me for *New York* magazine. We became fast friends and teamed up to speak out on racism, sexism, and classism.

By 1982 I had begun to seek other ways to make a living, and I decided on entrepreneurism. I tried to get a small-business loan to start a company. But no bank would risk its money on me—black, female, and, particularly, with a plan to start a business in Harlem. I was determined to open a fully equipped store providing school supplies, office supplies, and office furniture. By offering the same quality, prices, and service as midtown stores, I was going to ensure that no one in Harlem had an excuse not to buy their goods within the Harlem community. I paid the mortgage on my home late and used the money to rent a storefront for the first store.

Based on my previous experience, I knew that being a black woman in Harlem wouldn't work to my advantage in opening a business. I knew it would be more difficult to get business loans, establish credit, and get top supply vendors to work with me. So I prepared to open the store without getting credit lines by saving enough money to purchase my inventory through cashier's checks. My foresight was correct. I soon began negotiating contracts with hospitals and city agencies and going for loans that I never got.

One might say, here, that pretty much all one needs to get a loan is a good business plan. But even with a good business plan, containing all the correct phrases, there are other factors that you must be aware of. Without knowledge of these factors, or if you are in denial about them, you will not develop the survival techniques needed to maintain and mainstream your business. We have some great role models. These people are featured in magazines each year. As we go beyond the headlines and pictures, we realize that they did not get to where they are without a struggle. Black business owners face racism, classism, and sexism at every turn. To ignore these factors is to deny yourself the right and the opportunity to entrepreneurship if you are black in America.

Before opening my first store, Harlem Copy, Printing and Stationery Company, in 1983, I researched where Harlem's private and commercial companies spent their dollars. By my estimates, large city and state offices, schools, and local residents spent at least $1 million a month outside of the community on office supplies. I thought that if some of that money could be captured within the community to fund jobs and create new businesses, the Harlem community could begin to get on its feet economically.

Seven years later I opened Harlem Office Supply, Inc. (I had finally reached my goal of having a fully equipped store) just a few blocks from where I had established Harlem Copy—on Harlem's famed 125th Street. By then we employed a total of seventeen people—for several of them, removing their dependency upon welfare.

My daughters Delethia, Patrice, and Angela supported my efforts and had worked with me in opening Harlem Copy, sometimes seven days a week. Together we made a decision to draw an active blueprint for economic empowerment. My three daughters assisted me in every phase of the establishment of Harlem Office Supply. They have engaged in the fiscal day-to-day operations, in the meetings, and in the folding back of the paycheck in the interest of the long-term goal. But while I endeavored to establish a family business that would support my family and teach my daughters about self-determination and empowerment, my determination to find solutions for the entire community hadn't diminished in my career as an entrepreneur. Although it was a different path from building day care and schools, I was back into my activism role as a community organizer trying to gain economic empowerment for the people.

I formed the Invest In Harlem Committee, which brought community members together (in my living room at first) to examine ways that local business and industry spent its dollars, and ways to get those dollars to work for Harlem. I began to work, with others, to try to impress upon the people of the community that we have the means to sponsor our success.

Reverend Dennis Dillon, a Brooklyn minister who preaches Black Economic Empowerment, was of great assistance to me a couple of years ago in bringing this point across to nearly five thousand of Harlem Office Supply's shareholders at a shareholders' meeting. He repeated over and over in his sermons, "Where we spend our money is where we give our power!"—a phrase I have adopted, and vowed to repeat as many times as I can.

CHRIS ROCK AT THE APOLLO

CINTRA WILSON

From Salon.com (1999)

Cintra Wilson's impressions of the Apollo and its atmosphere stand in stark contrast to those of Elvis Presley's in an earlier generation. While Elvis spent night after night in the famed theater during several visits in the fifties, admiring the artists he would later imitate to great success, Wilson may never venture there again, and certainly not to see Chris Rock.

Late into the set, in a way that almost made it seem like comedy relief from the bludgeoning reality of his comedy act, [Chris] Rock degenerated into an antique, battle-of-the-sexist blue rant à la Redd Foxx. No sensitive new-age puss-male, Mr. Rock. This material was weak, offensive without being particularly funny, and had already been chewed to death in the sixties and early seventies by every seedy hack-bastard comic who ever emceed a strip club. I'm not the type to get my panties in a wringer about this type of misogyny-lite, as long as it's funny, but this section was all shit we'd heard ad nauseam: how women should be willing to give more blow jobs; how women really need to shut the fuck up, because they talk too much; how women are mostly in relationships to get their bills paid. Blah blah blah. He also mused on the tried-and-true cliché of how all men are dogs, incapable of fidelity, if tempted. "A man is only as faithful as his options," sayeth the Rock.

It was all more or less a seamy look at the inner workings of Rock's agitated sex life and his surprisingly unenlightened relationships with women in general, and seemed, well (cough), beneath him. I didn't identify with it at all, but maybe I wasn't supposed to; maybe it was a black guy thang. But seriously, compared to Chris Rock, Richard Pryor is practically Dr. Leo Buscaglia.

What I found the most hair-raising in Rock's monologue, and which I've encountered a bit lately in other venues, is that there is a recent public trend of black people, in a relaxed fashion, outspokenly and without malice, to talk about how much they hate whitey. This isn't due to weird zealotry, white-devil rhetoric, or fevered militancy, but is the honest result of a simple, profound, multigenerational resentment, which has always existed, but is usually kept hidden under the mild social politeness that has always kept integrated society from dissolving into total mayhem. This hatred is well deserved and understandable, I reckon, but it will make you just the slightest bit uncomfortable if it is being brazenly acknowledged by a beloved comedian and you are one of fifteen white people in the entire sold-out Apollo Theater in Harlem. We weren't nervous, everyone was perfectly nice to us, nobody mad-dogged us at the bar, but there was definitely a "one of these things just doesn't belong here" vibe. It wasn't scary, but it was a real eye-opener. Harlem is a real eye-opener. As robust and fierce-humored and vivid as the inhabitants are, if you have any kind of sensitive, bleeding heart, Harlem will bust it right in the chops and knock your privileged liberal world view sideways: It's just so goddamned poor. Even the walls of the legendary Apollo are peeling.

"There's a policy here at the Apollo," teased the warm-up comic. "If you're white, and you've never been here before, welcome—just remember to give all of your money to the nearest black person upon exiting the theater. We call it 'reparations.'" The Apollo audience erupted into the deafening white-noise blur of claps and howls louder than any audience I've ever heard; a sound so thick and round it feels like you can walk off the balcony onto it. We clapped too. Heh heh heh heh heh, ho ho. Ahem.

Rock, at this point, for all his expert funniness, is like a severed head on a post: eloquent, but above all a warning, and evoking a marrow-deep chill. Maybe there just isn't room for really funny material nowadays. Maybe that would just be unforgivably irresponsible. Maybe things have just gotten way too unfunny, at this point. It's a shame to feel denied a totally unencumbered Chris Rock, a soaring, radiant talent that didn't have to be weighed down with all that socially important shit. But, well, things need to change. If the world were a nicer place, Chris Rock would be a funnier guy. Whoomp. There it is.

ETHNIC CLEANSING COMES TO HARLEM

MAMADOU CHINYELU

From *Harlem Ain't Nothin' But a Third World Country* (1999)

Drawing on a number of social, political, and economic factors, Mamadou Chinyelu makes a strong and disturbing comparison of Harlem to Bangladash and other backwater cities and countries of the world. Of particular concern for Chinyelu is the Upper Manhattan Empowerment Zone, which he sees as the Trojan Horse devised to displace black residents and businesses in Harlem. But a key phase in what he contends is "ethnic cleansing" is the eradication of low-income housing.

It is important for Harlem to be cleansed of low-income African-American households for one very basic reason: The meager annual earnings of low-income households are not substantial enough to support the retail and entertainment establishments that are currently being developed in Harlem. And if your income is not high enough to support the business establishments of the masters of capitalism, then you must be removed to make room for moderate-, middle-, and upper-income households that can afford to support those businesses.

Playing politics with the housing market is the means by which a community is cleansed of its low-income households. When the purchase price and rental price of the housing stock of a community is significantly increased, low-income households are priced out of the communities in which they may have lived for decades. Such a policy, which is currently being implemented in Harlem, has been in the making for some time. For example, in August 1983, David Rockefeller, who by that time had stepped down as chairman of Chase Manhattan Bank, when attending the reception for the kickoff of Harlem Week in the capacity of chairman of the New York City Partnership, announced that an offshoot of his organization was launching a five-year plan to build thirty thousand units of housing for moderate- and middle-income families.[1] It was not clear whether all thirty thousand units would be built in Harlem or throughout the city. At any rate, there was no mention of building housing for low-income families. Statistics for the first seven years of the last decade of the twentieth century prove that cleansing Harlem of low-income families has moved well beyond the planning stage and has reached the stage of full implementation. From 1990 to 1997, for example, the number of households in Harlem with annual earnings of less than $10,000 has decreased by 26 percent. On the other hand, during that same period in Harlem, the number of households with annual earnings of $75,000 or more has increased by 80 percent, the largest increase for all income categories.[2] In fact, there were also increases in the other upper-income categories, including an increase of 13 percent in households with annual earnings of $35,000 to $49,999;

---

1. Owen Moritz, "Rockefeller Sees a Rebirth of Harlem," *New York Daily News*, August 11, 1983.
2. "Harlem Rising," *Kip Business Report*, August 1998: 12.

and a 46 percent increase in households with annual earnings of $50,000 to $74,999.[3]

Besides annual income, there are other indicators of who will be removed from Harlem. According to 1997 figures, there is an 18-percent unemployment rate in those census tracts in Upper Manhattan and South Bronx that are specifically designated as the federal empowerment zone. That rate is twice as high as the city's overall unemployment rate of 9 percent. Also within the federal empowerment zone, almost 14 percent (13.7) of the residents at least twenty-five years of age have less than a ninth-grade education, as opposed to slightly more than 9 percent (9.4) of the same age group having the same educational background in the city overall. Equally disturbing is that 43 percent of the residents of the federal empowerment zone live below the poverty level, compared to slightly over 19 percent (19.28) for the city overall. And 55 percent of the households in the federal empowerment zone make less than $15,000 per year.[4] By all indications, Harlem will be cleansed of those who are unemployed or undereducated, the working poor, and, in some instances, the fixed-income elderly.

In Harlem, the stage has already been set for a massive displacement, relocation, and ethnic-cleansing program that will uproot long-standing Harlem residents. To where these Harlemites will be relocated, nobody seems to know. And the city government, which is engineering the reloca-

---

3. Ibid., 11.
4. The statistics in this paragraph are either raw figures or computations based on the raw figures from "Data Center: Demographics," Upper Manhattan Empowerment Zone, www.umez.org, April 5, 1999: 1–4.

tion, appears not to care. As many as 25,000 occupied housing units in Harlem, currently owned by the city government, are designated to be sold to private developers. Those developers will then be able to charge market-rate rents for units that are currently rented under subsidy. Current residents of these Harlem units will be asked to relocate to allow for renovation. Supposedly those residents will be allowed to return either to their present building or to a building that is within a cluster of buildings where their present home is located. However, it is not guaranteed they will be returned to their same unit or to the same-size unit they may have occupied for ten, twenty, thirty, or forty years. For example, one husband and wife who have lived in their four-bedroom unit for thirty-seven years, raising three children, have been offered a studio or one-bedroom apartment after the renovation process has been completed. The wife said most of the people in their twenty-four-unit building were long-standing residents. She asked, "What are we supposed to do with all the things we've accumulated over thirty-seven years? Many of the people in my building purchased their own refrigerators, stoves, washers, and dryers."[5] Although she didn't pose the question, it must be asked: After making a thirty-seven-year investment in her home, isn't she entitled to maintain a unit size that will accommodate visits from her children and grandchildren? The actual investment made by many of the residents of these 25,000 units is immeasurable. Nia Mason, director of Action for Community Empowerment, a Harlem-based organization advocating on behalf of the

---

5. Author's telephone interview with Mrs. Maxine Newman, April 5, 1999.

tenants, said, "These tenants made investments in their apartments and in their buildings that the city refused to make. Some tenants have totally redone their apartments. In some cases, the tenants have taken responsibility for getting drug dealers out of their building. They have a stake in their buildings.[6] According to Mason, the city implemented the program without seeking input from the tenants.

6. Author's telephone interview with Nia Mason, April 6, 1999.

UNFORGETTABLE SUMMER FOR HARLEM LITTLE LEAGUE

HOWIE EVANS

Amsterdam News (2002)

No matter the sport or the season, Evans is on top of things as the long-time sports editor for the *Amsterdam News*, Harlem's most esteemed newspaper. On this occasion, Evans captures the Harlem All-Stars' return from the Little League World Series of 2002, where the team surprised everyone with a sensational tournament. They didn't go all the way, as Evans notes, but the future looks very promising.

If they never swing another bat, commit an error, throw a wild pitch or hit one beyond the playing field, Manager Morris McWilliams and the Harlem Little League All-Stars will forever remember the summer of 2002. These kids didn't just capture the attention and love of Harlem and the city of New York, they made headline news around the world. From coast to coast, the exploits of the team were the feel-good story of local and national news.

They didn't go all the way, slugged out of competition by a kid named Ryan Griffin and his three-run, Hank Aaron–like shot that gave his Worcester, Mass., team a 5–2 win in the Little League World Series semifinals. Then Harlem was defeated by the 2002 champions from Louisville, Kentucky.

Monday, the li'l guys came home to a rousing Harlem

reception at the historic Marcus Garvey Park, with every notable politician and community leader in attendance. Then they were escorted downtown to meet Mayor Michael Bloomberg. Boy, will they have something to talk about when they return to school in another week, and the teacher asks them what did they do over the summer!

And so will the Raifords, Dwight and Iris, the league's founders. As will Jeanette Spencer, president of the Harlem Little League, and her husband, Tony, who have been there from the get-go. And let's not forget Assemblyman Keith Wright and State Senator David Paterson. They were there before the wagon began moving toward Williamsport.

From their improbable ride to Williamsport, Harlem didn't come home empty-handed. Their bags contained some impressive items that are now and forever a part of Little League history. In the summer of 2002, the kids brought home a district, a regional, a New York State and a Mid-Atlantic championship. That's four championships. It's never been done better.

HARLEM IS MY HEART

YEMISE CAMERON

Yemise was selected as the first-place winner in the Harlem Children's Zone Essay Contest. The following is her winning essay as it appeared in *Harlem Overheard* (vol. 5, no. 18, 2001), published by the Rheedlen Centers for Children and Families.

It's six A.M. Here I am, small and humble, peering out my window to see the sun rise and glow on the East River over the rooftops of Harlem. Gazing at a community that has seen struggle and fear and risen above it all, I now see the hopes of the past, triumph of the present, and dreams of the future.

Harlem. A place where great people like Langston Hughes, Duke Ellington, and Marcus Garvey and many others created positive influences. These people came from a time when jazz was really hip and black folks were smiling. Harlem was born again and black folks were saying to the world, "I, too, sing America." Writers were writing, poets rhyming, politicians were politicking, and academics were studying. This was the Harlem Renaissance.

The Harlem Renaissance was the turning point for many blacks. I wonder, though, could we be experiencing a second renaissance in the twenty-first century? Looking around the neighborhood, I see many new changes in Harlem. There are new buildings everywhere. People are watching 125th Street. There are new buildings such as Old Navy, the Disney Store and even a Magic Johnson Theater. Harlem is on the rise again—and lots of people have questions.

Why has it taken so long to rebuild Harlem? Where are all the old businesses? Is the money coming back to the community or just going out?

As Harlem rises, people are stopping to watch the shaping of a new history—for the good and bad. "I think the fact that we don't have to go all the way to 34th Street to go to Old Navy or the Disney Store is good, but the bad part about it is, who did they build it for?" So says Shawnea Walker, a resident of Harlem. She has a good point. If this whole change is not for Harlem, then who is it for?

Regina Cameron, another Harlem resident, said, "To me this is great for Harlem. When I was growing up, we didn't have any of this. It's about time things changed."

What do I think? Well, I'm just glad that I get to be in a community that is starting a new life. Harlem is my heart. And to see it grow and change brings me so much joy. I know my ancestors are proud. I know you might be thinking that even if the outside has changed, we the people, the heart of Harlem, still need to find a better us. We will one day; that future is not so hazy.

The future. This will be a time when Harlem won't be just be a place of beauty, but a community with a lifted spirit and soul. I hope that one day people won't just see Harlem for its bad times but look at it for the good times and new accomplishments. Remember, no matter how hard your struggle, you can rise above it with dignity and pride.

Seeing the promise for tomorrow through my window, I walk away with a clear mind and warm heart that tells me Harlem will be okay. The love we, the children of Harlem, have for Harlem, will live forever.

HARLEM READER VIGNETTES

HERB BOYD

Amsterdam News (2002)

REVEREND AL SHARPTON

Keeping up with the Reverend Al Sharpton requires the speed of a sprinter and the endurance of a marathoner. While his presidential exploratory committee is busy weighing his possibility of seeking the White House in 2004, the minister is as ubiquitous as ever with a press conference at the National Press Club in the nation's capital and an autograph session for his latest book at the Book Expo in Manhattan.

Last week was a typical week for Sharpton, with a brief appearance at the "Blacks in Technology" summit at the Jacob Javits Center on Saturday and an hour-long interview with Gil Noble on *Like It Is*.

Flexing his diplomatic muscles, Sharpton responded to questions from Noble on the crisis in the Middle East, the war in Afghanistan, and the coup-counter-coup in Venezuela. He also lashed the Bush administration, particularly the repressive atmosphere stemming from the actions of Attorney General John Ashcroft.

And Sharpton was no less insightful on issues closer to home as he discussed the ramifications of economic plans on the Harlem Community. When asked to deliver his report card on Harlem and the advent of gentrification, he said he was disturbed by certain developments. "A lot of what we're seeing in Harlem today is resources being put into national retail chains, especially along 125th Street," he began. "What is happening is that these stores are being set up to provide a marketplace for them and to improve their economic picture, rather than providing economic possibilities for the people of Harlem.

"Now, this is not to say we don't want outsiders," Sharpton continued, "but if you're going to use the natural resources and the tax base of a community, then a large portion of that ought to be used for the indigenous population, so that they can open their businesses and develop economic entities."

On the controversial issue of the Upper Manhattan Empowerment Zone (UMEZ), Noble asked Sharpton about the widespread rumor that many of the small, local businesses were finding it difficult to get support from the UMEZ. "It makes no sense whatsoever to endow people who are already wealthy," Sharpton said. "The only thing we get out of this is that we can get jobs as sales clerks for these new stores. This is the real challenge of accountability. . . . I was under the impression that the UMEZ was set up to include community businesses, not to exclude them."

But Sharpton said all the blame should not be placed on the retail chains. "There are disturbing trends that we must challenge in our own community," he asserted. "I was upset to learn that after the sale of BET to Viacom, the company moved out of our community, along with hundreds of jobs. The idea must be to build economic entities in the community under our control, and to use our capital for development."

Sharpton was equally outspoken about the housing situation in Harlem that is witnessing an explosion of rebuilding and renovation, but to the exclusion of minority contractors. "There are all kinds of unfair practices going on in this realm in which people who live in the community can't get these jobs," he said. "They can't become part of the building trades, can't break the grip of certain exclusionary unions . . . can't get the contracts. And in the end, can't even get the apartments. What we're seeing are a number of people coming in with higher incomes and taking the property that was supposedly set aside for the community residents in the first place."

As for the blame for the inequity and unfair practices, Sharpton includes the city, the state, and the unions. "It is the legitimate role of community activists to put the spotlight on them and not be demonized for doing it," he charged.

Asked what he thought of the Bloomberg administration, Sharpton said that he was willing to let such City Council members as Charles Barron and Bill Perkins lead the way in this critique. "But, clearly, he's been in office more than one hundred days and the honeymoon is over," he said. "I disagree with some of his budgetary concerns. As for his desire to control the school system, well, I've always been one to believe that the community ought to control the schools. The more our parents are involved, the better it is for the children."

Sharpton said that rather than having the mayor take over the school system or abandon it altogether, "we should seek ways to fix a flawed community control policy. To give these schools to one entity leaves room for too much political manipulation and patronage." Sharpton added that he was not in favor of vouchers, which would allow only a few chosen students to be educated while the majority are left behind.

MONK

Activist. Nothing happens in Harlem without Monk in the audience, at the rally, or passing out leaflets.

I came to Harlem in 1947 when they had a snow storm so large that it stopped the city. I was about fourteen or fifteen. This community means a lot to me. It's a community where there are so many black people that it helps you expand your awareness of who we are as a people. I don't want to see the gentrification of Harlem where they move people out because this is our community. We might not own a lot of business here, but we built it up to what it is today. It was our efforts that have made Harlem known all over the world. One of the things that bothers me is that the leadership has sold us out; they went for the money, the fine clothes, the fine houses and partying and forgot all about us—the common folks. They were suppose to represent us but they only ended up representing themselves.

CAMILLE YARBROUGH

Author, community activist, griot, actress, and teacher are a few strands of Camille's résumé, but they reflect only a portion of her deep connection to the community.

I came to New York City in 1961 and was downtown in the theater. I moved to Harlem in 1984–85. As soon as I arrived in the city, I got on the A train and headed uptown. When I was a little girl growing up in Chicago, I heard about Harlem—and it was everything I hoped it would be. Just walking the streets, passing the Apollo or Michaux's bookstore, that used be where the State Office Building is now, was a treat. This community has been like a dream to me, a source of inspiration that has inspired all my books. It's a place where Langston and Malcolm walked. I once taught a course at City College called "The Harlem Community" and I usually started it by relating the first arrival of African people on the island back in 1626. Since then we have been pushed up the island from Little Africa, to the Tenderloin in the twenties and thirties, then to San Juan Hill where Lincoln Center is today, to Seneca Village in Central Park, and finally to Harlem.

People forget that Harlem was not opened for us, but for Europeans. We came here because we were pushed into this place. The question now is, where do we go? When the vendors were moved, it made me very sad because they brought a certain vitality, creativity. And there was Mart 125; it's gone too. But corporate America has taken over, the rent's gone up. Things are changing rapidly. But I'm hopeful that, as in the past, the spirit of our people will always manage to create new worlds.

PRESTON WILCOX

Few residents rival Wilcox's involvement in Harlem's political and cultural affairs. Once a close associate of Malcolm X, he continues to document the community's history as he monitors organizations and institutions.

I first came to Harlem in 1943 when I was in the military and sent here to pick up a prisoner from Welfare Island. I was only here for a brief moment then, but I will never forget stepping out on 125th Street. I had never seen that many black people in one place in my life. You see, I came from Youngstown, Ohio, where you know just about everybody in town. I knew after that one visit that I would return and spend the rest of life here. In some way it was decreed years ago. In fact, I was born on Harlem Street in Youngstown, so, in a sense, it was predestined. So, when I got out of the army in 1946, I headed straight to Harlem and I've been here ever since.

One of the high points for me occurred in the sixties when I was involved in the community control of our schools. We ran all the white school principals out of here and installed black ones. I am convinced that the powers that be don't want us to control our own destiny. The situation today in Harlem is that we have a bunch of gate-keepers who do not identify with Harlem. They are being paid by people outside the community to provide leadership for us, most of them still trying to find their way to 125th Street. You never see them in Showman's, 22 West, or Londel's. These leaders ought to be required to own a home in Harlem; and they ought to be required to send their children to schools in Harlem. In that way they will see our kids as their kids and take an active part in improving the school system. The one big thing that's missing in Harlem is the day-to-day contact among all classes of Harlemites. Once upon a time here in Harlem you had a basketball player, a parking-lot attendant, and a doctor all living in the same neighborhood, so their children came up together and had an opportunity to learn from each other. That day, I'm sad to say, is gone, but I hope not forever.

**HERB
BOYD**

PERCY SUTTON
Attorney and Chairman Emeritus of Inner City Broadcasting.

Looking ten years down the road, I am confident that Harlem will survive and thrive. And contrary to reports about gentrification, not all the newcomers are white. Black people are buying homes, renting apartments and what have you in Harlem. The restaurants and bakeries, owned by black people, are sprouting all over the place, not only on 125th Street. I think it's going to thrive and it all began when a crazy guy named Percy Sutton in 1980 bought the Apollo Theater, when every other store on 125th Street was vacant, and then got libeled and slandered. These people who assailed me were not there when the theater was eighteen inches filled with sewage, muck, and mire, with rats swimming around in the water. They were not there to help restore it, to paint the peeling walls. But that was twenty-some years ago; now what folks see is the legacy of things we did back then. What they are doing now, I tried to do when I owned the theater, but then there was no such thing as the Empowerment Zone. Back then there was widespread insecurity from visitors who were afraid to venture uptown. Things had begun long before Bill Clinton moved here, but it's good that he's in Harlem.

ELI KINCE
Artist/writer/teacher.

I see Harlem as a disconnected concept from the romantic notion that I once had of Harlem as the black or African-American capital and the historical place that cradled the Black Renaissance and other important movements and moments. I see too many healthy men, women, and children standing around discussing the actions of others while Harlem is being sold and bought right from under us. But I also see a strong influx of black professionals, young and old, who are moving into the neighborhood and who seem to want to be a part of the rebirth of Harlem. As new services and amenities are developed for the people who live here, Harlem will be even more wonderful. It is nice to see many of the older buildings refurbished, remodeled, and occupied. Much like a forest that has been burned down and has begun its regrowth, the rebirth of the Harlem cityscape is beautiful and also suggests a greater sense of security and hope for the future. I believe that the influx of other people will create a rich texture of ideas, goals, and solutions that will inadvertently effect a greater good for the majority of Harlem's inhabitants and the city of New York.

ELINOR TATUM
Publisher and editor in chief of the *Amsterdam News*.

Looking at the current situation in Harlem, particularly all the discussion about gentrification, I'm very concerned that the people who have invested their lives in this community will be left out. As the major retail chains move into the community, the small businessmen and women are forced to close their stores. They just can't compete with these large chain stores, with their greater volume of goods and cheaper prices. The only benefits of all this may be an improvement of services and more jobs, but the possibility of ownership is disappearing. But even with the increase of jobs, there must be training that can lead to managerial and supervisory positions. And we can expect the current pace of change in Harlem to accelerate in the next few years. The challenge we face is how to redirect this change so that the community can be a larger benefactor. Now, we, as a newspaper, can take advantage of these new developments by getting ads from the stores, but thus far this is not happening. What has to happen in the long run, and it is my hope, is that the companies invest not only in the property of Harlem, but in the people and their livelihood.

YUSEF SALAAM
Salaam's essays, articles, and creative writing have captured the passion and energy of the increasing number of Muslims in Harlem.

Harlem is currently experiencing a vital blooming of religious diversity. This predominantly Christian community has, in the last twenty-five to thirty years, witnessed a flowering of Islam. The population of Muslim, Continental Africans, and Muslim Diaspora Africans in Harlem is growing tremendously, and they are influencing the community's cultural, social, economical, and political life.

Muslim African-Americans and Muslims from African countries such as Senegal, the Gambia, Guinea, and the Ivory Coast are part of the melting pot of African descendants that gives Harlem its dynamic presence and potential. Muslims are vitally contributing to, and participating in, the flow of Harlem life. All over Harlem, Muslims operate numerous restaurants and specialty shops, are vendors on the streets, drive for and manage cab companies, work as security guards, teach school, etc. There are Muslim barbershops, a butcher shop, door-to-door restaurants, a dry cleaners, two book stores, and an array of other Muslim small businesses.

There is also a new, built-from-the ground-up, open-air mart managed by Muslims. The rehabilitated affordable apartment buildings that now replace the blighted tenement buildings were built with the assistance of Muslim labor. Muslims manage an initiative for home-ownership in an area where home ownership is virtually nonexistent. It is this dynamism driven by Islam that will inspire the Muslims to continue to contribute to the current growth and development of Harlem.

CREDITS

Houghton Mifflin: "116th Street" from *The Street*. Copyright © 1946 by Ann Petry. Reprinted by permission of Houghton Mifflin.

Dorothy Pitman Hughes: "Making Harlem My Business" from *Wake Up and Smell the Dollars* by Dorothy Pitman Hughes. Reprinted by permission of the author.

Kensington Publishing Corp.: "The Abyssinian Baptist Church" from *Adam by Adam: The Autobiography of Adam Clayton Powell Jr*. Reprinted by permission of Kensington Publishing Corp.

Mustard Seed Press: "Ethnic Cleansing Comes to Harlem" from *Harlem Ain't Nothin' but a Third World Country: The Global Economy, Empowerment Zones and the Colonial Status of Africans in America* by Mamadou Chinyelu. Reprinted by permission of Mustard Seed Press.

Oxford University Press: "We Return Fighting" from *When Harlem Was in Vogue* by David Levering Lewis. Reprinted by permission of Oxford University Press.

Penguin Books: "Witness to the Harlem Renaissance" from *Along This Way: The Autobiography of James Weldon Johnson* by James Weldon Johnson. Reprinted by permission of Penguin Books.

Random House, Inc.: "Minister Malcolm X" from *The Autobiography of Malcolm X* by Malcolm X and Alex Haley. Copyright © 1964 by Alex Haley and Malcolm X. Copyright © 1965 by Alex Haley and Betty Shabazz. And "Castro in Harlem" from *The Heart of a Woman* by Maya Angelou. Copyright © 1981 by Maya Angelou. Reprinted by permission of Random House, Inc.

State University of New York: "The Harlem Fox" from *The Harlem Fox: J. Raymond Jones and Tammany, 1920–1970*. Copyright © 1989 by John Walter. Reprinted by permission of State University of New York.

Third World Press: "Zora" by Laurence Holder, from *New Plays for the Black Theatre*, edited by Woodie King Jr. Reprinted by permission of Third World Press.

Thunder's Mouth Press: "Harlem" from *Goodbye Sweetwater: New and Selected Stories* by Henry Dumas. Edited by Eugene Redmond. Reprinted by permission of Thunder's Mouth Press, 1988. Copyright © 1968–2003 by Henry Dumas Estate by permission of Loretta Dumas and Eugene Redmond.

Verso Press: "Memories of a Sixties Girlhood: The Harlem I Love" from *Invisibility Blues: From Pop to Theory* by Michele Wallace. Reprinted by permission of Verso Press.

Warner Books: "The Harlem Rens" from *A Hard Road to Glory*, Vol. 2, by Arthur Ashe Jr. Reprinted by permission of Warner Books.

Wesleyan University Press: "Harlem in the Spotlight" excerpted from "Harlem's Neglected Opportunities: Twin Sources of Gin and Genius, Poetry and Pajama Parties" in the *Amsterdam News*, November 30, 1927, as reprinted in *A Hubert Harrison Reader*, edited by Jeffrey B. Perry. Reprinted by permission of Wesleyan University Press.

CREDITS

ACKNOWLEDGMENTS

Among the first to be cheered, honored, and acknowledged in this project are the contributors. Without them and their concern to document portions of the legendary Harlem community there would be no book. Of course, selecting from countless articles and commentaries on Harlem was no easy task, but I think these choices are representative of the community's storied history, the warp and woof that continues to make it a compelling venue for residents and tourists.

Four people must be thanked again and again for giving me my first real lessons on Harlem: Dr. John Henrik Clarke, Dr. Charshee McIntyre, Howard "Stretch" Johnson, and James Baldwin. It was the conversations with the late Dr. Clarke, Stretch, and Charshee that stimulated my scholarly interest; Baldwin touched me very early from afar in a visceral way through his essays. Later, it would be the contact with the Harlem community that I have covered as a journalist, mainly with the *Amsterdam News*, that has nourished my fascination, given me deeper insight of the people and the events that the contributors so brilliantly profile and evoke.

There are a number of treasured informants, some of them denizens of Harlem, who were as charitable with their time as they were patient with my inquiries—Preston Wilcox; Una Mulzac; Gordon Parks; Esther Walker; the Tatums; Clarence Atkins; Robert Allen; Elombe Brath; Mildred Green; Jules Allen; Sam Anderson; Playthell Benjamin; J. E. Franklin; Sybil Williams-Clarke; Sylvia Alston; Lonnie Youngblood; Ron Daniels; Robert Van Lierop; Rev. Dino Woodward; Percy Sutton; Sharon Howard; Gil Noble; Delilah Jackson; the Dinwiddie clan; Phil Lasley; Evelyn Cunningham; Ron Lockett; Yvonne Bynoe; the Blakes; Timothy Wong; Ward Cunningham-Rundles; Robert Dillon; David Levering Lewis; David Ritz; Bill Katz; Katherine Brown; Corliss McAfee; Charles, Catherine, Johnny, and Maya Boyd; and the Rojas family, to mention a few who have helped me navigate Harlem's history or provided ballast to my sanity.

A trio of beautiful and highly informed women was a constant source of counseling whenever I veered off course, most particularly my wife, Elza, my agent, Marie Brown, and my editor, Rachel Kahan. The ship has made it to shore only because of these wise helmswomen.

And now, moored and stabilized by Howard Dodson's foreword, it can only be hoped that The Harlem Reader provides at least a glimpse into what has been, and continues to be, a glorious patch of America's history. Perhaps the youngest contributor to the book, Yemise Cameron, says it for all of us: "Harlem will be okay."